# DIVERS CAPITALISM

## Profiting from Diversity, Inclusions, and Equity

**OLAV HARALDSEID &
WINIFRED P. LOUM JOHANSEN**

Published by Orchard Publishing Consultancy

A catalogue record for this book is available from the British Library

ISBN 978-1-9162861-6-0 (PB)

ISBN 978-1-9162861-2-2 (HB)

Cover photos: Maria Tatsi
Cover design: Muhammad Aslan
Book Layout: Muhammad Usman Shahid
Illustrations: Constance Beaugeard

# Dedication

*'Just because a man lacks the use of his eyes doesn't mean he lacks vision'*
*Stevie Wonder.*

This book is dedicated
to all of us outsiders,
though we are different, we are able.
It is our differences that when blended move
the human race forward.

*To my boys Loum and Lalwak,*
*and my lioness Adiero.*

# ACKNOWLEDGMENT

We would like to take this opportunity to thank the following people who have provided valuable guidance in the process of writing this book.

- Sigmund Håland, Fund Manager
- Trond Riiber Knudsen, CEO TRK Group
- Line Fransson, Journalist Dagbladet
- Anders Hectorlinde, Senior Advisor Assessio International
- Marit Øimoen, Content manager
- Lars Erik Lund, EVP Strategy and Sustainability at Veidekke-
- Kurt Mosvold, Managing Director at Mosvold & Co Ltd
- Elin Hauge, AI and Business Strategist
- Hon. Justice Norma Wade-Miller, Retired Puisne Judge of the Supreme Court of Bermuda
- Jennifer Vessels, Innovator, leadership and Growth Strategist
- Pat Shepherd, Editor and Publisher at Orchard Publishing Consultancy
- Kristel Antine Helland-Hansen, Psychologist - Working Environment specialist
- Johan Brandt, Founder and Entrepreneur @ Kahoot, We Are Human, EntrepreneurShipOne

You have challenged us and given constructive guidance, encouragement, and direction along the way which has been of invaluable support. Thank you for helping and supporting us during this hectic time.

A sincere thank you to friends and family for your support during the writing process, we would not have made it otherwise.

# FOREWORD TO DIVERSITY CAPITALISM

By Trond Riiber Knudsen:
Founder TRK Group and former Senior Partner McKinsey
& Company

'Diversity' is all around us, thrown around as a 'management idea' in line with 'agile', 'lean' or 'innovation'. Everyone agrees its relevant and, perhaps, even important, but few feel mastery, and even fewer know where to go for advice and apprenticeship on becoming an excellent Diversity Leader. That's why I was so happy to read through the first draft of *Olav and Winifred's* holistic guide and roadmap to becoming a leader comfortable with getting the most out of more diverse teams and organizations. Thus, this is where *Diversity Capitalism* is unique, on one side a passionate contribution and plea for the argument that diversity is not only to be tolerated, but rather needs to be celebrated AND that the very best leaders and organizations in the world have 'cracked the code' on getting true synergy and profitability out of diversity, and that this is a leadership skill that can be acquired.

## Diversity Capitalism – Celebrating Diversity

*Olav and Winifred*, themselves, by reflecting the potential in diversity on so many dimensions, are generously sharing concrete experiences and case examples as they walk us through a comprehensive roadmap to excellence in diversity leadership. A key observation is that achieving leadership excellence is a journey encompassing both awareness and knowledge, insights that can partly be acquired by this book; as well as 'the school of life', what you learn from your daily life, but in a professional and a private setting. As pioneers in the diversity leadership arena, it's my impression that *Olav and Winifred* have had to rely primarily on practical experience and experimentation. The benefit to us as readers is truly battle-hardened practical advice that often comes out of their own experience, such as when *Winifred* describes growing up in Norway as a child raised by African parents, having both an African and a Norwegian identity, an exciting blend that was seldom appreciated. It becomes apparent that's where *Winifred* developed her appreciation for each individual's uniqueness and her acute gut feeling against any type of stereotyping.

Through *Olav and Winifred's* stories, our biases and blind spots come alive, exposing our own history as if we suddenly see our self in a new light in the mirror. Several times I am forced to reflect, 'how did I react in a similar situation? Why did I struggle as a leader? What could I have done differently? With their characteristic blend of theory, practice, and storytelling the team makes it come alive in an eye-opening way. This is the case for me when *Olav*, apparently then a 'happy-go-lucky 'creative retail executive with a strong personality moved into Statoil's super stringent zero-fault tolerance culture. At first *Olav* is in denial mode and exposes many of the well-known barriers to individual change and shows a lack of appreciation for the opposing point of view. We are all, by definition, 'change-resistant' and enabling individual change is also part of diversity leadership; on some important themes there is zero-tolerance for 'diversity', like compliance with Statoil HSE strategic objective of zero faults, counting big and small events. *Olav* learned this the hard way, when Statoil threatened to take away his accumulated bonus unless he fell in line immediately.

Even diversity has its limits.

Interestingly, the book is full of examples of diversity thriving *within* well-defined boundaries, which might be why high-performing organizations and companies with strong values and cultures excel at driving profitability and growth from diversity. This was clearly what I saw both in McKinsey and with many of my best-performing clients.

In addition to helping me reflect on my own behaviour in similar situations, the stories in the book also helped me get a deeper appreciation of issues I have not directly experienced myself. In that regard, it helps to broaden your 'antennas' for types of diversity challenges and opportunities that can arise in the future. The book is thus a turbocharger of awareness, sensitivity, and empathy and accelerates your appreciation for differences as sources of strength and profitability. More and more I started to think about the book as my '*Handbook to Empathy*', helping me see and partly understand differences and profiles beyond my immediate experience and comfort zone. This is the case when *Winifred* describes her leadership role for contractual negotiations in West Africa, where people of widely different cultures, background, capabilities, and language skills are brought together, and *Winifred* learned to appreciate their differences and play her leadership role more as bridge-builder and intense listener, as opposed to the leadership approach she often takes in a less diverse and more familiar context. Another good reminder is that all good leadership is situation-specific and that most of us have too big a mouth and too small ears. Listening more is an often forgotten leadership virtue. As put in the book:

'We *should regulate the desire to speak and become better listeners.'*

In this case, and many others, *Winifred* makes me reflect on my own behaviour as a leader of diverse teams, hopefully making me more situation-aware for the future, and more likely to shut up and listen.

In addition to the need for both schooling and experience to achieve excellence, *Olav and Winifred* are reminding us that Diversity is a much wider canvass than most of us consider and understanding both the visible and invisible areas of diversity, is required to address our own white-spots and biases. Only then can we learn to appreciate the full complexity and beauty of a more diverse society where we as leaders are skilled at creating opportunities for all to develop and shine, in a context where their uniqueness and difference is celebrated as a source of value. This is the future model we should all strive for; an inclusive and healthy society that embraces *Olav and Winifred's* ideas of *Diversity Capitalism.*

## Gaining My Own Appreciation for Diversity

Like with most leaders, for me embracing the phenomenal upside of diversity has been a long and winding road, where every success has been followed by a revelation of how hard it is to truly get the 'magic' out of diverse organizations. Thus, Diversity has been an area where the more I believed I was 'getting it', the more I realized how little I truly understood. However, along this journey experiences and markers have helped to build my strong conviction that embracing diversity is a 'hidden goldmine' for organizations if every leader learns to get the best out of every single individual and knows how get the amazing 'synergy and music' that results from you as a leader mastering leadership under diversity.

Early on as a leader of the Marketing and Sales Practice in McKinsey, I launched initiatives aimed at 'filling capability gaps' and 'broadening the talent base'. We started recruiting talent with much more depth of expertise in more narrow areas than the typical broad and integrative McKinsey consultant. The old profile was of a 'Renaissance Man' who could master everything, now we added to that with expertise capabilities, and brought these people together in 'Sandwich-teams' with blended profiles. Creating 'magic' in these more diverse team settings was a new challenge for us as team-leaders in a rapidly diversifying McKinsey, and it proved to be much harder than we had expected. We all got a crash-course in diversity-leadership and started to get exposed to the difficulties and many hidden barriers to excellence in truly getting the best out of more diverse teams. What kept us going, though, was the amazing results and impact we delivered when combining our unique integrative skills with functional depth; this 'T-shaped' delivery model enabled by more diverse teams soon became a hallmark of our distinctiveness. Therefore, as *Olav and Winifred* describe in Part 1, I got early confirmation that diversity well managed can be a driver of competitiveness and profitability, and much more than a 'counting exercise'.

## Leveraging diversity as a source of strength in the venture world

As I later moved from advising top leadership teams at Fortune500 companies with McKinsey, to supporting tech start-up founders through my venture platform TRK Group, I realized that these small, fast-growing companies were better at leveraging the potential in diversity. With one of our companies in Oslo, Norway, the workforce of 40 hails from 22 countries, a level of geographic and cultural diversity I have never found with larger incumbent companies in the Nordic region. Clearly, for start-ups to succeed, they need to attract the very best talent independent of gender, religion, culture, and personality; and with the new 'post-pandemic' work model, remote teams mean you can truly tap into a global talent pool. Again, my experience on the ground is that the startup world is quicker at leveraging this source of talent and better at managing such a diverse workforce.

But of course, the venture and start-up world also have major diversity challenges; perhaps the most prevalent is the lack of female founders and female investors. This means that a major source of entrepreneurial leadership capacity is blocked from providing value in the entrepreneurial industry thus keeping important potential product and services away from being realized.

It's a gap we must close.

Personally, I have seen supporting female founders both as 'the right thing to do', but even more so a major investment opportunity. As an investor, being 'different' and 'contrarian' is required to drive outsized results. Thus, in TRK Group, more than 1 out of 3 of our 100 + portfolio companies have a female founder, and surprise, surprise they perform amazingly well.

And I've learnt to embrace new types of diversity. With my 25 Years of background from *Harvard Business School and McKinsey & Company*, I was clearly bringing a bias towards educational excellence, CV quality, analytical stringency, and personal grooming. That kept me from engaging with very different Founder profiles. For the first couple of years as a start-up investor, that stopped me from investing with some of the most amazing growth companies in the Nordics. For no good reason, like with Olav when he moved from retail to Statoil, I could not change my own expectations and preferences, before I learnt the hard way to open my eyes and appreciate true diversity among excellent Founders; that success here has more to do with your attraction to the right talent, being authentic and passionate, have the right networks, often being different from the 'corporate world'. My bad for not understanding that earlier.

If only I had access to *Olav and Winifred's* book at that time, I might have changed both my mindset and my expectations of successful founders much earlier, also picking up helpful tools and approaches to leadership under new types of diversity, where just doing 'more of the same' would not suffice. This book is a great reminder of that. Don't run on autopilot, open your eyes, be curious, have empathy, show real interest in every individual, and then magic truly can happen.


★          ★          ★


*Oslo October 17, 2022*

*Trond Riiber Knudsen has 30 years' work experience with McKinsey & Company as a director and senior partner from 2002-2015. He is also the founder of TRK Group – an Oslo-based active ownership firm aiming to catalyse growth from promising entrepreneurial ventures across 3 domains – disruptive technologies, digital service transformation and emerging Africa.*

# CONTENTS

# HOW THIS BOOK WORKS

**Part 1:** Diversity provides a general introduction to the concept of diversity and profitable and necessary. It makes a case for diversity and inclusion as something to be sought after and not simply tolerated. It goes on to offer some practical advice on how to build a diverse team and get the best out of the team. For this matter, the section introduces the importance of character strengths that enable inclusion as well as strengths needed for successful leadership and navigation in a diverse landscape.

**Part 2:** Visible Diversity discusses the profitability of diversity looking at it through the lenses of visible diversity. It covers gender, ethnical, social, age, and cultural diversity.
This section explores existing and foundational theories on inclusion as performance-enhancing across boundaries exploring the differences between Norway and USA when it comes to successful gender diversity.

**Part 3**: Invisible Diversity of the book focuses on invisible diversity, the traits, and characteristics that are often not visible and hence less obvious for consideration. Here we make a case for personality diversity and Neurodiversity. Different diagnoses come with their own sets of challenges yet at the same time offer superpowers that when well accommodated are vital for business idea generation, and entrepreneurship.

**Part 4**: Offers practical tools and advice to help managers build and lead diversity. It addresses key issues in diversity management such as recruitment for diversity, and obstacles to diversity and inclusion.

# Introduction:
## THE COMPLEXITY OF DIVERSITY

Today, diversity is described by most companies as an important social responsibility tool for building a reputation that helps to present a positive view of the organisation's values. In many companies' annual reports, diversity is often given a fixed spot in the columns for this very purpose. In other words, it has merely been about strengthening the company's reputation internally and externally. The statistics normally focus on the gender balance and in some cases the number of different nationalities within the company. Diversity, however, is much wider than this. In this book, we would like to explore the different facets of diversity. We will make a case for diversity as being profitable in a measurable and non-measurable sense for organisations and society. The first question to ask is, what exactly is diversity?

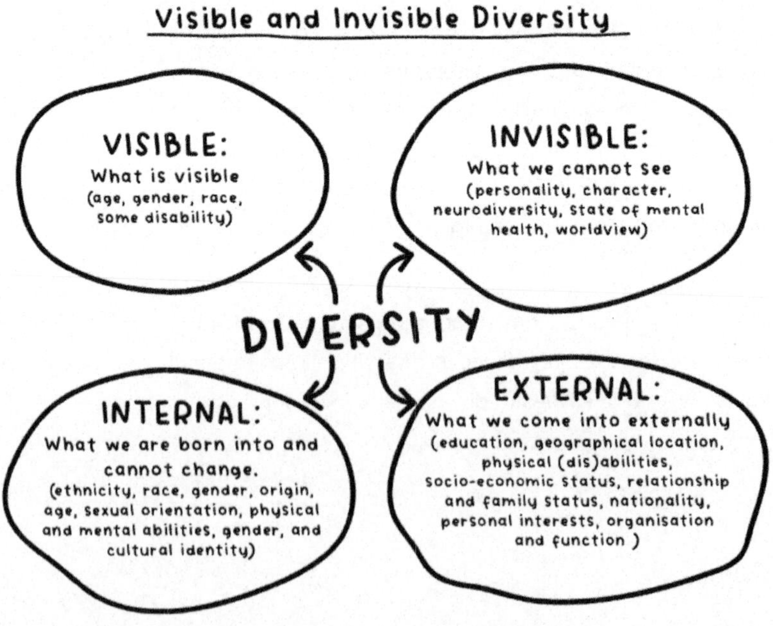

## Visible and Invisible Diversity

**VISIBLE:**
What is visible
(age, gender, race,
some disability)

**INVISIBLE:**
What we cannot see
(personality, character,
neurodiversity, state of mental
health, worldview)

## DIVERSITY

**INTERNAL:**
What we are born into and
cannot change.
(ethnicity, race, gender, origin,
age, sexual orientation, physical
and mental abilities, gender, and
cultural identity)

**EXTERNAL:**
What we come into externally
(education, geographical location,
physical (dis)abilities,
socio-economic status, relationship
and family status, nationality,
personal interests, organisation
and function )

*Figure1: The different faces of Diversity*

It would be so much easier if our diversities could be neatly parcelled into categories. Unfortunately, or perhaps, fortunately, people fit into lots of different categories, and one cannot be distinguished from another.

Diversity is complex. Some elements are visible, while others are not. Invisible diversity characteristics are those which cannot be seen with the naked eye, while visible ones are those we can see.

As can be seen in Figure 1, the human spectrum of diversity is complex because while we can see some of what separates us, such as race, age, sometimes faith, disability, and gender, some of the most critical elements are invisible. Elements such as personality, neurodiversity, gender with which we identify, sexual orientation, physical and mental abilities along with cultural identity. An important, yet another often taboo part of our internal diversity, is our state of mental health and wellbeing.

One could say Olav and I are diverse. He is male, I am female. He is white, I am black, our educational backgrounds were dissimilar, and our lived experiences through our formative years were very different.

Yet, in many ways, Olav and I are very similar. We share cultural norms, customs, traditions, and some personality traits. We can laugh wickedly at the same things because we share a world vision.

So, would you say we are diverse or similar?

And there are many more examples of this.

*Many years ago, I travelled to a meeting in Singapore. A lady walked into the meeting room; she looked Korean, but she walked in so confidently and purposefully that she did not fit into my biased opinion of the person I was expecting.*

*To me, in Singapore, although Korean in appearance, she carried herself like a Norwegian businesswoman so when she sat down, I greeted her in Norwegian.*

*She was surprised and delighted as I was right in my guess. She was, indeed, Norwegian.*

In my own case, I often see the surprise on people's faces the first time they meet me. I have the name of an old English woman – well there were very few Winifred's under the age of 75 - I have a Scandinavian surname, yet I happen to be a black woman, not old, not white, with a view of the world shaped by my multicultural upbringing.

Another example would be a white male in what appear to be, a seemingly homogenous group of white men but he may not feel that he belongs. So how could this be? His view of the world may be different, he may not identify himself as being male, his personality may be very different from the rest of the group, or he may be neurodivergent. In other words, his diversity is invisible. While visibility is important in inclusion, the invisible elements of diversity are the bigger part of the iceberg as they cut across all the visible elements and are crucial for our well-being and mental health.

The point here is that when looking at diversity, even cultural diversity, one should be aware of the invisible aspects of it, even what one might think is visible. For example, in gender diversity, I have known women who are more masculine than men by virtue of working in very male-dominated occupations. They have become more like a man to fit in, to adapt, to blend in, or even assimilate, in order to advance their careers or be more accepted in the workplace.

And so simply saying we have a woman in our ranks may only be a physical manifestation of a diversity, but cognitively, this woman is more male than female and is lacking the feminine traits that are needed. The cognitive diversity in that case, is still pretty low because the dominant traits are still predominantly male, even though she is female. It is important to look beyond visible diversity parameters and consider personality, character traits, and skillsets.

We have internal diversity characteristics that pertain to situations we are born into, with no personal choice, which we cannot change. These include ethnicity, race, gender, origin, age, sexual orientation, physical and mental abilities, gender and cultural identity.

Internal diversity may be visible, but it also may not. External diversity deals with external characteristics that influence a person's abilities. This could be education, geographical location, physical (dis)abilities, socio-economic status, relationships, family status, nationality, personal interests as well as lived experiences which shape our view of the world.

*I went to school with a girl who was adopted from Chile when she was three years old, and spent her entire life, or most of it at least, in Norway with Norwegian parents. If you simply looked at her you would see a Chilean girl with long black straight hair and the facial features of what you might feel is typical of many Chileans. However, language, culture, and worldview wise she was no different from someone born and raised with Norwegian parents. Her sense of cultural belonging is Norwegian - she is Norwegian.*

We often judge people based simply on appearance and, therefore, expect, her to identify herself as South American. Maybe that is what she looks like, but it is not who she is, internally. This is an example of what one may consider a discrepancy between internal and visible diversity.

I may culturally look one way and identify myself differently based on my own circumstances. A child born and raised by African parents in Norway will still look African yet will have a Norwegian and African cultural identity which will vary according to the context. They may possibly identify half the time as African and at other times as Norwegian. Within the family, with the family traditions and customs they may behave or act and identify as 'African'. At school or with friends, they will behave as 'Norwegian'.

I can already see that in my family with my younger siblings who grew up navigating between two cultural contexts - one at home and the other at school.

As a mother of bi-racial children, I can also see their challenge fitting in with two worlds. While they are very much Norwegian, they still get asked questions like 'Where do you come from?' while in Norway simply because of what they look like.

## Worldview Diversity

Several internal and external factors shape our view of the world. Our life experience is the critical factor in conceptualizing how we see and make sense of the world.

As our experiences change, so does our view of the world, this includes our moral compass, our political views, our outlook on life, and the criteria by which we can know what does and does not constitute warranted, or scientific knowledge. Epistemological diversity takes on a transactional subjectivism view where concepts of 'reality,' 'truth', and 'fact' are all relative and semiotic signs that are relative to the person(s) who hold particular sensemaking, constructions, or meanings (Lincoln et al., 2013).

Looking through a diversity lens, I may look very different from my friend, Isabel. She is a white female. We are almost the same age but look so different that one could be forgiven for considering us to be very different both culturally and ethnically. However, we both went to similar boarding schools in Africa, though in different countries, we both grew up during a civil war. In our formative years, we possibly had a similar curriculum and many of the same experiences that shaped the way we think. This makes the two of us quite unique in our understanding of each other.

We click, we see life in a rather similar way. We 'get' each other internally because we are culturally formed by the same philosophy and thus share the same view of the world. We look different and yet we are extremely alike. We had such a good laugh at people hoarding toilet paper at the start of Covid-19. Our civil war experience taught us that access to toilet paper was the least of your worries in a real-life threatening crisis.

Then there is my much younger sister, who spent most of her life in Norway, went to a regular Norwegian school, took hardly any of her education in Africa and does not share any of the same experiences as me. Her cultural or inner background setting is based on the Norwegian culture, curriculum, and school system. My sister like me, is black, but much younger. Seated side by side you would think we are very alike because we should be - we are family and therefore should have the same background. Yet, she and I are less alike than Isabel and I are.

## Organisational/Functional Diversity

This category deals with the different roles assigned to people within the context of the organization which distinguishes one role or employee from another. Assigned roles within an organisation are important as they shape one's life experience and view of the world. These could be job functions, seniority within the organisation, employment status, management status and physical job location and union affiliation.

## Diversity as a Reputation Token

Reputation building is important for organisations, and there is huge potential for boosting one's reputation by taking aspects of diversity and social responsibility seriously. However, many organisations don't realise just how the profitability of diversity is grossly overlooked. It can be incredibly profitable to exploit the enormous economic potential that lies within improving organisational performance through enhancing diversity. That is the concept of performance-enhancing diversity.

This is, today, an untapped resource and probably one of the biggest business opportunities for companies and organisations in the future. We should therefore shift the focus from 'just tolerating diversity' to 'profiting from diversity'. It is far more likely that we will move towards tolerance and inclusion as a society if we focus on the monetary value and profitability of diversity.

Diversity can no longer be just a goal or matrix used to measure and strengthen the company's reputation. Diversity is, first and foremost, an important tool for strengthening the performance of a company or organisation. With a properly composed team comprising people with different abilities, competencies, personalities, geography, gender, age and attitudes, diversity has enormous potential. If we manage to exploit inequality in such a way that we capitalise on the differences, we are better able to strengthen the organisation's performance, competitiveness, work environment, employee loyalty and profitability.

*'Where all think alike, no one thinks very much,'* said the American journalist and author Walter Lippmann. In Liberty and The News, he goes so far as to say, in his critique, *'Americans are willing to die for their country, but not willing to think for it.'*

The danger of narrow-mindedness, discrimination and stupidity increases with the erosion of critical thinking. There is a great danger in seeking to create environments which justify our own beliefs and to recruit people based more on homogeneity rather than the company's need for complementary skills in the workplace.

We must make a conscious effort to improve our performance by enhancing diversity, otherwise many will tend to act consciously or unconsciously in the direction of maintaining the status quo. After all, it is pleasant and comfortable to associate with like-minded people.

Let us take a quick look at PWC's annual Directors Survey for some recent findings:

*Companies are facing disruption from new technologies, geopolitical turmoil, cyber threats, increased regulation, and more vocal investors. Overseeing a company in today's challenging business environment can be difficult. Boards must be able to manage internal and external pressures to be effective. The changing business landscape means boards have more to understand and more to oversee. So they need to have the right people sitting at the table, diverse people with the best skills and expertise for the company to help steer the company toward a successful future.*

*(PricewaterhouseCoopers., 2016)*

*And even while making some improvements in boardroom diversity, directors aren't always convinced of how important that diversity is. While this crisis presents new opportunities for change, the onus remains on directors to make the most of these times.*

*(Price Waterhouse Coopers., 2020)*

# Conceptualizing Performance Enhancing Diversity

It is important to note that not all types of diversity are performance-enhancing. One can easily imagine that too great a spectrum of differences and opposing values can create tension, contradictions, and disharmony that will work against the sought-after cooperative climate in a group. For this reason, it is essential to find out what promotes and what inhibits performance related to diversity as well as find good examples of companies that have succeeded well with performance-enhancing diversity in practice.

Finally, increased globalization, migration, and percentage of women in the workplace, along with a wide range of different attitudes and personalities or people in different phases of life or with special needs; these place greater demands on future leaders to address workplace diversity differently. There is an urgent need for change that must be driven from the top right down through the organisation. It requires a fast discontinuous change to re-create directive change that will radically challenge existing practices.

According to Kurt Lewin, one of the modern pioneers of social, organisational, and applied psychology in the United States, for organisations to succeed in such change, it must be driven by management and be well communicated. There must be a 'felt-need' and understanding in the entire organisation as a collective to accept that this change is necessary for it to succeed (Lewin, 1947).

In short, it starts with the management team and how they see diversity.

Does the management team reflect the desired diversity? There are already many indicators to show that leaders/ or companies who introduce and manage a high range of diversity within their teams are tomorrow's winners.

Initially, having diversity in the workforce was considered to be a corporate social responsibility[1]. However, this has now changed; discrimination in the workplace is no longer just a question of social responsibility, it is now a legal requirement in many countries.

There is limited company data on inclusion based on ability and personality while gender and ethnicity are frequently reported in company annual reports. The focus of this book is to present diversity, equality, and inclusion as performance-enhancing steps which companies must take to thrive. We present the importance of character strengths that can support leaders in enhancing diversity and inclusion. While it cannot cover all the elements of diversity, it touches on gender, culture, personality, and (dis)abilities. Finally, it offers leaders guidelines on how to create great high performing diverse teams. Key research and references have been provided in the book for those who may be interested in going into more depth in particular topics.

---

[1] Social responsibility is defined as *'acting in the interest of others even when there is no legal imperative.'* (De Wit and Meyer 2010 p. 604)

# PART 1
# DIVERSITY

# 1.1: WHY DIVERSITY MATTERS

Recently the photograph of a business leaders' lunch at the Munich Security Conference (MSC) sparked a massive storm of outrage. The picture was taken and shared on Twitter by Michael Bröcker, editor in chief of The Pioneer, a German media group. It showed around 30 older white men in suits seated around a large table. There were no women and from the looks of it, no racial or visible faith diversity that might have been identifiable.

*This picture is like something from another world. But it is not another world. It is a reality in 2022'* Social Democrat lawmaker Sawsan Chebli tweeted. *'There is power here and women are missing here. We still have a lot of work to do.'*

A British academic, Jennifer Cassidy retweeted the image, saying, *'This is the CEO lunch at #MSC2022. This is reality. This is where the power lies. Where some of the most consequential decisions are made.'[2]*

Photograph 1: An all-male business leaders' lunch at the Munich
Security Conference Photographer: Michael Bröcker

---

[2] The picture was widely published. In this book, we reference:
https://www.thestar.com.my/lifestyle/family/2022/02/21/all-male-business-lunch-at-munich-security-conference-triggers-uproaron several media

# Why is diversity still an issue to be addressed instead of the norm?

Diversity is a fact and is part of us being human. After all, no two individuals are identical. Management has always dealt with the coordination of groups and individuals who are different, whether in terms of job, function, organisational role, personality, or other demographic variables. However, there are wide gaps and grey untapped zones when it comes to diversity. For example, there is a big difference between one management team consisting of only older men with financial education and another consisting of a mix in terms of gender, race, education, personality and more.

Since the publication of *Diversity Matters* (2015) and *Delivering through Diversity* (2018), McKinsey & Company has conducted further extensive studies in the period from 2010 - to 2019 looking at the relationship between diversity on executive teams and the likelihood of financial outperforming over time. The findings encompassing fifteen countries and more than 1,000 large companies is published in their latest publication *Diversity Wins: How inclusion Matters* (McKinsey, 2020a).

The results from the first two studies were startling and clear across all geographical areas. It showed the relationship between more diverse management groups and improved financial performance. In this context, diversity was defined as a larger proportion of women and a larger proportion of culture/geography in the management groups. This reaffirmed that there is indeed a strong business case for diversity, not just in terms of gender but also in terms of ethnic and cultural diversity in corporate leadership.

Companies in the top quartile for gender diversity on executive teams were 25% more likely to have above-average profitability compared to companies in the fourth quartile—up from 21% in 2017 and 15% in 2014.

There is substantial evidence that diversity leads to better financial results, and there are strong indications that companies who are aware of improving the diversity in management teams are, on average, more successful because group diversity determines group processes and outcomes.

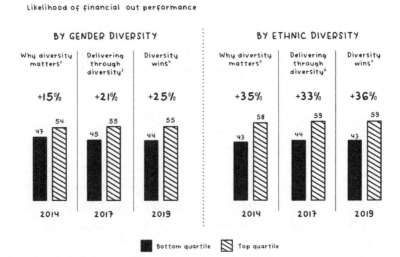

### The business case for diversity in executive teams remains strong.

Likelihood of financial out performance

| BY GENDER DIVERSITY | | | BY ETHNIC DIVERSITY | | |
|---|---|---|---|---|---|
| Why diversity matters[2] | Delivering through diversity[3] | Diversity wins[4] | Why diversity matters[5] | Delivering through diversity[6] | Diversity wins[7] |
| +15% | +21% | +25% | +35% | +33% | +36% |
| 47 / 54 | 45 / 55 | 44 / 55 | 43 / 58 | 44 / 59 | 43 / 59 |
| 2014 | 2017 | 2019 | 2014 | 2017 | 2019 |

■ Bottom quartile  ▨ Top quartile

*Figure 2: Significant correlation between diversity*
*(gender and ethnicity) and financial performance*

In Norway in 2017, Marte Cecilie Wilhelmsen Solheim defended her doctoral dissertation at the University of Stavanger. The research question was:

*'How do diversity and space affect innovation?'*

Her study found that Norwegian companies with a higher percentage of immigrants amongst their employees had better international cooperation and a higher degree of innovation. However, this only applied if the foreign employees had higher education. Organisational psychologist Roger Schwarz, in an article in the Harvard Business Review (2015) entitled *'What the Research Tells Us About Team Creativity and Innovation'* writes about how creativity and innovation require <u>different individual skills sets, team structures, and processes</u>.

Both divergent, as well as convergent thinking, are necessary depending on the innovation stage.

He pointed out that diversity within a creative team only had a positive effect on creativity if the members were able to take on the perspective of others, and had a shared vision, otherwise, the level of conflict increases and destroys the cohesiveness which an innovative team depends on to get results. A common platform of understanding is crucial, especially in a diverse team. Team success will depend on a clear and common understanding of the objectives and tasks. Innovation effectiveness and shared vision are reciprocally and longitudinally related and that shared vision and team dynamics are also reciprocally and longitudinally related (Pearce & Ensley, 2004).

*You can get both the least efficient and most effective teams with diversity – it all depends on how they are led.*

*(Dr Carol Kovach)*

This is shown in the figure below.

## Cross-Culture vs. single culture group effectiveness

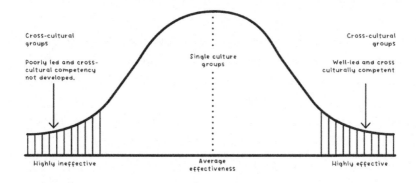

*Figure 3: Significant correlation between diversity (gender and ethnicity) and financial performance*

Diverse teams are both the most and least effective. The ability to lead diversity is crucial to the outcome. There is therefore little reason to measure how diverse a company is. It is what you get out of it that matters.

Today, some companies measure the number of women and the number of people with ethnic minority backgrounds in the company and have these as KPIs in an account of the company's sustainability. What we really should be measuring is the quality of leadership, their competence, the company culture and the effect it has on the performance-enhancing diversity within the company.

## Is Diversity Profitable?

According to a 2018 World Bank paper, Africa alone lost 2.5 trillion Dollars in human capital due to gender inequality. What would be the global figure? What are the effects of such loss on society, business and individuals?

How profitable or loss-making diversity is, cannot be measured on the diversity metrics of a company. What is important to look at is, how being inclusive affects the performance of every level of the organisation right down to the individuals. How does it affect the perception of the company outside its own walls?

Profitability is the result of the combined enhanced performance of every member of the team and the company's relationship with the external environment.

It is the objective of this book to bring to light how diversity is, or can be, profitable. It addresses the pertinent issues, hurdles and obstacles that today render diversity difficult to navigate. It offers practical advice on how to create and develop not only a diverse organisation but rather an inclusive one where people thrive, henceforth enhancing their passion and performance. We note that there is a strong will in most organisations to have inclusive workplaces, but few know just how to do this. In biblical terms, *'The spirit is willing, but the flesh is weak'*.

# Making sense of diversity

Making sense of diversity and inclusion in interpersonal and intrapersonal relations is not an easy task. Taking a simple philosophical approach, one can look at it as a phenomenon. Phenomenology is concerned with how people make sense of the world around them, essentially it is the study of lived experience or the life world[3] (Van Manen, 1997). Our perception of the world is based on the complex mix of our personality, capabilities, competencies, history and experiences. This is not only how we perceive the world but also how we perceive others, and how we execute our jobs.

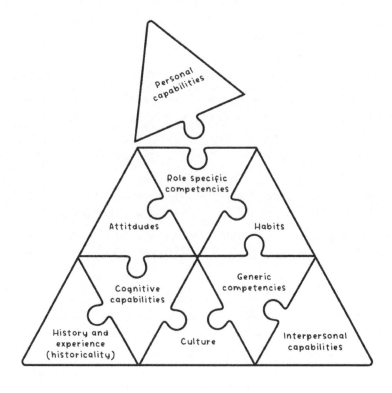

*Figure 4: The pieces of the puzzle of how we see the world the way we do.*

---

[3] When it comes to lived experience, objectivity and facts are not meaningful concepts because meaning is given to the understanding of human actions (Bryman, 2016, p. p. 27). The focus is on peoples' perceptions of the world or the perception of the 'things in their appearing' (Langdridge, 2007).

As a black woman with skin a rather unclear shade of brown, finding cosmetics, especially cosmetics that match my skin tone has always been a struggle. Either I am too dark as is the case most times, or too light for the shades. This made buying cosmetics a necessary evil I endured and never looked forward to.

One morning I walked into the Van Baerle Shopping Gallery by the Conservatorium hotel in Amsterdam and found a store called Skin Cosmetics. I had arrived on a late flight, and in the stress of the journey, I had left my toilet bag on my bed back at home and now had to endure the gloomy affair of sorting myself out. I went into this store just looking for a day cream, toothpaste, toothbrush and hoped to find the bare necessities for a hygienic existence for the two days I would be in the city.

I did not expect, perhaps because of my own prejudice regarding where black women can buy suitable makeup, that I would get anything beyond the day cream, toothbrush, toothpaste, and deodorant. Judging from the location and clientele, I suspected it was an expensive store targeting white women of a certain financial standing.

As I looked at the different face creams, hoping to find one on sale, a very polite, friendly and superb professional young white woman with a beautiful set of teeth behind a genuine smile approached me and asked gently if I needed assistance. Frankly, that was unusual as I am used to being ignored in high end stores.

Possibly because she saw I was stressed and uneasy in that setting, she stood and listened attentively as I told her what I needed. She offered me a seat, a glass of water and returned with a cup of tea.

As I relaxed with the tea and water, she put together a little basket of the products I needed, based on my specifications. We made light conversation through which she picked out key information about my requirements, and perhaps, the need to look my best for the events of the day. She offered to put make-up on me.

*While I was particularly sceptical about how this young white woman in an up-market white store was going to 'paint' me, I was so tired and in need of some care that I accepted her offer. After all, it was free of charge. How bad could it be?*

*When I finally held up her mirror for me to see what she had done, I was in utter disbelief. I had never looked better in my life. The make-up was spot on and beautifully toned.*

*The foundation colour was spot on, the powder was flawless, never mind the rest.*

*How was that possible in a store that did not reflect any traces of 'blackness'?*

*There was no black person or black product brand in there (well, what I know as black) and yet the results were amazing.*

*In short, I bought all the products she had used on my face. I had never heard of the Laura Mercier brand before that moment and because it was such a beautiful experience, I have stuck to the same brand for over five years now.*

*Whenever I am in Amsterdam, I return to that store to buy my skin care and make-up products or the nearest brand distributor.*

*We buy lived experience, and we make sense of our world based on our experiences. I would never possibly have used this make-up or made the irrational decisions to go through the trouble of staying true to the brand for all these years otherwise.*

*Figure 5: What is a profitable client?*

Why does one choose to buy a Samsung phone or an iPhone? Why do you choose between a red or blue dress? What helps you decide on your next make of car? It boils down to how one experiences them. Look at the highlighted words in the figure below: Without diversity, you cannot understand the subtle, unconscious motivations that shape your client's behaviours. How then, can you get the insight to make the valuable transformations grow and profit?

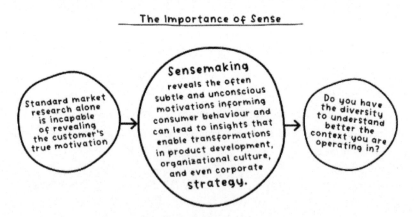

*Figure 6: The importance of Sense making*

This applies to where we want to work as well. We are motivated to work where we are made to feel good about ourselves, where we feel safe. This feeling is by itself not objective. There exists a personal bias resulting from one's own sum of experiences[4].

In my case, why take a detour through Amsterdam to buy make-up there when I can order the same thing online or simply find another store in Oslo? The answer is I felt good, safe and well taken care of in Amsterdam. The sales lady discovered my unmet needs through conversation and met them without any stress for me.

*How do we make sense of our world,*
*our work, our level of safety?*

Acceptance or inclusion in our workplace, in life in general does not occur in a vacuum but rather in the social context of the organisation or society. It is in the context of who we meet, how they respond to and us, and how they are similar or different from us. Every encounter involves an interpretation influenced by an individual's background or 'historicality' (Laverty, 2003).

When my family moved to Norway, my mother insisted on living in a small town, preferably with no immigrants, away from the capital. It was important to her that we were met, judged, included or excluded in the community on the basis of who **we** were, what **we** did and how **we** related to others and **not** on the reputation of other foreigners. And then it was important to her that we were good members of the community because how people experienced **us** would influence how they would then treat others who looked like us.

## Capitalism is the goal

This book is primarily aimed at managers and middle managers who want to improve performance through capitalizing on performance-enhancing diversity. In the business world, performance is largely about creating good profitability over time. The title 'Diversity Capitalism' is chosen on the basis that diversity has a greater potential to be profitable - and not just something you have to

---

[4] This is what Merleau-Ponty called experience through lived mind and body and interactions (Schutz, 1967)

learn to live with. Our intention with the title is to make people take a step back, open their eyes and understand that diversity is vital for future value creation.

Capitalism is a word that is not usually associated with diversity, nor is it a distinctly positively charged word in many places. Diversity, on the other hand, is modern, politically correct, and sounds like social responsibility. For many, capitalism is a word that may be associated with cynicism, abuse of power, and its side effects of divided societies as examples.

The bottom line today, however, is that capitalism exists in various forms in all countries of the world except for North Korea. All countries in the world practice capitalist principles - even those that consider themselves socialist. The classic conflict of interest between labour and capital from the last century is a bygone stage and is unlikely to return.

In capitalism, it is ultimately the customer who decides what is good and bad, what has the right to life, and what has a future. They decide the shape, colour, taste, brand, price, whether they want to buy in-store, or online, have it delivered at the door, in the mailbox, at the post office, and in some cases delivered by drone or printed on a 3D printer. In other words, customers are the market's sovereign chief judge.

The nation-states can to a certain extent set rules, restrictions, customs barriers, taxes and so on, but by and large, it is the customers who ultimately decide. Lower tariffs and cheaper transport make the competition more global in scope. Larger international companies such as Starbucks, Coca Cola, and McDonalds are, in principle, little hindered by the nation-states, although tariff barriers between China and the USA have recently been stepped up somewhat and the war in Ukraine has entailed economic sanctions. International companies have a recipe and a concept and run with this with small adaptations across geographies regardless of what the politicians may like to think.

## Diversity attracts top talent

Greater diversity in a company's management team can provide easier access to top talent across genders and ethnicity. This is because such diversity gives clear signals to potential job seekers. It increases the talent pool by capturing the interest of, for example, more female and more different ethnic talents.

Diversity, inclusion, and equal representation are among increasingly important factors that job seekers are considering when they are looking for employment. In other words, diversity, and inclusion up to and including board level makes your organisation a more attractive workplace.

There is an emerging trend among our job seekers; they want to know about the hiring company's diversity, inclusion, and representation statistics data. More and more candidates have this as one of their criteria when they are researching potential companies. For every ten job seekers on our site, six to seven of them are women and they are interested in the female representation in the company from the board, management, and respective sections in which they may work.

For a long period, there were only Norwegians in Equinor ASA's management team and many of the foreigners I spoke to thought there were limited career development opportunities for non-ethnic Norwegians. Equinor was then largely seen as a politically controlled company with great influence from the largest owners which was the Norwegian government.

However, following the appointment of foreign executive vice presidents, this perception of the company changed quickly. It was also accepted that one could work from England and the USA and still sit in the company's group executive management team.

This change opened up new opportunities and changed perceptions, perspectives, and the narrative around Equinor. The company was seen as inclusive and the motivation for foreigners to work at, or remain in, Equinor changed in a positive way. Equinor was no longer a 'Norwegian company', but a 'multinational company' with great opportunities for everyone including foreigners.

Now they were able to, to a greater extent, recruit far more widely with larger parts of the world as a target area and through this they could get hold of the best qualified and skilled people available. Without sufficient international recruitment, there will soon be a large gap between the need for talent and the access to it. This has a severe impact financially in the form of increased costs, poorer quality of job performance, and increased time spent.

## Diversity strengthens customer service

The development of our understanding of lifestyle, socioeconomic, cultural, or religious drivers and expectations will enable organisations to better adapt their systems and procedures to meet these diverse expectations more fully.

Building a diverse team which is a genuine reflection of the customers you serve, supports a deeper understanding of their needs and increases the opportunities to form those all-important human and more personalized connections that customers seek and value. These exceptional customer experiences in turn produce a virtuous cycle of increasing returns.

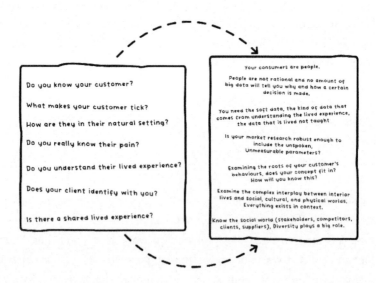

*Figure 7: Diversity as a source of soft data influencing customer behaviour*

A management team needs to have a selection of managers who to a certain extent represent the customers the companies intend to attract. Understanding customers is perhaps the most important skill any company can have. Women account for far more purchases than men as they are most often the primary facilitators for the family. Because of this, it seems reasonable to assume their perspective is also the most important customer perspective.

According to Mark Gungor the speaker, advisor, and comedian who has published several studies on the differences between women and men as customers, women make decisions based on emotions, while men make greater use of facts and data. While men are more loyal to brands, women are more loyal to good customer service (Van Aswegen, 2015). Based on such customer insight, it is better if the management teams do not only consist of men which they often do, especially within retail.

While this may seem like a gender-based simplification, the underlying principle can be translated to other areas of diversity and inclusion as a lived experience.

You could ask, why do people buy a certain product or service?

Perhaps being an engineer puts me in the middle of the stereotypical male/female principles of how we buy what we do. I normally have a set of specifications for what I want to buy, and the idea of general window shopping and trying on various clothes for the fun of it does not exist in my world. However, I will shop where I feel comfortable if I am able to.

In his bestseller 'The Power of Humanities in the Age of Algorithm', Professor Christian Madsbjerg, researcher and philosopher, helps us to better understand sensemaking and how it reveals the often subtle and unconscious motivations informing consumer behaviour and can lead to insights that enable transformations in product development, organisational culture, and even corporate strategy (Madsbjerg, 2016).

Olav had an experience when out shopping for gifts for friends and family which affected his future buying from a particular store which he shares below:

*I was in a small store in our local department store to pick up a gift. I knew the owner well, and she had my loyalty. However, on this particular day, she was not in the store and there was an assistant I had not met before. I went in and politely asked her to take down a beautiful large Kosta Boda plate.*

*She kindly declined to do so. In her words, the plate was too expensive for me to afford and so taking it down was a waste of her time.*

*According to the sensemaking approach, focus is on peoples' perceptions of the world or the perception of the 'things in their appearing' (Langdridge 2007). In this girl's perception of the world, I did not 'appear' rich enough to buy this product. That is something that happens to me rather often, I am afraid.*

*I decided long ago that my money must buy me some joy, that is, it must be joyful to spend it. I walked to the store's competitor and bought all the birthday gifts I needed for that month, spending over 4000 NOK. It was their loss not mine, and for months, I boycotted not just that store but all the franchises.*

*I had left the store feeling judged as wanting and did not return there for some months. However, because I knew the owner to be a kind and inclusive lady, I went to her one afternoon and told her my story of meeting her new assistant. Needless to say, she was mortified to hear it. She then used the experience to send all new employees for customer care training on biases, prejudices, and customer profiling.*

*I was very pleased with how she handled the situation, and I have now remained a faithful, happy, and profitable client.*

How much business is your company losing because some individuals in your organisation have not been open to diversity or acted with prejudice?

How do you know the experience of minorities when it comes to the use of your products or services? Most minorities feel powerless and have been victims of prejudices so often that they no longer bother to report such incidences. Instead, they quietly boycott a product, store, or service.

To get that insight and better understanding, one must seek complexity of views rather than narrow meanings. One must have the diverse experiences, the lived experiences, some of which are never openly discussed. In order to get such customer insight, it is essential that the management teams do not consist only of white men who have little or no understanding or lived experience of the extended customer base beyond market data.

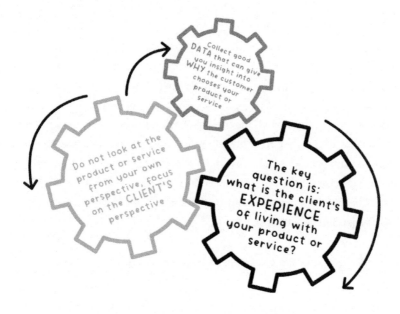

*Figure 8: Diversity and the Lived Experience*

Diversity in management teams helps companies to identify changes in the market faster and more efficiently. Greater diversity in management groups increases the understanding of the varied end users, and thus the response time for adaptations to new trends and customer needs is improved. In other words, a diverse workforce contributes to understanding different customer groups, meets communication more broadly, and captures the needs of different customer groups better.

In the last thirty years, the evidence of creeping diversity in staff and management of the major Norwegian food stores is in their product selection. While there is still a big segregation in the food market with foreigners having their own food stores that bring in the food stuff they desire, the clientele of the foreign shops is changing. The wide selection of fruits, vegetables, lentils, spices and other exotic products draws in the younger Norwegian population, turning areas like Tøyen and Grønland into multicultural food shopping hubs.

In order to compete with this trend, one sees more exotic products making their way into Rema 1000, Joker, COOP, Menu etc. There is more diversity amongst the cashiers and store management too. As an immigrant, I am happy to buy my beans and korma in my local store, it saves me a trip to Oslo. Hence the diversity in product selection also draws in the client group that was left out or increases the range they buy from their local supermarket.

Cultural values and traditions influence the attitudes and behaviour of our customers as well as managers. The values internalized and reflected by every one of us and how we interact with each other are so strongly influenced by culture and identity.  If we don't tap into that internalised influence of culture through diversity in the management group, then better understanding of our diverse client groups will be lost.

H&M has tried to mirror the customer group among its employees locally.

> When customers are diverse, so must we be. It formulates the difference between women and men and the way they shop. Men are on a mission, women on a journey. Men want a fast and efficient trade, while women are looking for a unique experience. Women make purchasing a lived experience.

International companies have often made the mistake of going too far in standardising products and services across geographies. Amongst other things, I well remember that Circle K tried to standardise a coffee concept across nine countries in Europe without considering local preferences for taste in the Baltic countries. In this case, they were forced to reverse this decision as the coffee did not sell there. With a little more international expertise, one would avoid such and similar mistakes.

'Think global - but act local'

as it is so nicely put.

## Diversity Increases Employee Satisfaction

It is not just customers and their different needs that are better served if the diversity of employees is better understood and taken care of by a more diverse management team. Several studies show that diversity in management groups strengthens employee satisfaction and influences positive attitudes and behaviour in the workplace.

For example, it is not surprising that employees from minority groups and/or women in male-dominated occupations get a 'boost' in self-esteem if management groups have a higher degree of diversity: in other words, someone who represents them. In his research, Van Manen (1997) looks at how we create meaning from a lived experience. In this case, the experience of feeling represented in the management team gives a sense of belonging and inclusion.

At the same time, a more diverse management team will also help to break down prejudices in a company.

Employees are often pleased to see one of their kind in the management. There is a very strong symbolic importance of leadership, that 'one of their kind' walks as equals with the bosses, breaking the invisible walls between the majority and minority.

I recall from the discussions in calibration and disposition meetings in Equinor ASA that an employee almost got labelled as a 'nerd' by a manager, in the negative sense, while others felt he was amongst the most valuable resources in the company. It is important to have a broader perspective than one based on individual experiences and/or prejudices.

*❝ Only the wearer knows where the shoe pinches. ❞*

*(Old English Proverb)*

Slightly different perspectives on the part of managers gives greater leeway to be able to see a 'profitable difference' in a company. I am also convinced that a diverse management team has a greater influence than policies on equality, discrimination, etc. in promoting diversity and employee satisfaction. The saying 'Seeing is believing' - probably applies to most of us.

# Diversity Enhances Decision Making

Extensive research shows that there are cognitive limitations and biases in every individual that precludes that individual from making fully value-maximizing choices when making decisions. In their landmark publication in 1974 entitled 'Judgement Under Uncertainty: Heuristics and Biases', Amos Tversky and Daniel Kahneman's 1974 paper reshaped the study of human rationality, and 'behavioural economics.' They investigated human decision-making, and how the brain dealt with uncertainty or complexity. Based on extensive experiments carried out with volunteers, they discovered that humans made predictable errors of judgement when dealing with ambiguous evidence or make challenging decisions as a result of 'heuristics' and 'biases' (Kahneman, 2011; Kelman et al., 2017; Tversky & Kahneman, 1974).

Therefore, greater variation in background and experience within a management team provides a broader approach to different types of issues, counters inherent biases, and thereby strengthens[5] both the ability to innovate and the opportunity to land well-balanced decisions with a higher degree of quality. The level and diversity of skills required in a management team to successfully manage are so wide that they require a good level of diversity, particularly during periods of change and crisis. Here again, it is important that the team members can listen to and take each other's perspectives.

---

[5] As pointed out by Schwarz (2015), even the most diverse teams will fail unless they are willing to listen to each other.

When a group is too homogenous there is a tendency for everyone to strive for consensus. It also implies that even when some members may disagree, rather than override an opinion, members will remain silent, setting aside personal views. It is what the social psychologist Irving L. Janis termed 'groupthink' and 'wilful blindness' (Janis, 1972, 1982). It is an advantage to have some contradictions in a group as this stimulates the discussions and sharpens the concentration which stops the team from acting in this way. In addition to this, the perspective usually becomes more nuanced and holistic when the range of inequality is present.

Some of the most fruitful discussions I have been involved in are those where there is a fundamental disagreement on the issue. Most of the time, these discussions have created a lot of commitment and temperature, but then they have also ended with more nuanced and better decisions; in other words, a high-quality decision-making process and better decision making. This is an example of what Janis (1989) called 'vigilant' decision-making.

In commemoration of the tenth anniversary of the collapse of Lehman Brothers, the US investment bank, Christine Lagarde the leader of the International Monetary Fund (IMF), stressed the need for more gender diversity in the banking sector. She called the collapse of Lehman Brothers a 'sobering lesson in groupthink'. She also wrote that:

> Greater diversity always sharpens thinking, reducing the potential for groupthink'. She added: 'This very diversity also leads to more prudence, and less reckless decision-making which provoked the crisis.
> (Lagarde, 2018)

When I was in the Norwegian management of Statoil Retail Norway, we received information from some 'unfaithful servants' in Shell saying that they intended to launch V-Power, the first quality petrol of its kind in Norway. After a quick discussion, we in the management team agreed to launch our own quality petrol 'Ultima' with nationwide advertising in all newspapers the day before Shell's 'secret' launch date. The fact that we only managed to get Ultima petrol at two stations by the launch date was of less interest. The objective was obviously to cast a shadow and sabotage the competitor's launch.

We did succeed in sabotaging Shell's launch campaign. As they were gathered for the big launch at Fornebu, they were confronted with full-page ads about Statoil's quality petrol Ultima in all the country's national newspapers.

Management needs to be able make snap decisions things as they are unfolding, and in this situation, we certainly were able to make a quick decision. However, this particular decision is not something we are proud of today. Had we had greater diversity in the management team at the time with someone who had challenged our thinking we might have decided differently and better and not fallen victim to groupthink and 'wilful blindness'. It's actually not about winning such marketing stunts, but rather about winning customers by delivering quality and customer service over time. That said, I must admit that we enjoyed it and had a good laugh that sat well in the walls for a long time.

## Diversity as a Driver in Innovation

The first crucial step in any innovation is to create opportunities. Generate ideas and innovative opportunities by identifying gaps, trends, threats, or unmet needs. To get to the great ideas, it is often useful to have a pool of ideas. This supports the premise that the greater the number of people in an organisation who have different life experiences and cognitive diversity, the greater the number and quality of different ideas and solutions that will be generated. There will be more people thinking outside the box to generate solutions and ideas which are better quality.

❝ Diverse and inclusive cultures are providing companies with a competitive edge over their peers. ❞

(Dieter Holger (Wall Street Journal 2019)

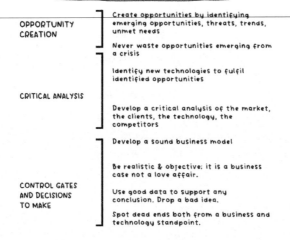

Figure 9: The value of Diversity in Innovation

*❝The best way to have a good idea is to have a lot of ideas.❞*

*(Dr Linus Pauling)*

This quote summarizes conclusions from The Wall Street Journal's first corporate ranking that examined diversity and inclusion among S&P 500 companies. The Journal's researchers' work joins an ever-growing list of studies by economists, demographers, and research firms confirming that socially diverse groups are more innovative and productive than homogeneous groups.

## Critical Analysis in Diverse Teams

A diverse group is better able to critically evaluate the market fit; with diverse life experiences they are able to map the unmet needs and provide better market data for good decision making. Diverse teams are more capable of addressing market segments with demographics similar to the team members. A 2013 Harvard Business Review article by Hewlett et al (2013) reaffirms the known fact that when at least one team member shares a client's ethnicity, the team is more than twice as likely to understand that client's needs than teams where no member shares that trait.

When members of diverse teams see things in a variety of ways, they are poised to recognise new and different market opportunities, and they can better appreciate unmet market needs. Expanded market awareness produces results.

Research provides compelling evidence that diversity unlocks innovation and drives market growth—a finding that should intensify efforts to ensure that executive ranks both embody and embrace the power of differences. Note however, that for innovation, cognitive diversity is crucial. It is of no value to line up diverse people who all think the same or have the same background and hope for diverse ideas.

In this research, which is based on a nationally representative survey of 1,800 professionals, 40 case studies, numerous focus groups and interviews, we scrutinized two kinds of diversity: inherent and acquired.

Inherent diversity involves traits you are born with, such as gender, ethnicity, and sexual orientation. Acquired diversity involves traits you gain from experience. For example, working in another country can help you appreciate cultural differences while selling to female consumers can give you gender smarts. We refer to companies whose leaders exhibit at least three inherent and three acquired diversity traits as having two-dimensional diversity.

By correlating diversity in leadership with market outcomes as reported by respondents, we learned that companies with 2-D diversity out-innovate and out-perform companies with lower levels of diversity. Employees at these companies are 45% more likely to report that their firm's market share grew over the previous year and 70% more likely to report that the firm captured a new market.

2-D diversity unlocks innovation by creating an environment where 'outside the box' ideas are welcomed and heard. When minorities form a critical mass and leaders value differences, all employees can find senior people to whom they go to bat for compelling ideas and can persuade those in charge of budgets to deploy resources to develop these ideas.

Six behaviours, we have found, unlock innovation across the board:

a) Ensuring that everyone is heard.
b) Making it safe to propose novel ideas.
c) Giving team members decision-making authority.
d) Sharing credit for success.
e) Giving actionable feedback.
f) Implementing feedback from the team.

Leaders who give diverse voices equal airtime are nearly twice as likely as others to unleash value-driving insights, and employees in a 'speak up' culture are 3.5 times as likely to contribute their full innovative potential (Hewlett et al., 2013)

Figure 10: Six behaviours that unlock innovation across the board

# Diversity and Reputation

Reputation building and social responsibility have received a higher focus now than ever before. In addition to being perceived positively by potential jobseekers and customers, it will also be perceived positively by authorities and organisations, which in turn can have an impact on the organisation's framework conditions. We see clear trends for companies to go much further than authorities' requirements and take greater social responsibility in many areas. They want to emphasise that they contribute something positive towards society to get 'goodwill' back, amongst other things.

You gain access to a more diverse talent pool when you are seen as an employer that embraces diversity. Employees are not the only ones who have expectations regarding diversity; customers do as well. Diversity is critical to your brand reputation, from both a workforce and customer perspective.

NorgesGruppen ASA is the biggest wholesaler and retailer in Norway. They have realised that they are such a large player in the grocery trade that they can no longer go under the radar for society as the media's critical spotlight is on their dominant position.

NorgesGruppen has the ambition to become 'climate neutral' by 2025 with owners who are willing to go to great lengths to make it happen and who are very conscious of taking a lead in health and welfare. They all agree on strengthening their attractiveness as employers for people with a minority background and they are among the best in class in the area with as many as 47 different nationalities employed.

KIWI, a soft discount chain in NorgesGruppen was the first to get the Hijab as part of the work uniform in the country. This was very positively received and meant that they gained a competitive advantage in recruiting people with a minority background.

# 1.2: FROM AFFIRMATIVE ACTION TO PROFITABILITY

Diversity in business is a word that has a screaming need for more practical content. Performance-enhancing diversity is a position white spot no one has properly taken. We all talk about tolerance and social responsibility related to diversity, and that we should generally be more tolerant towards each other. The intention is certainly good, but tolerance is not a positively charged word in my world. Tolerance probably says something first and foremost about how many side effects one is willing to accept. For example, how many side effects can one live with when using a drug, and how much difference can we tolerate?

Tolerance tends to pacify us. People talk about it, but little happens in practice. We must act – and the motivation to act is greater if something is profitable. In other words, motivation is linked to expectations of a positive return. For us to have a positive return, the sum of the advantages must outweigh the disadvantages and costs. In other words, we need to know how diversity can be profitable if we want to do something about it.

Understanding the concept of diversity is about acknowledging similarities, but also appreciating differences. The business community in most countries faces two parallel challenges: to expand the diversity of top management in companies and organisations and to develop knowledge about shaping and utilizing the resources and skills that a diverse workforce possesses. The focus in recent years has been on increasing the number of women in top management, while the real needs in the business world go far beyond this. The most important element of performance-enhancing diversity may not be what we can see, but what is in the minds of everyone.

Diversity is more than simply women and culture. It also deals to a great extent with differences in what is in the brain of everyone such as competence, personality, attitudes, and more.

# The Downsides of Diversity

Increased scope of diversity does not necessarily have positive effects in all contexts. Robert Putnam found in a study of more than 30,000 interviews in the United States that a greater degree of diversity in a neighbourhood meant that fewer people used the ballot, fewer participated in volunteer work, fewer contributed to non-profit organisations, and health among the population was generally poorer (Putnam, 2007). It is worth noting that several scholars (Abascal & Baldassarri, 2015) have challenged the interpretation of the research data by Putnam.

When it comes to trust, or likely, lack of trust, it is rather an issue of prejudice rather than diversity per se (Abascal & Baldassarri, 2015; Grewal, 2016).

Modern societies are becoming increasingly multi-ethnic, spurring debates, tensions, challenges, as well as opportunities. That increased diversity in societies due to factors such as migration poses challenges, is a reality that is not necessarily politically correct for those of us who want to see the benefits of diversity. Nevertheless, this is relatively solid data from a comprehensive survey that we simply cannot ignore.

Good social networks in neighbourhoods are built up of commitment to common interests, friendships, religion, and much more and, according to Putnam, such similarities and common interests will strengthen 'social capital'. Neighbourhoods with less diversity lived longer, had better health, better trust in each other, used their right to vote more often, had better health, and were far happier with their lives.

With Putnam's research as a starting point, how can we explain that economic metropolis such as New York, London, and Los Angeles are the most innovative and profitable multicultural centres; in neighbourhoods where people seek out and relate to diversity to a lesser extent, diversity will not necessarily strengthen the social environment and the closeness between people. It takes listening, trust, respect, and acceptance of different perspectives.

# Diversity without Trust is Dead

It is said that faith without work is dead, and so is diversity without trust. Trust is a critical element in the interpersonal and group dynamics in every workplace. Without trust, it is difficult to work towards mutual goals, as individual goals and intentions will override any collaboration and cooperation. Trust is easier in a homogenous environment, however with increased diversity, some inherent biases and prejudices hinder trust. As humans, we are more willing to share information and accept being influenced by people we trust.

| What to do: | Why you should do it: |
| --- | --- |
| Make the Connection. | **To reap trust, you must sow trust.** Trust is a willingness to accept vulnerability based on positive expectations of trustworthiness. |
| Be Transparent and consistent in behaviour | **Building trust is a continuous process** Trust is a dynamic ongoing process. Outcomes of trusting behaviours affect perceived trustworthiness. |
| Be honest and truthful | **You are only as good as your word.** Propensity to trust is based on expected ability, integrity, and benevolence. |
| Take blame and responsibility, give credit where it is due. | **For people to depend on you, you must be dependable.** Cognitive-based trust is based on the available knowledge about the trustee's competence, reliability, and dependability. |

| | |
|---|---|
| Empathy and compassion go a long way | **Lead with the heart.** Affective-based trust is based on emotional investments, genuine care, and concern for the welfare of others and the belief that these sentiments are reciprocated. |
| Be just | **Don't play favourites in a team.** Trust in teams involves a continuous social process of sensemaking, interpreting, signalling, and reciprocity. |
| Lead not command | **Be encouraging not commanding** You catch more flies with honey than with vinegar |

*Figure 11: How to build trust*

Where there is a low level of trust, we are more likely to see conflicts, withholding information, and further deepening the level of mistrust. The symbiosis between the crocodile and the Egyptian plover bird in the photograph below only exists because of deep trust between the two parties. One may consider the organisation as the crocodile, powerful, in control, and an individual with a minority background as the plover bird. The bird trusts the crocodile not to devour it as it cleans the crocodile's teeth.

*Figure 12: The Nile Crocodile and the Plover*

Professor Ana Cristina Costa has researched the role of trust extensively in the workplace. Trust is a psychological state based on the expectations, perceived motives and intentions of others, as well as being a manifestation of behaviour towards others. According to the research, our willingness to trust others is rooted in our personality, cultural background, education, and several other socioeconomic factors. Our perceived trustworthiness is the expectation and considerations about motives and intentions underlying our actions and trust behaviours. In short, we trust because we see trustworthiness, once that trust is abused, or violated, it is hard to re-establish it. Without trust, we cannot get out of our defensive positions. Without trust, we cannot build team coherence and good performance.

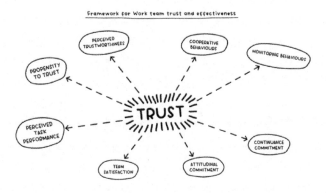

*Figure 13: Framework for Work Team Trust and Effectiveness (Costa, 2003)*

To build a working diverse culture, one must build trust between everyone. Researchers looking at the effects of demographic diversity on trust in teams in terms of nationality, age, and functional background, concluded that diversity was negatively associated with team trust and perceptions of trustworthiness between members. We are, as people, afraid to trust people who are different from us. Hence, the most important job managers can do is to promote trust within diverse teams to harness the most value and enhance performance.

In neighbourhoods, we largely seek out attitudes and interests that correspond to our own. On the other hand, within companies comprising highly competent personnel, diversity becomes the cement that strengthens performance. Different perspectives provide better insight, better breadth of expertise, and strengthens competitiveness. In a diverse company you activate innovation, perspective, and competence.

Boston Consulting Group (Lorenzo et al., 2018) has also looked at the extent to which diversity affected financial performance by looking at 1,700 companies in eight different countries. They found a statistically significant correlation between diversity in management teams and innovation with consequent financial performance in all countries. This can be attributed to the improved understanding of the market through life experience and soft data.

## Performance as a Criterion for Selection

Diversity is crucial for future competitiveness, but before you get to that point, you must have a good foundation in place. Diversity won't help completely if the sum of individual skills is not good enough in the team or group. In other words, differences can only, to a small extent, compensate for the lack of individual performance.

Basic high performance at the individual level must be at the foundation and is in many ways a prerequisite for a high-performing group or organisation. Having a football team consisting of good interaction and good complementing skills does not help much if the average of the individual skills is only on a par with non-professional players. In other words, complementary skills must come as an added value beyond good individual skills as a basis, if one is to capitalise on diversity in practice and be competitive in a demanding and competitive market.

Differences are also not a good enough argument in a recruitment process if the individual skills are not sufficient. Good and different, on the other hand, are not to be despised. It is the combination that makes it explosive. Let us, therefore, take a closer look at the foundation (the individual skills) before we look at the composition and group dynamics.

# Individual Versus Group Performance

People perform differently in different roles, stages, and parts of society, at all levels of an organisation, and across different geographies. At school, in sports, and in a job situation, there is a normally distributed curve consisting of individual performance variations. This is not something you can sweep under the rug for ideological reasons or because for some reason you do not like it that way. It is a reality we must deal with, and an opportunity we can use if we are to be better than the competition at recruiting and, most importantly, retaining skilled employees.

Of course, it is more difficult to measure job performance than it is to declare a winner in a high jump competition. However, this is not a valid reason for not measuring performance variations in business. Through my various roles as HR director in larger Norwegian companies, I have carried out many measurements of what performance variations cost in monetary terms.

*Poor performance is a costly affair.*

The difference between a good and average general manager at an average petrol station in Norway is measured at approximately 100 000-dollar per annum EBIT (In Circle K we had 2200 petrol stations in Europe).

The difference between a high-performing and an average store manager within the grocery trade in Norway is somewhere between 100 000 and 500 000 USD in EBIT per year depending on the store's size and turnover.

If the worst 20% of store managers had performed on a par with the 20% best, NorgesGruppen as a group would have earned 50 000 000 USD more per annum in profit before taxes.

This says a bit about the potential that lies in having the right man or woman in the right place in business-critical positions, and it is not surprising that the cumulative effect over a year is so high. If you go into a grocery store where the vegetable department looks cluttered, you immediately realise that the store is poorly managed which results in falling sales, food wastage, low customer satisfaction and numbers, reduced profit, and other factors which over time constitute a significant loss of profit.

It is not only at the management level that large performance variations were found.

We also found differences between:

1) Great and average sales personnel at a Statoil petrol station measured in average sales per customer. The top 10% bestsellers had an average sale per customer that was as much as 70% higher than the 10% lowest performing, and that is only on average sales. In addition, there is reason to believe that the best sales personnel also generate higher sales through good customer care and more.

2) The best and the average prescriptions for care sales in a large pharmacy chain. The best percentage of prescription customers who buy something in addition to the prescription is 84%. The lowest performers are about 12%. In other words, it amounts to a substantial difference not only with the prescription customers. An average shopping cart in Apotek1 was 16 dollars for the best employees compared to 9 dollars for the lowest-performing employees. This makes a huge difference in revenue over time.

# Competence, Motivation, And Financial Results

There are competent and motivated people behind all the good results an organisation has generated and will generate in the future. If this is the case, we must be better than the competition at recruiting, developing, and retaining competent and motivated people.

This is a prerequisite for being able to create good results in an organisation. In addition, if you manage to spice up the team with performance-enhancing diversity, as an organisation or group you will most likely go from good to best.

We should ask ourselves:

- Are we as an organisation better than the competition at recruiting competent and motivated people?
- Do we have better objectives, strategies, processes, systems, tools, tests, etc. that make it probable that over time we are better than the competitors at this?
- Are we better at training our managers and employees so that they develop faster than the competition in critical areas of competence?
- Can we keep the best in a world where head-hunters make good money from the best job changers?

# 1.3: BRING OUT THE BEST

## It Starts with Culture

*There is no good or evil. Performance depends on the fit between strategy and culture. First, you need to know where you want to go but where you want to go has to fit with your culture. Both depend on each other. You cannot generalise it.*

*(Geert Hofstede)*

There is often an ideological discussion about how to invest in bringing out the best in the organisation's human resources. Some focus mostly on talent development while others are more concerned that everyone should participate, and that there is talent in all of us. In the USA, the focus is to a greater extent on talent development, while in Scandinavia there is traditionally a greater focus on the development of all the organisation's employees. This difference is what is described as a means-oriented culture (Scandinavia) where the way (how) we work is important versus the goal-oriented (what we achieve) culture in the USA. We would argue that both ideologies have their strengths and weaknesses, and they should be able to co-exist in a divergent and inclusive organisational culture.

*The core of the matter lies in organisational culture.*

*How can we create good culture*

*where everyone is able*

*to thrive and grow?*

In a diverse organisation, one will find employees who are highly driven, and task oriented as well as those who are not. There will be some who are focused on control, punctuality, discipline, and structure, which is vital for some roles such as accounting, finance, and management of change to name but a few. Yet, you will also find those who have an easy-going, fluid, responsive, unpredictable but creative style of work. This too has its place in certain innovative roles.

Knowing that people differ in the way they work and see the world and the ability of an organisation to be open and accessible, particularly for underrepresented members, is a vital ingredient in determining how inclusive it becomes.

For example:

1) How are newcomers welcomed into the organisation?
2) Does everyone fit in or are there two camps with one for the insiders and one for outsiders?
3) When an employee faces challenges, do they feel supported by the organisation?
4) Is there empathy?
5) Does the organisation have a heart?

At the heart of the matter is the organisational culture. Is the organisational culture motivating and empowering to employees, allowing them to take the actions necessary to achieve the business strategies?

Geert Hofstede, the father of modern-day Organisational Culture defines it as how members of an organisation relate to each other, their work, and the outside world in comparison to other organisations.

It is the *'That's how we do things around here'* of your organisation. It refers to how your company conducts itself, which includes the unique ways in which it drives business activities, processes, and philosophies.

We believe organisations must develop trust in the working environment, particularly where there is a need for a high level of Interdependence between departments, close cooperation, teamwork, and flexibility. No talent will remain in a bad organisational environment.

If you want to bring out the best in human resources, it is probably most appropriate to think of two things simultaneously. You need to facilitate the development of everyone whilst also taking care of the greatest talents. If you do not take good care of the talents, it is highly likely that others will do it for you, especially your competitors and that really is not good for business.

Ideology is a very bad starting point for making good business decisions as it tends to overshadow the sensible and more pragmatic vigilant decision-making process. It is not good enough that something works in theory, if it is to have any tangible effects, it must work in practice. An organisation without heart or empathy is likely to lose the individuals who not only possess, but also value, soft skills leaving behind only a harsh competitive workplace which will eventually lose all the other top talent.

As a leader, it is essential to create the arena where your players feel safe, build trust that can get everyone performing. The question is how?

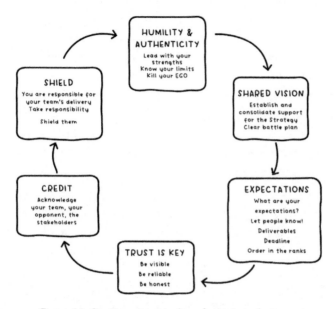

**HUMILITY & AUTHENTICITY**
Lead with your strengths
Know your limits
Kill your EGO

**SHIELD**
You are responsible for your team's delivery
Take responsibility
Shield them

**SHARED VISION**
Establish and consolidate support for the Strategy
Clear battle plan

**CREDIT**
Acknowledge your team, your opponent, the stakeholders

**EXPECTATIONS**
What are your expectations?
Let people know!
Deliverables
Deadline
Order in the ranks

**TRUST IS KEY**
Be visible
Be reliable
Be honest

*Figure 14: Creating a team culture for high performance*

# 'A' player in 'A' position – the right person in the right spot at the right time

One of the most important things you can do to contribute to greater value creation in an organisation is to get the greatest talents into the most business-critical roles ('A' players in 'A' positions). First, you must identify the greatest talents in the organisation based on well-thought-out criteria. Because talent is evenly distributed in the population, by focusing on talent as a key criterion, you have a good starting point for a less biased organisational constellation. Second, plans must be made to get the best people into the most business-critical positions. It does not help to have identified a talent if you are not able to use the talent where the person gives the best return for the company and has true job satisfaction.

You lose a lot of money by having a 'B' player in an 'A' position as then the company loses money, but it is just as bad to have an 'A' player in a 'B' position as then you do not utilise the capacity that exists in the organisation in the best possible way.

Many people struggle a little to differentiate people based on their performance, and some even believe that the vast majority perform at the same level. Some managers give their employees the same salary regardless of their performance and base promotions more on seniority, competence, and experience than on good performance over time. One could say a lot about this but would rather refer to a more poignant wording from Richard Beatty known for the book 'The Workforce Scorecard' (Huselid et al., 2005) in a lecture at a business partner programme in Utah.

> If you don't differentiate on performance,
> you will win the losers and lose the winners.

(Richard Beatty)

There is little to suggest that there is good economics in winning the worst and losing the best people over time. Therefore, managers must dare to differentiate on performance assessments, salaries, career development, and more.

In 2005, Equinor ASA introduced a new performance management system. This system assessed managers on a scale from 1-5 on deliveries and 1-5 on behaviour. With this as a starting point, one could put the leaders in 25 different 'boxes' based on their different achievements.

Before the first calibration meeting with the new system in the company, we saw a 'plot diagram' of how all the managers had been assessed. What that plot diagram showed was that we as leaders were terrible at differentiating. As many as 97.5% ended up in 4 out of 25 possible boxes. I recall that the CEO, Helge Lund asked us to redo the job with clear expectations of a higher degree of differentiation.

The ultimate performance principle for companies is to work to get the best people into the most business-critical positions. The principle is as follows:

1) Define the organisation's greatest talents based on clear overall criteria.
2) Define business-critical positions, which is to say the positions where performance variations have the greatest impact on the company's financial results.
3) Plan how to get the company's greatest talents into the most business-critical positions.

In other words, have the right players in the right positions.

# Diversity Without Inclusion Is a Waste

However, having the right players in the right positions does not guarantee a win if the team is not playing as a team. To play as a team, you need to go beyond looking at diversity and start working on inclusion and building trust in the organisation. Diversity is not synonymous with inclusion, although many organisations hold this view which is erroneous.

In the 2018 September Gallup report, Ella Washington and Camille Patrick (2018) go on at length to dissect diversity and inclusion and agree that diversity represents 'the full spectrum of human demographic difference', both the visible and the invisible.

Putting a broad spectrum of people together and then just expecting enhanced performance is pointless without inclusion, and inclusion is that feeling of belonging.

- Do I as an employee feel included in the team?
- Does my opinion matter?
- Am I respected and valued?
- Am I treated with acceptance and respect so that I can let my guard down, and trust my environment enough so I can be myself?

> ❝ Fish rots from the head down. ❞
>
> *(African proverb)*

As with diversity, inclusion requires that the management has clear goals and values set out. The CEO should spearhead diversity and inclusion goals, and these must be anchored in all levels of the organisation.

It is said that actions speak louder than words. The behaviour of the management and their teams sends a clear message to the rest of the organisation. The passivity of leaders and a lack of reflection on inclusion and diversity at the top may influence subordinates and others to believe that passivity is the appropriate response. Often, it is unclear who is responsible for diversity and inclusion in a company. It is assumed that it is something HR must handle, often without clear strategic goals. Diffusion of responsibilities in the top management often leads to passivity and chaos in the subordinate teams and mid-level managers because defuse roles and responsibility creates a lack of psychological 'ownership' of a problem. When there is no 'ownership' of a problem, there is automatically a sense of diminished perception of available support when it comes to that problem. (Mueller, 2012)

Without the clear intention of management to create an inclusive and accepting environment, it is unlikely that inclusion will happen automatically. The goals for inclusion must be actionable, measurable, and evidence based. The challenge for many managers will be how to monitor and promote inclusion. Because inclusion is a life experience that varies from person to person, managers must use multiple ways to assess the work environment.

Miles and Huberman (1994) promote qualitative research as a source for well-grounded, rich data and identification of processes within a local context (p.1). When it comes to human experience, managers are encouraged to gather qualitative (soft) data such as employee narratives, conduct interviews, surveys, observations etc. The sustained period of continuous monitoring of change in the workplace and data collection needs to be firmly established in the locality. Experience is subjective, and it is important that managers collect information from the right people. If you want to know how a certain minority are doing in your workplace, ask them. They know what constraints, hurdles, and challenges they come across.

# Continuous Improvement

## Why everyone needs to get 10% better at their job every year

In addition to getting the best people in the most business-critical positions, you need to work systematically to bring out the best in everyone. Not everyone in an organisation can be top talent and that would hardly work in practice either. There is no conflict of interest with investing in top talents whilst bringing out the best in everyone else as well. It is possible, even desirable, to have both. It is this pragmatic approach that is the most profitable over time.

All employees and managers must in collaboration, create a development plan that aims to make them at least 10% better at their job each year. Development can take place through strengthening work experience, knowledge, and skills as well as regulating/strengthening one's behaviours which are important for job performance. In this work, it may make sense to draw inspiration and learn from the best by reducing the performance variations in the company.

## Comparison and measurement as a source of inspiration

We are not all cut from the same cloth, we are as people diverse and excel at different things. It is like the story of the hare and the tortoise who were competing in a race. While the hare had the speed, the tortoise had endurance. As the story goes, the hare ran fast, then fell asleep under a tree close to the finishing line. Meanwhile, the slow tortoise persevered, slowly but steadily until he crossed the finishing line and subsequently won the race.

If you want to get inspiration from top performers, you must use the comparison as a source of inspiration for everyone otherwise the comparison may well make people feel inferior. Unfortunately, many companies have fallen into this trap. The yardstick is not recommended even though it seems to be a popular tool for some leaders.

My mother was probably not the best educator in the world, narrates Olav, she made me aware of the fact that my sister had far better grades than I did in high school. Though she had the best of intention by trying to motivate me, instead I felt inferior and lost any motivation to make changes. If, on the other hand, she had used the comparison as a source of inspiration, this could probably have influenced the desire to work harder.

She could have said:

*'She has managed it, I'm sure you can do it too. If you just set aside a little more time for your schoolwork you will get there too.'*

Such encouragement and belief in my abilities would have made me more motivated with better results as the outcome.

# 1.4: ENHANCING PERFORMANCE

It is, of course, essential to be able to tell someone which qualities and skills help performance in an organisation. Economic results are, after all, a reflection of the sum of human achievements over time, no matter how you turn it around. There is not necessarily an unambiguous answer to this in research, but some character traits and skills seem to be more important than others.

Having examined ethical leadership, servant leadership, and emotional intelligence through the analysis of published studies to ascertain any shared characteristics contributing to effective leadership, Lumpkin and Achen (2018) concluded the following 10 shared characteristics were vital for effective leadership.

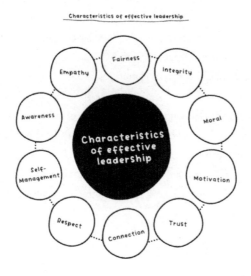

*Figure 15: Ten shared characteristics vital for effective leadership*

They concluded that leadership effectiveness increased when leaders demonstrated integrity, trust, and respect, served others with empathy and fairness, and were personally and socially competent.

In this section, we will take a closer look at the role of character strengths that are not only important for the leadership of a diverse team but for enhancing diversity within the team as well.

# The Importance of Character

Why is character important in all this? Well, a growing body of research, documents that people with certain traits are performing better in work life, making more money, or excelling in their core activities such as competitive sports. Because character governs day-to-day lives, and performances, it is worth looking at it and trying to get a deeper understanding not just how we function as individuals but how this subsequently affects how we function as a group, and a diverse group at that. We believe this understanding will contribute greatly to the performance of the organisation.

Character is particularly challenging in diverse teams, especially at the start when there is a low level of trust as there will be biases and fear. The pattern of interaction will influence the group dynamics.

Christopher Peterson and Martin Seligman, pioneers in positive psychology, put together a theoretical framework on character strengths and virtues based on extensive research that reveals these traits are good in all cultures, throughout history, and across all diversity boundaries. In their book Character Strengths and Virtues (2004), the duo presented 24 character strengths organised into 6 virtues:

- Wisdom and strength
- Courage
- Humanity
- Justice
- Temperance
- Transcendence.

According to Peterson and Seligman (2004), character strengths are defined as 'habitual actions' (p. 76) that are 'stable yet malleable' (p. 12) and are 'shown to have tangible consequences' (p. 85).

Character strengths can be acquired and contextualised, we can learn, mould, and master character traits (Peterson & Seligman, 2004; Seijts et al., 2018) gives us a simplified presentation of the different components that come together to determine character strength.

Character reflects our inner habits of cognition, emotion, volition, and behaviour such as personality traits, and values, that enable sensemaking, leadership, judgement, good decision making, and subsequently performance excellence. (Crossan et al., 2017; Seijts et al., 2018).

In their extensive research, Seijts et al (2018) found that despite the importance of character traits, leader character was not a topic well discussed or researched. This is despite a plethora of corporate crises that can be linked to inadequate or weak corporate governance such as the banking sector issues that led to the 2008 financial crisis, the Volkswagen emissions scandal, and the collapse of Enron, to name but a few. Leaders with bad character traits are often associated with toxic, coercive leadership. In such organisations, fear of the toxic leader means that negative feedback will not be shared openly due to fear of reprisals or reprimand.

We can look at character from two perspectives: performance character, and moral character. While the focus of this book is on performance character traits, moral character is critical too for ethical leadership and compliance and is discussed further down. As such, we focus on the character strengths that promote good leadership, which is judgement and what constitutes good judgement.

# Judgement

At the heart of the framework of Crossan et al (2017) leader character shown in Figure 16 is judgement. The ability to make sound and timely decisions requires more than just intelligence. Good judgement is the foundation on which good leadership is built.

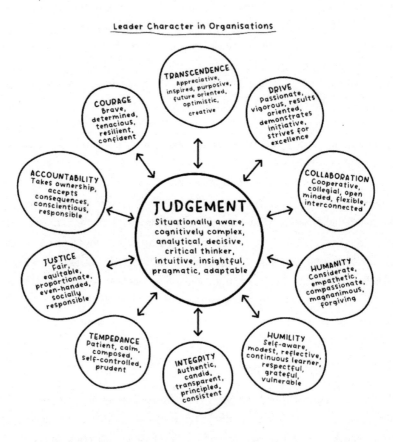

*Figure16: Revised Framework of Leader Character in Organisations (Crossan et al., 2017)*

Good judgement is itself based on good situational awareness. Managers need to understand their environment, both internal and external. Often, organisations are great at top-down communication but terrible at the bottom-up feedback loop. Hence management may maintain policies they believe to be working while in fact, they are detrimental to the strategy. In some cases, all the procedures, frameworks and processes may exist, made with the best of intentions, yet fail miserably because management did not have a good enough understanding of the 'low simmering' issues that never made it to the management meetings.

It is obviously better to think fast and right rather than slow and wrong. The individual's ability to think is often a success factor in both a leadership role and an employee role. Relatively high intelligence is an advantage in working life in many types of positions. Among other things, it says something about how one can master complex issues, how quickly one can solve different tasks, and with what precision.

Research shows that to manage complex situations and teams successfully, leaders must be adaptive and flexible to be able to deal with cognitively and analytically complex problems and challenges. Part of the complexity is rooted in how they handle the diversity of views, cultures, personalities, competencies, abilities, and working styles. It all starts with listening.

In order to make good judgement, leaders must be able to gather, analyse and make sense of information. Such information should come from multiple sources to reflect different views, experiences, and scenarios. Based on this information analysis, they make sound decisions. Unfortunately, we live and work in constantly changing environments and situations yet decisions must be made under these highly dynamic, uncertain, and complex decision-making environments (Alison et al., 2015; House et al., 2014).

This requires that the leaders be not only intelligent but possess good social and cognitive skills, those often-called soft skills which are vital for human relations such as a good dose of common sense, curtesy, decency, humility, and empathy. Simply put, likeable and approachable. These are the type of skills needed to promote interpersonal communication, understanding and make judgement calls towards the goals set out. This requires intelligence.

# Intelligence

Intelligent people tend to be more creative, better problem solvers, and better at understanding highly difficult issues. It is especially important when it comes to keeping a good overview when planning and solving complex issues under time pressure. They are likely to be decisive and critical thinkers who can act intuitively, and insightfully.

Hard work and great commitment can, to some extent, compensate for intelligence. You do not have to have a high IQ to be a good leader either. It can work well with a strong will, the interest, and hard work. However, many believe that the intelligence of a leader should preferably be slightly above the average of the population, for example somewhere between 110-125 (100 is the average for the total). As a result, it has now become more common for recruitment processes to use different variants of cognitive proficiency tests as one of several 'selection criteria', an important supplement in a comprehensive recruitment process.

Intelligence corresponds significantly to job performance. New studies refer to correlations between 'General cognitive ability' and job performance of as much as 0.62 (Salgado & De Fruyt, 2017)), and it is almost a little scary. In practical terms it means that you explain performance in business with approximately 35% based in general mental abilities. No other recruitment method has a higher match with job performance. Do we envisage an increasing sorting society in the business world in the future?

It is not necessarily the case that extremely high intelligence such as Mensa candidates over 131 is only beneficial to working life. Often, highly intelligent individuals want to immerse themselves in a narrower subject area. Therefore, they often become a little too intellectual and theoretical, finding it difficult to fit into a defined corporate culture. Nevertheless, they can function well in demanding professional positions and come up with ingenious solutions in important areas.

I once tried to find the 'success profile' of managers in a grocery chain by testing the 10% highest performing and 10% lowest performing in terms of financial parameters, up to personality, cognitive abilities and more. Above a certain level (100), it did not appear that higher IQ led to better job performance. On the other hand, it was clear that performance fell quite sharply at levels below 90, and that is perhaps not so strange. In addition to not being as good at thinking fast and correctly, a leader with a lower IQ might feel 'threatened' by 'smarter' employees?

One can imagine that this in turn affects both self-confidence and leadership style. Perhaps low-intelligence extroverts become more authoritarian while low-intelligence introverts tend to be more withdrawn? For example, there is reason to believe that it is more difficult to explain decisions rationally with poorer reasoning capacity and that it can quickly develop into; *'It will be like this because I say so'* - which is probably not automatically perceived as trustworthy or acceptable by the employees.

In a study by Flynn and Shayer (2018) that was widely circulated in online newspapers in December 2017, the average IQ in western European societies has fallen quite significantly since 1995. If the trend continues, the average IQ will have fallen by as much as 6.5 points over a generation (30 years). They wonder if this may be related to the enormous influence of technology. More time, from four to five hours a day with more on weekends, was spent on TV, computer games, and mobile phones, all of which weaken the ability to pay attention and solve problems.

❝ *Never underestimate the power of stupid people in large groups.* ❞

*(George Carlin)*

There are probably still many who do not take IQ tests seriously, but if you doubt that they are a highly relevant measure of important abilities in a human being, you are far beyond what is a scientific consensus. The higher the IQ you have, the higher the probability that you earn well, have good health, have high life expectancy, and generally score well on most of life's success indicators.

There is reason to believe that a fall of 6-7 IQ points will be reflected in the degree of innovation in society in the future. This will lead to fewer highly productive taxpayers. If it reflects a general decline in intelligence, it will, amongst other things, give us more crime than we would otherwise have, and poorer health in society. In total, this is likely to cost our society billions.

# Courage

*Courage is the most important of all the virtues.*

*(Maya Angelou)*

Without courage, one cannot consistently practice all the other virtues. Without courage, it is difficult for leaders to make high-quality decisions. It takes courage to step outside of the cognitive limitations and biases that enable the continued existence of segregation and discrimination.

It is that courage which allows us to make difficult decisions that we may be criticised for by our peers. Leadership is not a popularity contest. Especially for leaders in the public sphere, there will be a level of fear of public judgement and crucifixion.

Research shows that for example, politicians, whose power, reputation, and future careers are in the hands of the voting population, have a strong incentive to avoid blame (Kuipers & Brändström, 2020; Moynihan, 2012). It also showed that the biggest fears were particularly related to those actions that are public, irrevocable, and hard to undo or disown (Boin & t' Hart, 2003; Weick, 1988).

Racial discrimination, slavery, or emancipation of women would never have ended or come through without the courage that those pioneers had or would not have endured for so long if perhaps some leaders had dared to go against their peers and the public.

While the modern-day leader may not face such huge issues, introducing change in any organisation will be met with resistance, hence one must have the confidence and courage to execute the right quality decisions such as to enhance the diversity in the workforce.

Because the world is getting borderless, conducting business across cultures introduces a level of complexity that demands diversity in the organisation and in the leadership. It is courage and humility which enable good leaders to listen to their teams and advisors across cultural boundaries. It takes good listening to make good decisions and take timely action. It then takes courage to follow up to ensure the implementation of the decision, especially where there has been resistance and opposition happens.

In their research, Alison et al (2015) found that decision tasks which are not time critical, involved multiple agencies, and with no clear strategic direction had a higher likelihood of failure. One may say that this is symptomatic of large organisations, political and bureaucratic processes with unclear roles, strategies, and task communication. The organisation will have visions, goals, and strategies, but the more people who are involved in the implementation then the more likely it is to fail. The company becomes like a huge tanker which by virtue of its size takes a long time to turn or change direction compared to a small motor cruiser that could turn immediately.

Many companies have diversity and inclusion goals and strategies but with minimal implementation. This is partly due to 'everyone' being involved in the strategy and no one person taking decisive action and stepping into the unknown.

As a hiring manager, it will take courage to hire a person so different from the majority. It is a risky thing to do. Many questions pop up in the process along with a genuine fear of making a mistake.

At the individual level, it takes courage to step into the unknown, to be that minority struggling to prove one's worth and one's capabilities. It takes courage for the majority to be accepting and inclusive of an 'outsider'. It takes courage to also express one's fears constructively and show vulnerability when facing the unknown. It takes courage to trust, particularly where trust has been broken before.

As you can see, courage is a crucial trait for diversity and inclusion.

# Drive (Grit)

*❝It seems impossible until it is done.❞*

*(Nelson Mandela)*

Drive or grit describes the passionate vigorous, result-oriented strive for excellence. It is the ability to take the initiative, be self-motivated, and pick oneself up time and time again in the pursuit of a long-term goal.

A person who can be said to personify grit was the late Nelson Mandela. Throughout his 27 years in incarceration, he remained true to the vision of a united South Africa. The vision of a society not governed by discrimination, prejudices, and hatred. In his words, "Everyone can rise above their circumstances and achieve success if they are dedicated to what they do.'

That is grit and courage combined.

The psychologist Angela Duckworth at the University of Pennsylvania has researched grit and performance extensively. We have talked about the importance of intelligence in good decision-making, creativity, and all that, but little has been said about perseverance, drive, and will power.

In their research, Duckworth et al demonstrated that grit was a strong predictor of success beyond IQ. In other words, it is not enough to have a high IQ; to achieve difficult goals, one must have the drive/grit for sustained and focused application of that intelligence. (Duckworth et al., 2007). Talent without grit is only potential that will not be realised.

Beauty and perfection come through perseverance, hence the saying:

*'No grit, no pearl'*

I did my master's thesis at the Norwegian Sports Academy where the purpose was to uncover what distinguished the best from the second-best in sports with special emphasis on attitudes and motivation. It was a comparative analysis of Norwegian and Swedish table tennis players at the national team level. Sweden was at that point top of the world rankings and Norway was in the upper-middle class.

The biggest difference I found was that the best players in the world were far more internally controlled than those who did not quite reach the top who were far more externally controlled. An internally focused person sees him/herself as responsible for his/her results and the subsequent progress in life.

*It is up to me and my efforts if I am to succeed in life.*

The externally controlled tend, to a greater extent, to place the blame for their performance on external conditions beyond their own control. There can, of course, be causal connections such as lack of help from others, lack of support structure, lack of finances, coincidences, lack of talent, and even luck. In the context of a lack of diversity, such excuses may be; a lack of applications from the unrepresented population, less than expected performance during interviews based on unrealistic criteria, and a lack of willingness in the organisation to accept minorities.

The best players were those who took ownership of their own performance and results. They were convinced by the extraordinary efforts and extraordinary results and focused on that rather than on the external factors.

Jan Ove Waldner is one of the world's greatest athletes of all time and he said when interviewed:

*I analyse my defeats so I can learn from them in order to succeed in the future.*

(Jan Ove Waldner)

If you acknowledge the relationship between your own efforts at one end and the results you create at the other, your expectations and motivation are likely to go in a more positive direction. If, on the other hand, you tend to place the reason for your success or failure as being out of your sphere of control by blaming others and not acknowledging your weaknesses, poor performance, or shortcomings, then your expectations will be low, and your motivation will follow suit.

To be motivated to embark on a task, you must expect a positive return at the other end. In other words, the long-term advantages at one end must outweigh the disadvantages and costs at the other.

Our experience is that we can see who is internally or externally controlled in the business world. The internally controlled take their responsibility and are solution-oriented, while the externally controlled are more likely to complain, look for scapegoats, and are more problem-oriented. Undoubtedly, one is best served by those who see themselves as responsible for their own results, and their progress in life reaches further than most and influences the people around them in a far more positive manner.

## Integrity

The Cambridge dictionary defines integrity as the quality of being honest, ethical, and having strong moral principles which you refuse to change. Ethics is the part of philosophy that seeks to answer questions such as 'What is good?' 'What is right?' and 'How should one behave?'

Ethics, in other words, is a norm on which an individual bases his words and actions. Morality is about how you behave, that is, what you do. To act morally means to behave according to the norms and rules that apply in the group to which one belongs. The group can be family, friends, or colleagues. Immoral behaviour often leads to negative reactions from others. Professional ethics is about the choices you make as a professional. These choices concern users and colleagues. Do you show respect? Are you taking responsibility, or are you trying to sneak away?

To create a working environment that is inclusive and equal, a leader must have the integrity to actively respond to, and challenge, discrimination, harassment, and exclusion in any way, shape, or form swiftly. It is the responsibility of leadership to ensure that differences are welcomed, and everyone feels a sense of belonging and inclusion.

Every so often, organisational scandals reveal that leadership knew of ongoing malpractices but did not respond promptly or simply chose not to respond for one reason or the other.

Why is integrity profitable and how is it relevant for diversity and inclusion?

First of all, ethical leaders help to create an ethical work environment which builds employee trust and enhances employee performance. In a recently published article in the Journal of Business Ethics entitled *'How Does Perceived Integrity in Leadership Matter to Firms in a Transitional Economy?'*
Wei et al (2019) examined the effect of perceived integrity in leadership on both subjective firm performance and objective employee productivity.

The results of their research showed that perceived integrity in leadership was an important driver for employee productivity in dual-strategy and non-strategy firms. There is a need for further research in this area but the fact remains that we are likely to trust people we perceive to be ethical. An ethical platform creates psychological safety. It is that sense of psychological safety that enables us to bond towards a mutual goal.

Addressing the issue of ethics in banking, the IMF chief Christine Lagarde wrote:

> *Ethics is not only important for its own sake, but because ethical lapses have clear economic consequences. Good regulation and supervision can do a lot, but they cannot do everything.*

*(Lagarde, 2018)*

Unethical behaviour has preceded many of the crises the world has seen, including the financial crisis.

79

# Collaboration

According to the Confederation of Norwegian Enterprise's main organisation 2015, among ten alternative abilities and attitudes, collaboration is the trait that most Norwegian companies attach the greatest importance to when hiring new employees.

But what are the qualities that are most seen in collaborative people? The keywords here are cooperative, collegial, open-minded, flexible, and interconnected.

Good collaboration is fundamental to an inclusive work environment. At the heart of it is good communication, and trust. One must be willing to be an active listener to one's colleagues. Diversity introduces different opinions, and viewpoints which may cause friction. Active listening is about listening to understand, listening with an open mind, not simply listening to respond.

> When people talk, listen completely. Most people never listen.

(Ernest Hemingway)

The art of listening and learning is essential yet complicated. Particularly listening to feedback that does not put us in a good light. Many people struggle to critique or give criticism, and the vast majority struggle to accept criticism, or critique of their performance.

As Winston Churchill put it, 'criticism may not be agreeable, but it is necessary. It fulfils the same function as pain in the human body. It calls attention to an unhealthy state of thing.'

Collaborative people are interconnected with others, better able to listen, better able to take criticism. They are more accepting, and respectful of others and are likely to stand up and be supportive if someone asks for help. They are generally more open-minded to the diversity of opinions and as such better at giving feedback, praise and constructive criticism as well as receiving them.

We have met many self-centred individuals who are most concerned about themselves. They often say the right things and express the right values with claims that they have good cooperation qualities yet in reality, they are more concerned about themselves and how they are perceived. Those who will, in practice, put the company's best interests before their own and contribute to the common good are not as prevalent as one might often wish. They may be present in words but certainly not in deeds.

This is one of several reasons why companies today seem to emphasise behaviour or the way you create results, to be just as important as the deliveries. A 360-degree evaluation is often carried out to ensure that employees and managers comply with the company's values in practice, including good collaboration.

## Motivation and accountability

There are tons of books on motivation so much so that one would never finish reading them all in a lifetime. This is testimony to the importance of it. The corporate environment of today is more complex and diverse than ever before, requiring a high degree of motivation and accountability to systematically implement or develop inclusive workplaces. Motivation is known to play an important role in employee satisfaction and subsequent retention. Various studies have shown that unmotivated employees were less productive compared to highly motivated ones.

So, what tools would you say are available to motivate employees in a diverse working environment?

A combination of motivation and competency will make a person more efficient which in turn will increase the productivity of the organisation. Performance motivation is, the need for and the joy of, performing; that is, the desire to succeed. This is closely linked to grit. Without ambition, you are unlikely to get far despite a large dose of intelligence. It helps little to be clever if you are not willing to go that extra mile. Effort and consistency are needed to create good results and the inner driving force is the engine that will create them.

During my career, I have met many people who have all the skills in place, but simply do not want to put in the time and energy needed to perform beyond an 'acceptable' level. This can of course be a value choice, but it can also be that their level of ambition is simply below average.

What motivates an individual varies greatly from one individual to the next. Some people are motivated by feeling the joy of mastering difficult tasks, and by constantly setting higher goals. This trait is what is labelled 'the love of learning' in the Value in Action Character strengths (Peterson & Seligman, 2004). Others are motivated by beating a target such as in a competition and getting precise feedback on their performance. This is linked to grit, the urge to keep getting better. Some people are motivated by exciting work tasks and/or a good working environment. Promotion, good pay, and social recognition can also promote the motivation of some. Either way, it seems that most crucially one must have a strong inner drive to succeed as well as an inherent interest in the content of the job.

In the financial sector, there are on average more competition-oriented employees than in the health sector. It would appear that certain types of people are drawn to a certain type of job in a certain type of industry which best aligns with their character strengths. In addition, industry culture and industry-specific tasks inhibit and promote specific motivational aspects. An employee with high flexibility, independence, and competitive orientation will presumably apply for jobs where he/she can apply these qualities best.

Some scientists are overly concerned that people should have the right inner motivation, and that one should not be concerned with, for example, external motivational aspects such as money, career, and social recognition which are deemed to be less politically correct motives. As a leader, I have gradually developed a more pragmatic attitude. I am more concerned with what people achieve in practice over time than what the driving forces are behind the achievement. They do not always even know it.

An employee once told me in a confidential conversation that he was interested in making an impression on the ladies at work and was motivated to put in a higher effort for that reason. He delivered phenomenally, so I found no basis for saying that his motive was necessarily wrong. Another person was motivated by being the best sales representative every month – he was a very competitive guy without being egocentric. He delivered fantastic results although, in fact, social recognition was his most important motive. He just loved to get positive feedback and recognition for high performance delivered.

## Humanity and empathy

Empathy comes from 'empatheia' from the Greek language and means understanding or emotionally experiencing, how another person is feeling by entering their world.

However, there must be an understanding of the other's premise so that you do not interpret the other's emotional life as if it were one's own. In other words, you must have the ability to live in another person's thoughts, feelings, and needs.

*Many years ago, while conducting contractual negotiations in London, I happened to get stuck in a traffic jam on my way to Heathrow airport. It was a Friday afternoon, and mine was the last flight to Oslo.*

*By the time I got to the check-in counter, my seat had already been given to someone else. The plane was full. I was completely devastated. Not making that flight meant that I would not be there to make it for my son's birthday. I had, despite a hectic job never missed important days in my children's lives. Needless to say, it would not have been easy for my then husband to host twenty ten year holds for a party in the house without some help. I was so desperate and stressed that I phoned my manager who was on the same flight and asked him if he would give up his seat for me. He understood my situation, and being a parent too, he disembarked, and spent the night at the airport so that I would be able to make it home that evening.*

*Because of his empathy, I remained a faithful ally for as long as we worked together, always going the extra mile to make sure we nailed our contracts and met our group objectives.*

It is important to distinguish between empathy, which is to be able to understand the emotional life of others, and sympathy, which is to have a positive attitude towards another. You can have a positive attitude towards someone without being able to understand their emotional life, and conversely you can understand someone's emotional life without having a positive attitude towards them.

Empathy is an important prerequisite for being able to help others, and as a leader you need to bring out the best in those you motivate. Empathy can be the key to good communication and to building good relationships. Therefore, this property is important within organisations and businesses.

Empathy is also an important trait for inclusion. Being able to understand the emotional life experience of not belonging is a positive driving force towards including others. As society becomes more diversified, tensions are rising between perceived different groups, cultures, faiths, races, and so on.

In their extensive research on empathy and inclusion among Norwegian students, Solhaug and Osler (2018) examined the emotional and cognitive aspects of empathy: feelings and expression of empathy, empathetic awareness, acceptance of cultural difference, and empathetic perspective-taking (Solhaug & Osler, 2018).

The conclusion drawn from their study was that Intercultural empathy was particularly important when individuals perceived significant cultural differences. The study also found that intercultural empathy may be learned through experience, and that information and understanding of cultural diversity was an important predictor of intercultural empathy.

Another study conducted in Norway and Denmark showed that female students showed substantially higher intercultural empathy and awareness than their male counterparts (Solhaug & Kristensen, 2020).

Therefore, it could be argued that having more females in a predominantly male environment is more likely to improve inclusive citizenship and participation of those who traditionally do not fit in.

Empathy can also be exaggerated. It is not the intention of a man as a leader to end up as a social worker. As a woman, perhaps my empathy weighs heavy in my decision making. I must admit that I have, in the past, worked very hard to support others, or cover up for their weaknesses because they were struggling with life. My office is often the 'emotional support corner' where colleagues come in for emotional and practical support.

While this is not a bad trait, being overly supportive is also draining, and can inhibit us from having clear boundaries on performance or completing our own tasks.

During my MBA as well as the taught modules of my DBA studies, I often found myself stressing to finish my own submissions on time because I spent so much time supporting other students with their assignments that I nearly always ran out of time for my own submissions.

One is hired to do what is ultimately best for the company, not just for the individuals. One must also have a degree of common guidelines that are not necessarily optimally adapted to everyone's needs, and one will, at times, have to implement measures that are not necessarily perceived as very considerate and sympathetic to individuals. Nevertheless, one can communicate bad news in a considerate and good way, which will result in most people accepting it.

## Humility

Abraham Lincoln, the 16th president of the United States of America is known to have been a man of extraordinary emotional intelligence and humility.

> *I am humble Abraham Lincoln. I have been solicited by my friends to become a candidate for the Legislature. My politics are short and sweet, like the old woman's dance.*

*(Abraham Lincoln)*

He was open to listening even to those that did not agree with him, accepting his own shortcomings and seeking counsel even from his opponents. Compared to many leaders whose egos outshine their virtues, Abraham Lincoln''s humility and lack of personal importance shaped his leadership towards a more just and inclusive society. It was the humility to acknowledge that he was no better a man than any other, and all men were indeed equal hence the need to end slavery.

In a recently published study in the International Journal of Intercultural Relations, Mona Alsheddi (2020) examined the existing literature on humility and tolerance of diversity. The result of the study showed a positive relationship between humility and accepting people irrespective of their opinions, cultures, and religions. People with high levels of humility were likely to tolerate different opinions and cultural and religious backgrounds.

> *I recently witnessed a very arrogant expat manager at a tourist facility who not only racially profiled the clients but spoke to his staff in very belittling terms. He assumed such an air of racial superiority over his staff who were indigenous that it left a bitter taste in my mouth. One could tell how demotivated and uninspired the staff were by how they treated customers. There was a general sense of apathy and zero enthusiasm.*
>
> *I spoke to one of the staff members who said a lot of workers had quit over the treatment they received from that manager. Often, they quit without letting top management know of the arrogance of this manager. The company was spending a lot of money on training and onboarding of new staff due to high employee turnover, so eventually top management had come to acknowledge that there was a problem. Fortunately, it was his last week as a manager of the facility, he had been fired.*

Humility is a vital character strength for harnessing the best out of diversity. Inclusion builds on humility. Studies have shown a correlation between humility and multiple positive human behaviours and attitudes such as good cooperation, curiosity, tolerance, and charitable behaviour. In addition, humility has had negative correlation with right-wing authoritarianism or social dominance orientation (AlSheddi, 2020). When we are humble enough to accept each other and listen, we are less likely to want to kill each other.

There are multiple subcategories of humility but there are two main dimensions which are intrapersonal and interpersonal dimensions. Humility is often misunderstood being seen as submissive or downplaying one's own value.

The intrapersonal dimension of humility resonates around one's view of oneself, the clear recognition of one's strengths, capabilities, disabilities, weaknesses, limitations, and shortcomings.
The interpersonal dimension of humility is about understanding and accepting others' strengths, capabilities, weaknesses, and limitations. In a biblical sense of 'love thy brethren as you love thy self,' one could say true humility is accorded to self as to others.

Intellectually, humility in this sense is the wisdom and confidence to understand that no one knows it all, yourself included and that there are areas where others have better understanding, competence, and experience than you. It is not about denying validating your capabilities but giving others the same value.

Without intellectual humility, even the most intelligent group of people is likely to perform optimally. This explains why in innovation, highly diverse teams were only found to perform better if the members were able to listen to each other. In diverse groups, beyond intellectual humility, cultural humility which deals productively with cultural differences is vital in understanding the cultural dimensions of behaviour, character, and ways of relating.

It may be such that an individual is unable to challenge authority or speak directly to superiors due to their cultural upbringing. Understanding national cultures makes it easier to discern such subtle behaviour that may naturally not make sense seen from someone else's point of view. This is often the case where the communication is the top-down 'leader as the commander,' type of communication that was the dominant leadership paradigm during the scientific management movement, but it is less likely to function in today's modern world. One is more likely to succeed with effective participatory team communication between the members. Above all, there must be good listening between the top management, intermediate management, and right down to the team members carrying out the tasks.

That said, arrogance is destructive even in homogenous teams. When people are met with humility, and acceptance, they are better able to blossom in a role. The confidence and space allocated to them as a result are highly motivating. Humility to treat an individual on their merit is a prerequisite for inclusion which is performance-enhancing.

# Temperance

*You can't run the country if you can't run yourself*

*(Lady Bird Johnson)*

Temperance is often described as a virtue in religion and philosophy and is one of the six virtues in the positive psychology classification, together with wisdom, courage, humanity, justice, and transcendence. It deals with the complexity of self-restraint. Whether it is to control one's appetite, or emotions, or lust.

When it comes to leadership, temperance is much more, it is the ability to exercise clear, calm, and sensible, sensible judgement. Temperance is crucial during crisis leadership when emotions are running high, and the level of complexity requires that one is level-headed and self-disciplined. Complexity mandates one to act based on factual information and sound reasoning/evaluation instead of emotions, impulse, and personal feelings.

Difficult conversations require one to moderate one's feelings and choice of words as careless communication may have unwanted consequences. It is temperance that makes one put aside personal ambitions, vanity, pride, and ego to do what is right for the organization and hold oneself accountable for one's own mistakes.

Temperance is very important in a diverse team. When people can manage their emotions, they can listen more effectively and generally communicate better and are therefore better able to trust each other. People high in temperance are better able to control their reactions to negative emotions such as disappointment and insecurities. They have a sense of balance and order even in difficult situations. They score high in values such as modesty, humility, self-regulation, hospitality, decorum, abstinence, and forgiveness, all which are very important for trust-building.

Managers who are aggressive and threatening in behaviour are unlikely to get the best out of their employees in the long run. This impulsiveness creates a sense of fear and reservation which is counterproductive.

One can say lack of restraint has been a key factor in sexual harassment cases, bullying in workplaces, even embezzlement. Many people sitting in prisons are there because if a lack of self-restraint. Temperance is a key ingredient in creating psychological safety in a workplace and in life.

## Organisational commitment

To be committed is to be strongly emotionally connected to a cause you are in favour of or almost have a passion for. In other words, you will have 'your heart in the company you work for'. Commitment is not the same as being happy. Happy employees are not necessarily more productive. In other words, employee engagement is the emotional connection that an employee has to the company and its goals. You are passionate about what you do. From the company's point of view, commitment is important because it is known that increased commitment leads to increased productivity, growth, and profitability. At the same time your commitment seems to spread to others.

- What is organisational commitment?
- Why do some organisations retain people for a long time while others have a high turnover?
- Why is it important to reduce employee turnover and withdrawal behaviours?
- Why should you promote inclusion in the workplace?

Studies show that highly satisfied employees are more likely to be committed to the organisation than those who are less satisfied (Saridakis et al., 2020). Here, the researchers present three types of organisational commitment:

1. **A normative commitment** which is the desire to remain part of an organisation out of moral obligation like completing a task.
2. **A continuance commitment** which is the perceived costs of leaving an organisation, or the risk of losing values such as bonuses, perks, pension schemes.

And finally:

3. **An affective commitment** which is the desire to belong to and identify with the organisation.

When we talk about a profitable organisational commitment in the employee context, we are talking about 'affective commitment', something that is relatively long lasting and stable over time. This comes from experiencing a high sense of job satisfaction and emotional belonging.

As humans, we have a primal and evolutionary need to belong to a tribe. When we find an organisation where our values are mirrored and we humans are included, we will develop affection towards our job and our colleagues and develop the drive to perform better as our success and that of our organisation becomes synchronized.

# Execution Abilities – Going from Strategy to Implementation

*However beautiful the strategy, you must occasionally look at the results.*

*(Winston Churchill)*

Creating a diversity and inclusion plan or strategy is easy. Most self-respecting companies have a strategy which will be broken down into action plans and measures. Almost regardless of how good these plans are, it will ultimately be the company's ability to implement them that separates the best from the not-so-great companies. Diversity and inclusion cannot be simply about fancy strategic goals and plans, it must become the culture of the company and be part and parcel of its strategic thinking to enhance profitability and performance.

A good plan is only 5% of the job, the other 95% is implementation, that is to ensure that the ambitions and plans become concrete action throughout. This is the hard part. Rest assured, diversity and inclusion strategies are not always easy to implement which means they will fail to yield the expected results.

Many people spend a lot of time discussing whether the company's strategies are correct instead of focusing on and ensuring fast and good implementation. When it comes to diversity and inclusion strategies, it is important to garner commitment from all levels of the organisation to create a working environment that is conducive to all, and then, based on this, build a strategy. To succeed in the implementation, the strategy needs to be an integral part of the company culture accepted by all from the top management to the bottom workers of the company. It must not be a stand-alone strategy.

Companies want employees who are more action than talk - those who lead the 'balls to the finish' and who deliver on time and quality. 'Smart talkers' are in many ways the opposite. They mean a lot, but they do little. In our experience they are found in staff functions in larger companies where performance results are less visible.

The question remains, how can companies best connect the strategy to implementation?

In their well-acknowledged book *'The Knowing-Doing Gap'*, Jeffrey Pfeffer and Robert Sutton (1999) confront the challenges of turning the knowledge of how to improve performance into actions that actually produce measurable results. We know diversity and inclusion are performance-enhancing and profitable, now how do we close the gap between knowing that and taking the measures to act?

According to Pfeffer and Sutton (1999), organisations must do more than smart talk, and *'use plans, analysis, meetings, and presentations to inspire deeds, not as substitutes for action'*. In other words, execution is the key to success. The management must learn by example. If there is a strategy to increase the diversity in the executive and board, let management take the action required as it will inspire the rest of the organisation.

## Commercial mindset

People with a commercial 'mindset' are individuals who like to make money and seek out new business opportunities. They have inherent business acumen in them and are, on average, better at making money than those who do not have the same motive basis. Let us get this straight: diversity and inclusion are good for business, and so rather than look at it as an HR thing, it is time to quantify it and include it in the money-making mindset.

It has at times been surprising to see how little interest some may have in the company's financial results - especially in some staff functions. Some seem to be more concerned with processes than results, more concerned with subjects and theory than economics and results. Sometimes you could wonder why they chose to work in a commercial business in the first place. Many are stuck in the old ways and unable to keep up with the times. They have a fixed strategy mindset that is not capable of being responsive and adaptive to changing conditions.

For a company, it would probably have been best to hire people who are concerned with making good money on behalf of the company, but who have little interest in making money on their own behalf. It is an enticing thought, but not exactly truly relevant in practice. The problem is that these people only exist to a small degree. The rule is that those who are interested in making money (shopkeepers) are precisely this both on behalf of themselves and the company.

A commercial 'mindset' is not something you can easily turn off in some situations and on in others. It is more like you either have the grocery store mentality, or you don't. Ultimately, a business should deliver good returns to the owners.

Developed in the 80s, the HPI is one of the most used personality assessment tools used by HR and recruiters to assess key behavioural tendencies that can predict how:

- people will work together
- they will lead
- they are likely to fit into a certain environment
- they will get along with others
- they will get ahead of others

When building a diverse team, personality will matter. The best commercial mindset may be impossible to work with, meaning despite the talent, the organisation will not get the benefits in full as so much time and resource will be diverted to putting out fires.

It is undoubtedly an advantage to hire people who think like owners. High scores on a commercial motive basis are one of the dimensions of Hogan's Assessment - motives, values, preferences inventory, and correlate positively with job performance in business

It is worth noting, however, that both in the general public and among psychologists, personality tests are not 100% embraced as the true predictor of a person citing the impression management theory. Impression management theory describes the phenomenon of how during social interactions, most people will try to present better versions of themselves to maximize acceptance and status and reduce the chances of rejection and the loss of status (Hogan et al., 2007). This implies that people will paint themselves better during interviews, perhaps better than they really are.

Some earlier research conducted (Hogan et al., 1996) however, showed that:

(a) Well-constructed measures of normal personality were valid predictors of performance in virtually all occupations.
(b) They did not result in an adverse impact for job applicants from minority groups.
(c) Using well-developed personality measures for pre-employment screening was a way to promote social justice and increase organisational productivity.

## Self-confidence

Self-confidence is about perceived security about what one can realistically accomplish in different areas. In addition to various genetic preconditions, previous experiences of success and defeat are also of great importance for the development of self-confidence. Good self-confidence is crucial for many achievements both privately and in working life. Self-confidence is a good trait in meeting and integrating new people. Normally, self-confident people are not afraid to reach out to others and be open and inclusive without feeling threatened. Self-confidence is not the same as arrogance. The inclusive nature of self-confident people often makes them successful in working life.

Confidence is a very important trait in leadership in building credibility, motivation, team emotional state, affective tone, goal setting, inspiration, and drive in the team. Research from sports shows that a leader's confidence has a direct impact on team performance (Fransen et al., 2016).

*Would you follow a cowardly, uncertain, and insecure commander to war?*

From their research on sports and their team leaders, they concluded that there was a strong correlation between the team's performance and the team leader's confidence in the team. In other words, we want to imitate those we look up to and align our behaviour to reflect their behaviour, to socially align for acceptance. Confident leaders are thus in a better position to inspire change, transformation, and enhanced performance. A team leader who expresses confidence in the team's performance is likely to see good performance.

Likewise, a leader who is seen, known to be inclusive and has a divergent team is likely to speak about diversity and inclusion with more confidence and credibility which again produces the needed results further down in the organisation. It shall not be a case of 'do as I say not as I do'.

One sees the following gains with good self-esteem:

- People with high self-esteem often set high but realistic goals.
- They are good at selling messages, convincing, and negotiating.
- People with a high level of confidence and self-esteem withstand adversity and setbacks better as they have a history of success as well as failures and bouncing back.
- The faith in future success and experience enhances resilience.

It is not hard to motivate oneself when successful, but it requires self-confidence to motivate oneself in adversity. In adversity you show what you are made of. It is said that the dragon rises against the wind, not with it, implying if you deal with adversity and learn from it you have the best chance of success.

## As a leader, it is recommended to:

- Have a management team that reflects the diversity of the company's most important customers
- Illuminate issues from different relevant perspectives thus avoiding making bad decisions and choices
- Attract the best talents in your industry by having strategies, processes, and tools that secure the greatest talents into business-critical positions
- Have concrete and detailed development plans for each employee which will strengthen their performance by a minimum of 10% in the job each year
- Reward good performance better than bad performance.

# PART 2
## VISIBLE
## DIVERSITY

# 2.1: PERFORMANCE ENHANCING GENDER DIFFERENCES

## Gender Differences and Profitability

In the work on gender equality, one has naturally been most concerned with equal rights, and opportunities, which has been, and still is, sensible and necessary. Gender egalitarianism is the extent to which men and women receive equal treatment, and both masculine and feminine attributes are considered important, and desirable in society.

Unfortunately, generic differences between the sexes do not receive much attention as this is often seen in the light of conditions that may counteract the work on equality. Differences between the sexes have naturally had to give way to arguments about equality and gender equality.
With such an approach, however, one has missed out on generic differences between the sexes that can promote performance in a team or a group.

*❝Research shows that the biggest difference between men and women can be described in just one word: conscience.❞*

Quoting IMF chief Christine Lagarde on the issue of diversity,

*❝Our own research bears this out—a higher share of women on the boards of banks and financial supervision agencies is associated with greater stability. As I have said many times, if it had been Lehman Sisters rather than Lehman Brothers, the world might well look a lot different today.❞*

(Lagarde, 2018)

On average, men tend to take far more risks than women with the advantages, and disadvantages it entails. A slightly more balanced approach would perhaps yield better results over time.

All in all, female and male managers seem to come out relatively similarly from different types of management evaluations, however, there are some variances in different types of skills in the job situation assessed by variants of 360-degree evaluations. In other words, this says something about employees' perceptions of what female and male managers on average score highest on. There are many different studies here - but some common features of differences seem to be prominent:

**On average, women score highest on:**

- Ethical behaviour and honesty
- Good personnel management
- Ability to find good compromises
- Justice around pay and reward
- Involvement and coaching
- Being good role models
- The ability to collaborate
- The ability to listen.

**Men score on average the highest at:**

- Risk-taking
- Ability to conduct negotiations
- Ability to set requirements for skill
- Decision making
- Making unpleasant decisions
- Strategic capabilities
- The ability to compete
- Find technical solutions.

Regardless of whether this gives a correct picture of generic differences between the sexes or not, there are still few today who will not agree that there are differences between the sexes in terms of leadership style - differences you largely can capitalise on. It is about using the good foot for men and the good foot for women more often for the good of the company.

Performance and potential follow an almost equal Gaussian curve across gender differences. This implies that by not having an almost equal proportion of women in leading positions in the private and public sectors, society is missing out on many leadership talents and revenues.

Many women have ambitions, but it is still the case that fewer women than men want to reach the top in the business world, and there are many indications that there are still more barriers that contribute to this. However, if we manage to create a conducive working environment so that more women want to be leaders, we will have an overall better portfolio of good leaders over time.

It is a fact that we have not come far enough yet, in bringing out the full potential among women as employees, and there are still far too few female top managers in both the private and public sectors across geographies. From the universities and institutions of learning, the number of female students in what was previously seen as male arenas such as engineering and finance has seen a steady increase. This should mean that the increase is reflected in the corridors of power yet the percentage of females actually decreases with every elevated level in organisations.

So, where is the disconnect?

Although many companies try hard, we still see too many examples of outstanding female leadership talents stopping their career development at the middle management level or in typical staff positions. Perhaps we should ensure from the start of a career that not too many women start their careers in typical support functions such as Communication and HR. Not that there is anything wrong with support functions, but they do not lead to the top jobs to the same degree. A position as CEO and COO is rarely within reach without management experience and demonstrated performance with responsibility for the company's revenues and expenses. The uncertainty for a board will simply be too great if one has not been able to show solid financial performance in previous jobs.

The number of female top managers varies greatly in scope across geographies. If you look at Scandinavian companies, for example, they are among the worst in the world in this area. This is even though they have come a long way in gender equality work in many other areas. Today, only 5-7.5% of Scandinavian top managers are women in large companies, compared to 16-18% in the USA.

What are the barriers?

And why is the difference between Scandinavia and the United States so enormous?

We will return to this later in this chapter, but first I will look at the history of gender equality work. It is important to bring with us the perspective on how gender equality has been historical to understand why we are still lagging in this work. Many stereotypes and prejudices we still have today have their roots in history.

## The History of Feminism

The belief in the importance of gender equality has developed society in the direction of a more equal society, although this still varies greatly across geographies. The work on gender equality has had different ideological directions, but the common goals are that men and women should have equal rights, opportunities, and responsibilities.

Some may argue that in many modern Western societies, equality has long been achieved. In former 'Eastern Bloc' countries and 'in the third world', however, feminist ideas have only now begun to gain organised support, and in other countries, they have barely reached the agenda. Feminism is strongly opposed by religious fundamentalists in many countries. Even though feminism is strongly opposed, feminist ideology is still on the rise and is becoming increasingly worldwide, but there is still a long way to go in many places, including a few modern western societies.

The modern women's movement has its roots all the way back in the 15th century, but it would be a few hundred years before it really took off. Many consider Mary Wollstonecraft (1757-1797) to be one of the first pioneers of feminism. She wrote 'a defense of women's rights' and argued, amongst other things, for equal education of women and men. She became a great inspiration for many prominent feminists who would eventually prove to be successful.

In the 1850s, women in Britain and the United States began to form their own organisations. These became a social movement, which worked for the interests of women. The idea sprang from the Enlightenment's emphasis on the rights of the individual and was linked to the emergence of a more liberal and democratic, modern industrial society. The women's movement helped to change women's perceptions of themselves and their opportunities, brought them into politics, and helped change society in favour of women. Several social reforms were implemented, and women had better living conditions. Gradually, women became more and more aware of their low status in society and their lack of rights.

## Voting rights for women - wave 1

At the turn of the century came the first great wave of feminist activity. Many women, especially in England, took part in mass demonstrations to improve the situation of women. Women's suffrage was the number one priority, because women, like men, wanted to influence their contemporaries. Battles in favour of women were otherwise difficult to get through in a national assembly that consisted exclusively of men.

Women's work to gain the right to vote dominated much of the time before the First World War. New Zealand and Australia had already given women the right to vote in 1893 and 1902, respectively. But Women's rights started a lot earlier. Millicent Fawcett was a prominent British feminist and author heavily involved in the organised movement that worked for women's suffrage at the turn of the century between the 18th and 20th centuries. Mary Wollenstonecraft is considered one of the first and most important pioneers in feminism. A great inspiration for those who started the work with voting rights for women.

## The women's liberation - wave 2

World War I and World War II contributed to a delay in the further spread of feminism, but in the 1970s, women's struggle against gender discrimination became relevant again. The struggle for suffrage at the beginning of the 20th century was the first wave of feminism, this was the second. In the 1970s, feminism was replaced by women's liberation.

The liberation of women in the 1970s was a fight for women's right to decide over themselves and their own bodies. By this, they meant the right to control sex, pregnancy, and childbirth themselves. In the 1970s, it was still difficult to get statutory abortion. It was taboo to have children out of wedlock and unwanted pregnancies were often resolved with unsafe abortions. Women wanted to avoid objections from the authorities, employers, churches, family, partners, or priests when it came to abortion or general control of their own bodies.

Women's liberation - the second wave of gender equality at work. The poster 'We can do it' was originally made in the United States during World War II but later used in the women's struggle implying that women can do as good a job as men.

Part of the emancipation of women also applied to rights in working life. Men had access to most occupations which gave them status and were well paid. The common perception at the time was that 'male' occupations were more demanding than typical 'female' occupations. Traditionally, the struggle for equal pay for equal work has been important for a long time and it remains a pertinent issue today. Today's feminists are still fighting for the right to self-determined abortion and the right to decide over their own bodies. In addition, the focus is largely on violence, abuse, and sexual harassment of women. Universal struggles for feminism include the struggle against forced marriage and female genital mutilation.

# The #Metoo campaign - The start of the 3rd wave in gender equality work

The #Metoo campaign focused on men (especially in positions of power) who abused their power through sexual harassment in business, politics, sports, and other arenas. It is more than likely that this problem has been far more extensive than many have imagined, and many stories remain untold due to fear of repercussion. The men are still in power or have such influence that challenging them, though wise may have long term negative consequences for the women hence they remain silent.

The campaign has been mostly about men having to open their eyes and understand where the boundaries of sexual harassment go. #Metoo came as a statement of support to the many women who had dared to report harassment and abuse from film producer Harvey Weinstein, but the campaign has opened the eyes of many employers and created a great deal of engagement worldwide.

The #Metoo campaign has probably been an eye-opener for many women too. What many people thought they just had to accept because it was just that the way it was expected to be, was not acceptable. The campaign made it possible for women to see that one could speak out, and whoever spoke out would be taken seriously. The #MeeToo campaign has also been an eye-opener in another way. It has revealed that inappropriate behaviour, harassment, and abuse against women has a surprisingly large scope. It has thus become more legitimate to expose inappropriate behaviour, even if it is not necessarily illegal based on legal considerations. 'Inappropriate' is of course not a precise term, but it typically covers what is now referred to as 'unwanted sexual attention' and especially repeated attention when the person receiving the attention clearly states that it is unwanted.

It is extremely inappropriate for powerful people, often older, to exploit their position over people who are younger and have less power, and who may even be in a kind of dependency relationship with the person in power. Bill Clinton's affair with Monica Lewinsky is a good example - it was not illegal - it was not involuntary - but it was still very inappropriate.

The campaign has also been an eye-opener for men, who may have become more aware of where the boundaries are. To the extent that it has been, it probably first and foremost indicates that the judgement has in principle been too weak. It might well have rung a bell earlier if women were repeatedly given unwanted sexual attention. Some people tend to have manipulative traits, especially in combination with alcohol, and unfortunately need the threat of public humiliation to stay on the straight and narrow - since they lack natural moral fibre.

Alcohol is the elephant in the room in many #Metoo cases. Some men want to defend their privileges and access to women. High blood alcohol intake is the No. 1 risk factor for both exercising and falling victim to sexual discomfort and abuse. Nevertheless, one can naturally not use this as an excuse to behave despicably. One must know oneself, and know how to react to alcohol, and based on this take precautions.

## #Metoo and diversity

While looking at the #Metoo cases that made the news around the world, it is intriguing to see the lack of diversity in the victims. One may ask, do immigrant women not get sexually harassed? Do seasonal workers, females in low-paying jobs, and the disabled not experience unwanted behaviour? Outside of the political, entertainment, and power spheres, there were few or no stories to tell. Does that mean such conduct is contained within these sectors only?

The lack of stories should perhaps be a cause for alarm. This may in itself be an indication that many unspoken barriers hinder likely victims from speaking out. As leaders, our job is to ensure the safety of our entire workforce. It seems likely that the weakest in society do not have the energy, options, or protection to dare to report cases of abuse in their workplaces.

As a young immigrant employee, I too faced unwanted sexual harassment in my workplace, but I was afraid that I may not get another job easily as I had a mortgage and financial obligations, so I tolerated the abuse for a very long period. I feared his network and what it would entail to go to war with such a powerful executive. My fear of not being well accepted in the society, knowing that people like myself were often excluded during employment processes, and the perpetrator knowing this too made me the perfect prey.

# 2.2: CONTINUED BARRIERS FOR WOMEN IN BUSINESS

The vast majority will agree that women are, in principle, as professionally qualified as men to take on future leadership tasks. Based on this aspect, there should be far more female leaders than there are today in both the private and public sectors. Many male top executives expect women to be proactive in their own career development while disregarding the biases and obstacles that prevent women from doing just that.

There is reason to believe that companies should to a greater extent appoint managers at the higher level based on qualifications and suitability using, among other things, balanced performance management systems rather than this being a 'self-promotion game' based on internal and external job postings that are often prejudiced.
Various barriers still seem to be inhibiting getting more female leaders at higher levels.

## Not Enough Women to Choose From?

According to Organisational Psychologist Tomas Chamorro-Premuzic, the three popular explanations for the clear under-representation of women in management are:

(1) Lack of capability
(2) Lack of interest
(3) Though interested and capable, they are unable to break the glass ceiling (Chamorro-Premuzic, 2013).

Indeed, it is quite often claimed in recruitment processes that there are not enough qualified women to choose from and that women are not motivated enough to take on top management positions. It is also said that women prioritise differently.

However, international research makes it clear that the lack of female top managers cannot be explained by the fact that there are not enough qualified women to choose from. Nor is it because women are not motivated to take on such positions. It is most often simply women do not compete with men, a competition that is not necessarily fair. It must also be the business community's responsibility to ensure that it attracts the most talented women.

## Biases, prejudices, and hurdles in recruitment

In this context, it is obvious to look at what requirements are initially set for top managers. We must also look at which assessment methods are used in the selection process. The first obstacle comes already in the design of the requirements for the position. If a group of older male leaders is asked to list the requirements that should be placed on a top leader, this is not necessarily based on up-to-date knowledge of which leadership qualities seem to perform best over time.

If this is a position that is perceived as masculine, or that men determine the qualifications, the requirements will soon be accordingly. The concept of competence must therefore be expanded, and the empowerment of women must, to a greater extent count as criteria for evaluating candidates.

Many 'head-hunters' are primarily motivated by reducing uncertainty when hiring top executives, avoiding misses gives them better opportunities for repurchase – which they make a living from. The safest thing would then be to hire a CEO who works well in the role today into another CEO role. It is also the least labour-intensive rather than looking for leaders with a higher potential. As there are mostly male CEOs today (108pprox.. 95% in Norway), this means that it is mostly men who change roles in such processes, also described as the chair game in the old boys' club.

It has been documented that even in situations where women and men are objectively equally professionally qualified, it is usually the man who gets the position. There is thus an unconscious form of discrimination. If the interviews were also conducted by men, there are many indications that this effect is amplified.

While those who are hired at the bottom of an organisation often have to go through several very thorough structured interviews, tests, 'assessments' and more, top managers usually get away with it more easily. They are hired mostly based on references, reputation, and conversations. Such interviews, or conversations, are often conducted by men who unconsciously prefer people who are like themselves, also called the equality effect.

## Gender and stereotypes

In their extensive research on female leaders, Psychology professor Emeritus Eagly and Karau studied perceived incongruity between the female gender role and leadership roles, concluded that there were two forms of prejudice:

(a) Women being perceived less favourably than men as potential occupants of leadership roles.
(b) The evaluation of behaviour that fulfils the prescriptions of a leader role less favourably when enacted by a woman (Eagly & Karau, 2002).

Facebook boss: Sheryl Sandberg stated the following in her book *Lean In*:

> ❝ The more successful a man is, the better he is. On the other hand, when a woman is successful in business, she is less well-liked. ❞

*(Sandberg, 2013)*

To substantiate the claim, Sandberg refers to an experimental study conducted on American business students in 2003. The 'case' was originally based on Silicon Valley founder Heidi Roizen where a school class was divided into two equal parts.

Both parts got the same stories. One with a male protagonist Howard and the other with Heidi. The result of the experiment was startling. The students rated

Heidi and Howard as equally competent. However, they did not like Heidi, but thought that Howard was a core guy. They would neither work for nor hire Heidi and viewed her as selfish. Howard came out far better. The students wanted to both work for him and have a beer with him after work. Sandberg argued that this can have major consequences for women as we promote people who are competent, but also well-liked.

Similar studies have been conducted in Norway with the same result. The reason for these differences is probably strongly entrenched deep-seated gender stereotypes that turned out to be worst among the male students. There is thus no conscious desire to affect women, but they are still affected, unconsciously. For female leaders, likeability and success go hand in hand.

Sandberg's example is in line with decades of extensive research which conclude that women will face distinct social penalties for doing that which will lead to success.

The conclusion is that attitudes are less positive towards female than male leaders and potential leaders. Secondly, it is more difficult for women to become leaders and to achieve success in leadership roles (Eagly & Carli, 2019; Eagly & Karau, 2002).

## Seeing is believing

There are still very few women who end up as CEOs of large companies. There is also uncertainty amongst many young female leadership talents related to how dedicated a CEO and management are in practice in terms of the commitment to getting women up and forward. It helps little, for example, to talk about this if one cannot refer to examples of compliance with policy and intentions in practice. The power of example is important in this context. Concrete examples have a much stronger effect on women's motivation than 'empty words and hollow promises at the Christmas party'. Seeing is believing!

The onus is on those female leaders who have made it to the top, to lift other aspiring female leaders up too. Mentorship and encouragement are important yet relatively underutilised.

## Choice of lifestyle

Women generally want a career, but most also want to be the primary facilitator of children's upbringing. Therefore, many women choose to slow down their career development because of a generally stronger conscience and commitment to their children's development. However, a few years of reduced speed should not mean the same as stagnation in career development. Here, the company needs to make long-term career plans that motivate an accelerated development of female leadership talents when, for example, returning from maternity leave, and one should to a greater extent be able to share the leave between the parents.

Many leadership skills come with the role of parenting, but they are unfortunately overlooked in the workplace. An interesting question to ask a woman who has been taking care of her children is what task and time management skills she has learnt in the process. Many of the people skills acquired through parenting are important in the workplace and could be harnessed.

Long-term career planning for female leadership talents can be extremely profitable, but there is limited knowledge about how much this is used today. Potential related to the emergence of new technology and new forms of work that make it easier to combine family and career is also not currently being used well enough. In other words, the potential is far greater than what most companies realise in this area today. The Covid-19 Pandemic was an eye-opener when it came to working from home.

## Self-limiting beliefs

Self-limiting beliefs are the Achilles heel of many talented women and/or rather the greatest potential for mental improvement. The belief that one cannot do something is in many cases greater than the actual inability of women.

Men are far more prone to overconfidence and some to the extent of suffering the Dunning-Kruger effect (Dunning et al., 2003). The Dunning-Kruger syndrome is a cognitive bias about how incapable we are of knowing that we know so little. So much so that we have the tendency to hold overly favourable views of own abilities in many social and intellectual domains, totally, blissfully unaware of our incompetence. In another study by Pennycook et al on the Dunning-Kruger effects in high-level reasoning, those participants who made the greatest numbers of errors on the cognitive reflection test (CRT) were also the ones that overestimated their own performance by as much as a factor of more than 3 (Pennycook et al., 2017).

The opposite is often associated with high performing women. In 1978, two psychologists Pauline Rose Clance and Suzanne Imes developed the concept they termed 'imposter phenomenon,' to designate:

> ❝...an internal experience of intellectual phoniness that appears to be particularly prevalent and intense among a select sample of high achieving women. Certain early family dynamics and later introjection of societal sex-role stereotyping appear to contribute significantly to the development of the impostor phenomenon. ❞

*(Clance & Imes, 1978)*

This is despite outstanding academic and professional accomplishments.

There is a key statement worth looking into:

Certain early family dynamics and later introjection of societal sex-role stereotyping appear to contribute significantly to the development of the impostor phenomenon.

Boys and girls have historically been brought up differently. Boys are told to be brave, daring, and encouraged to do activities that build strength, resilience, and risk taking. Girls were encouraged to be mild, sweet, kind, and pretty and are often directed towards nurturing roles. There is no denying that the girl child stands at a disadvantage already from the start. Her confidence towards leadership is not being nurtured during her formative years.

The second element is societal sex-role stereotyping where men are more often seen as leadership material and with the lack of role models, women accept the biased societal standing.

In the context of diversity, we enter yet another sphere of women likely to fall even further away from opportunity and into imposter syndrome; the women from minority backgrounds. One is not just a woman, but a foreign woman in a workplace that is not inclusive.

In a recently published article in Harvard Business Review, Ruchika Tulshyan, the author of *The Diversity Advantage: Fixing Gender Inequality in the Workplace* and the founder of Candour, an inclusion strategy firm, addressed the role of the historical and cultural contexts, of systemic racism, classism, xenophobia, and other biases that were not addressed by Clance and Imes in their study of imposter syndrome (Tulsshyan & Burey, 2021). The point is that rather than focusing the view on fixing women, the emphasis should be on creating inclusive workplaces where everyone can thrive.

The onus is on society to create a level playing field for all, starting from early childhood, through education in the formative years to working life.

In parallel with being supported, facilitated, and encouraged, women must dare to take greater responsibility for their careers. They must be made aware of making their own career wishes visible and be 'selected' when interesting and challenging opportunities arise.

Taking responsibility for one's own progress in life is one of the most important qualities one must have to succeed in various areas regardless of gender, and here women, in general, have tremendous potential for improvement. However, it can be difficult to have a lot of self-confidence if there are too few examples of women reaching the top in business. It would have been easier to believe if the management jobs were a little more evenly distributed in the first place.

# Self-promotion, Self-praise, and Unconscious Discrimination

It has been documented that men, to a greater extent than women, tend to brag about responsibilities and tasks they have not had. With this as a starting point, it quickly becomes a fact that the entire assessment process can quickly favour men. While smart women often suffer from insecurities and imposter syndrome, the opposite problem of 'overconfidence' seems to be a more widespread phenomenon in men.

In an article in the Harvard Business Review entitled *'Why Do So Many Incompetent Men Become Leaders?'*, Organisational Psychologist Tomas Chamorro-Premuzic is of opinion that:

> *...the main reason for the uneven management sex ratio is our inability to discern between confidence and competence.*

*(Chamorro-Premuzic, 2013)*

He stresses what is in line with numerous studies that confirm that men tend to think that they are much smarter than women. Yet arrogance and overconfidence are inversely related to leadership talent.

Recruiters are not sufficiently aware of this and believe that those who are hired are the best qualified. If we really believe that the best qualified regardless of gender should get the job, we must ensure that we treat men and women equally. Then we must have a more gender-neutral selection methodology where women and men are assessed based on demonstrated competence.

It should be the content of achievements in current and previous roles as well as suitability and competence for new challenges that will drive promotions and not how good you are at marketing your own 'excellence'.

# Those Who Have Defied the Barriers

Despite the barriers, there are many good examples of women who have reached the top jobs. It can be interesting to learn from those who have succeeded in their ambitions, especially if there are any common denominators or general tips. There does not seem to be a success formula that is generic for these, but some similarities are still prominent such as:

- Most of them have had very rapid progression early in their careers.
- Most have had line experience early on.
- They have been willing to prioritise careers.
- Many have had a mentor and coach.
- Many have been helped to balance work and private life.

Beyond these more generic observations, there seem to be many different paths to the goal. These observations differ slightly from men. The success formula otherwise seems to be relatively similar regardless of gender.

# The Changing Faces of Powerful Women

For the 18th time, Forbes has published an annual list of the World's 100 Most Powerful Women. They are coming from 30 different countries and territories and work across finance, technology, politics, philanthropy, entertainment, sports, and more. There is a continued diversity development in this annual list which used to be predominantly Caucasian. Though slow, the changing faces of the world's most powerful faces are also an indication of a growing gender diversity trend across the globe. On Forbes' 18th annual list of the World's 100 Most Powerful Women, one finds 40 CEOs, overseeing a record $3.3 trillion in revenue.

These are some of the names which appeared on this list which shows how it is finally changing for the better.

#2 Kamala Harris: First US Vice President

#5 Melinda French Gates: Billionaire and Co-chair of Bill and Melinda Gates Foundation

#9 Tsai Ing-wen: First female leader of Taiwan

#27 Nicke Widyawati: CEO and President-Director of Indonesian oil and gas company

#45 Thasunda Brown Duckett: President and CEO of TIAA financial services

#68 Rihanna Fenty: Billionaire and Co-owner of Fenty Beauty

#91 Ngozi Okono-Iweala: First Director-General of the World Trade Organisation

#92 Raja Easa Al Gurg: Managing Director and Vice Chair of The Easa Saleh Al Gurg Group

# 2.3. GENDER AND DIVERSITY IN DIFFERENT COUNTRIES

There are startlingly large differences amongst employed women in top management roles across geographies. Why is it, for example, that in the USA you have 16-18% female top managers in large companies while in Scandinavia, for example, you only have 5-7.5%? There is always a complex picture of many different factors and probably not a single answer, but here are some explanations that may be useful to look at.

There are several factors that enable women to advance in the workplace. If you take into consideration such factors as equal pay, parental leave, and percentage of women working outside of the home as well as those in senior positions, then these are the parameters where Scandinavian countries are in the lead. Not surprisingly, the countries presenting the best conditions for women in the workplace are:

1.  Iceland
2.  Sweden
3.  New Zealand
4.  Norway
5.  Luxembourg
6.  Denmark
7.  Poland
8.  Finland

Let's look at what they each do to achieve this.

## 1. Iceland

Thanks to a strong women's movement and laws designed to improve gender equality, Iceland tops the list with the best conditions for working women. For starters, Iceland has mandatory gender quotas for company boards, ensuring that women have a voice and representation of at least 40% of the board. It also takes care of new mothers and fathers. Since 2000, it has given parents nine months of shared leave paid at 80% of their average salaries (up to a set amount).

The results are undeniable. For the last decade, Iceland has topped the World Economic Forum's annual gender gap report, and it continuously performs well in The Economist's Glass-Ceiling Index, which rates the best countries for working women. As a result of its efforts, Iceland has the highest female labour force participation rate and a large percentage with 42% of managerial positions occupied by women.

## 2. Sweden

Gender equality is a cornerstone of society in Sweden, and it has the numbers to prove it. In the public sector, more women than men hold management positions and in politics, 46% of parliament members are women. Sweden's Minister of Gender Equality, Asa Lindhangen, credits this representation of women in the legislature as a result of various initiatives, including improved childcare, better protection for pregnant women, and more opportunities for working mothers.

Further illustrating Lindhangen's point, Sweden is also known for having one of the most progressive parental leave and childcare policies in the world. Parents are entitled to up to 16 months of shared leave paid at 80% of their salary (with a cap). And as a result of Sweden's maximum-fee policy, childcare cannot exceed more than 3% of the family's income.

## 3. New Zealand

Known for its longstanding commitment to gender equality and enviable work-life balance, New Zealand is a desirable country for working women. As evidence of this, it regularly ranks at the top of the World Economic Forum's gender gap report. It has one of the lowest gender wage gaps at just 5.6%. And at 76%, it has one of the highest female labour force participation rates. Plus, parental leave is nothing to scoff at. Thanks to 2017 legislation which extended leave duration, parents can take 26 weeks of paid leave if their baby is due on or after July 1, 2020.

## 4. Norway

Like other Nordic countries, Norway is paving the way for gender equality. One of the first countries to introduce gender quotas, Norway started requiring public companies to have at least 40% female board members all the way back in 2007. Additionally, almost 40% of its parliament members are female, and 31% of senior managerial positions are filled by women.

Norway has one of the most flexible and generous parental leave policies. Mothers can take 35 weeks at full pay or 45 weeks at 80% pay, while fathers can take between zero and 10 weeks, depending on their wife's income. In practice, it is now frowned upon for fathers **not** to take paternity leave. In addition, when a child is being born, the father is entitled to two weeks of paid leave to support the mother during the first two weeks of adjustment.

## 5. Luxembourg

In recent years, Luxembourg has taken several steps toward enhancing gender equality and women's economic participation. From 2016 to 2017, the country successfully reduced its gender pay gap by 1.3%.

In part, they achieved this through policy. For example, Luxembourg requires companies with 15 or more employees to have an 'equality delegate,' or someone responsible for ensuring that male and female employees are treated equally when it comes to employment, training, promotions, pay, and working conditions. And as for parental leave, employers are required to agree to full-time parental leave of four or six months, without exception.

## 6. Denmark

Denmark has made significant progress towards closing the gender wage gap in earned income, with women earning just 7.8% less than men. The country is also close to closing the gap in labour force participation. With 77% of females employed, compared with 82% of men, there's less disparity than ever.

Denmark's government-subsidised day care along with one of the most flexible parental leave policies in Europe may have something to do with their success. Parents are entitled to leave of 224 days which equates to around 10 months, which they can share however they see fit. Day care is more affordable than in other countries Danes also prioritise work-life balance, with a 37-hour official work week and a minimum of five weeks' paid vacation for full-time employees.

## 7. Poland

Since 2000, Poland has made substantial improvements in reducing the female unemployment rate. The female unemployment rate dropped from 18% in 2000 to just 5% in 2017. And with a gender pay gap that's also only 5%, Poland is that much more attractive for female employees.

Perhaps it's the 22 weeks of full pay that women in Poland get for maternity leave or the strong economy that's contributing to the country's success with gender equality. Whatever the case, it's working. Women in Poland are more likely to have permanent employment than men and to work in professional occupations. And not only that, but the proportion of Polish women in management positions is relatively high at 36%.

## 8. Finland

According to The Economist's Glass-Ceiling Index, Finland is one of the world's best countries to be a working woman. Why? From 2016 to 2019, the Finnish government launched an action plan to promote gender equality by closing the wage gap, improving employment opportunities, and providing equal representation on company boards. They've also taken measures to improve life for working mothers. All children under school age are entitled to municipal day care, and the family's income level impacts day care fees. Affordable childcare makes it easier for Finnish women to maintain a work-life balance, which is a top priority in Finland.

# 2.4 WOMEN'S SUCCESS IN BUSINESS

With their favourable conditions and economic opportunities, these countries make it easier for deserving women to excel in business. As more countries make strides to improve gender equality in the workforce, more and more women shine as the natural business leaders they are. Here's why this powerful gender is naturally inclined to succeed in business.

## Effects of a Strong Focus on Profitability

Few would argue that there is too little focus on making money in the competitive business world in the United States. In relation to this strong "competition and profit pursuit", the Americans have to a greater extent than other countries found that it is profitable to invest in talent. As there is no reason to believe that there are fewer leadership talents among women than among men, it seems obvious that there is a lot of money to be made in developing the best female as well as male leadership talents.

Already early in a career, the potential is thoroughly assessed by employees and if it is considered high, you are bet on regardless of gender. One is a little more careful about proclaiming talents early on this side of the Atlantic, and in Scandinavia the 'Jante law' is probably also more prominent for better or worse.

The Jante laws are from a 1933 fictional book by the Norwegian writer Axel Sandemose entitled 'A Fugitive Crosses His Tracks' in which he writes about the social codes of a Danish town called Jante. These social codes are dominant throughout Scandinavia, and explains the Scandinavians love for equality or perhaps better said, equilibrium in everything. From how we work, to how we live, there is not a big divide. It also means however, that the incentive to perform better than others or strive for higher achievements is frowned upon, except, perhaps in sports.

**The Ten Jante Laws are:**

1. Don't think you are anything special.
2. Don't think you are as good as we are.
3. Don't think you are smarter than we are.
4. Don't convince yourself that you are better than we are.
5. Don't think you know more than we do.
6. Don't think you are more important than we are.
7. Don't think you are good at anything.
8. Don't laugh at us.
9. Don't think anyone cares about you.
10. Don't think you can teach us anything.

I recall how different it was to go to high school in Norway compared to my British education in Uganda when I moved to Norway after my O-levels. I was used to a competitive style where grades mattered. In my new environment, being ambitious was an ugly thing. It was more important to fit in, have fun, and get through high school. I really experienced the Jante laws up close and personal. When I was admitted to the technical university, two years after my arrival in Norway, I expected a pat on the back from old friends in the village, I was rather appalled to be met with 'You must not think you are better than others.'

## Greater acceptance of 'nanny' in the United States

In Scandinavia, there is a greater tradition and expectations are that women should be natural 'supermums' who should breastfeed their children for a long time, make baby food from scratch, master all roles equally well, sleep in the same bed with the child - and preferably manage all aspects of life without any help. There is a greater acceptance of paying for help and relief in the United States or in the UK.

For example, it is a common practice to pay a nanny to look after the child at night so that the mother can sleep and during the day when they are at work. The same cannot be said to be the case in Scandinavia. The strong position of the family in society means that it is not as socially acceptable to pay for assistance with a career in private business as justification. Paying for help so you can be both a mother and have a career goes against the 'Scandinavian model'. Perhaps some people may not 'approve' of it simply out of jealousy because that family can afford to pay for help and they can't. It also diverts from the socialistic model.

*When my children were small, I opted to have au pairs. Both my husband and I were commuting to Oslo for work, and both travelled with our jobs. To make matters worse, our three children were scattered in three different locations. One in school, another in a pre-school a few hundred metres away and the youngest, sixteen kilometres in the wrong direction from the office. The stress of navigating traffic across the country traffic to drop the children off, then the dashing madly through the city traffic in the morning to get to work, and the reverse in the evening left us exhausted and frustrated.*

*Getting an au pair to assist with the morning logistics and picking up in the afternoon was a welcome relief. However, when it became known to the extended family that we had hired an au pair, we were ridiculed and branded snobs. We were subjected to belittling comments at every opportunity.*

Norway is an example of a very conformist country where it does not take much to stand out. There is a broad consensus that 'this is how we do it in Norway', and if you choose differently, there are various forms of 'social sanctions'. It can be in the form of you being told how it should be or offered unsolicited tips and advice or even reprimanded. Norway is a welfare state with many social benefits that support family life. The pressure is on us in Norway to manage everything ourselves, even to the point of utter wipe-out or exhaustion.

## Shorter maternity leave

In Scandinavia, we have the world's longest maternity leave. Psychology professor Emeritus Eagly and Carly have carried out extensive research on women and leadership. In relation to maternity leave they imply that 'Dangers lurk in family-friendly benefits that are used only by women.' (Eagly & Carli, 2019). For while a long maternity leave is a good investment for the family and the children's upbringing, it can also be an inhibiting factor for career development in women to the extent that one is not able to divide the leave between men and women better than we do today. You gradually lose focus on the job, and it can take some time to 'get back into the rhythm' after a long maternity leave, especially if you do not update yourself professionally along the way.

There are large differences between countries, sectors, and occupational groups in the degree to which they offer jobs that make it possible to combine work and family.

In the United States, there are such highly educated jobs in various parts of the private business world. In Norway, such flexible jobs exist primarily in the public sector. This difference may also help to explain why Norway has a more gender-segregated labour market than the United States.

In some sectors, it may be that female leaders are preferred. In technology companies where a high rate of innovation is important, it may be that women are preferable as top managers. As many as 8 out of 10 top executives are women among the 10 largest technology companies in the United States, and that is hardly a coincidence. If one is to lead a wide range of diversity where many different points of view need to be heard, it is important that the leader has good listening skills. It is also important that a leader is not too headstrong, confident, and dominant in his or her leadership style. Perhaps it has been realised that there are more of these 'listening leaders' among women?

Here are some of the top women leaders in Tech companies around the world.

- Susan Wojcicki CEO of Youtube
- Anjali Sud Ceo of Vimeo
- Anne Chow ACEO of T&T Business
- Yamini Rangan CEO of HubSpot
- Ebony Beckwith CEO Salesforce foundation
- Aicha Evans CEO of Zoox
- Gwynne Shotwell COO and President of SpaceX

- Dr. Lisa Su Presidnet and CEO of AMD President
- Mary Spio Virtual Reality Founder/CEO of CEEK
- Paulette Rowe CEO of Paysafe

# More Objective Performance Management Systems

In the USA, it is more common to use relatively comprehensive performance management systems than in other parts of the world. There are lots of differing opinions about such systems, but they do seem to have some clear advantages. One of the biggest is that they contribute to fairer promotions based on a greater degree of objective criteria, and less on perception. Such an objective system is less beneficial to self-promoting people. Without systems that can document performance, then you can see that more subjective assessments, informal networks, and good self-promotion abilities will form the basis for promotions. Not only women but other minorities and other outsiders will thus benefit from such objective systems as they are usually not as good at self-promoting as men.

# Financial Compensation of Competence

In the USA, companies are willing to pay high salaries for competence or experience while in Norway, salary levels are more hampered by the equality principle. This means fewer variations occur on the salary scale even where competence is very varied where the roles are similar. As a Norwegian set on this mindset, I once challenged the high executive salaries in the US – then I got this crisp answer from a leader in Chevron:

> If you think competence is expensive, try incompetence.

Regardless of what one might feel about executive salaries in the US, they are significantly higher than in Scandinavia. In other words, they are willing to pay more for managers at higher levels regardless of gender because they believe, amongst other things, that they contribute far more than the salaries of those at the lower end. This can mean that more women are motivated to be leaders because they are willing to pay more for the extra effort being put in by a top leader. It takes an insane amount of effort – but you get more in return for it in the form of higher salaries and compensations.

## The Business Community Responsibility

Today, there are only 5-7% female leaders in Scandinavian Countries. The blame for this hardly lies with the politicians. There are just as many women and men taking higher education. There is also a good distribution in the ASA boards with a minimum of 40% being women. In other words, ideal conditions for a more equal working life are largely present here in Norway.

Within certain areas of society, such as politics, there is a much more even distribution of gender in relation to key leadership positions. This is even though key positions of trust in politics are at least as labour-intensive as, for example, being a leader in a large company. There are probably few who will doubt that prime minister, Erna Solberg's calendar looks as tough and labour-intensive as the calendar of the head of Equinor, Telenor or DnB – if not significantly tougher.

The business community must take responsibility for the fact there are only 5-7% female leaders in business. Plans must be made in each company to bring out female talent, and they must be willing to learn from those who have succeeded such as those companies in the United States. If you do not become more skilled in such areas in the future, you will probably lose out to those companies which have managed to capitalise better on gender diversity and therefore, have attracted and retained the most talented women.

Apple took responsibility for women in Saudi Arabia. Tim Cook recently demanded that the Saudi authorities invest in the country. They stated that men and women must be able to work side by side at all their outlets. Recently, Apple received guarantees that this would be possible and that none of their employees would be punished for breaking the restrictive rules which exist in the country today.

It is interesting that large companies can, if they make a stand, set the agenda for gender equality work in countries in which they operate. This helps to promote women's rights in a nation where this is not exactly at the top of the agenda.

Tim Cooke believes that diverse teams are a prerequisite for creating the best products for Apple's customers. This is an important principle for us that we must live by across all geographies.

## Recommendations

In order to attract and retain female talents:

- You must bring out the potential of female employees in your company.
- The company should bring female leadership talents into higher leadership positions.
- You must facilitate a good balance between work and private life for female leadership talents.
- You must promote complementary skills in your company.
- You must respond to customer diversity in terms of men and women.
- Important decisions must be based on a holistic approach.

# 2.5: ETHNICAL, CULTURAL AND SOCIAL INCLUSION

For many years, there has been an increasing degree of interaction across geographies within economics, technology, culture, and politics. This is a trend that has developed since the 1950s, well facilitated through trade agreements and significantly lower tariffs. In recent times, this trend has been further accelerated by the fact that transport over long distances is becoming increasingly cheaper, and easier. A journey that once took months, by ship now takes hours in flights. Low fare airlines have made flying more accessible and affordable to the masses. Larger shares of production and services are currently exported in low-cost countries. The rapid development in emerging markets means that many companies are becoming more global in their scope and uniqueness. With the European Union, and the Schengen agreement, for example, mobility within Europe has become much easier. Opening up the labour market also means that we are all able to work more internationally.

The potential for an economic upturn is great but the risk in the form of greater complexity, cultural crashes and unexpected responses from local competitors and the local community also increases the risk of potential downsides. High-performing global organisations are often less effective in engaging local employees compared to locally established companies. They also have greater difficulties in conducting innovative processes with a view to finding good adaptable solutions in the micro markets in which they operate, and they also often have greater challenges in working with the authorities and the government as well as various forms of social contact.

To overcome the challenges, companies need greater cultural understanding, and comprehension of local preferences and more. Through more international recruitment and career development, this will increase the likelihood of success globally. Despite this, there are still many examples of large international corporations being led by culturally homogeneous groups, often in the top 100 with the same citizenship.

# Migration

From a social political perspective, societies have seen several waves of migration recently that are triggered by political instability and wars. Some examples include the Mediterranean migration crisis, the migration caravans pushing towards the US borders, the Rohingya crisis to mention but three. There are several unwanted side effects of massive immigration and mobility that are directly linked to exclusion from participation.

Both researchers and politicians consider participation in the labour market to be the best way to integrate. Professional activity strengthens social interaction, improves language skills and counteracts the development of parallel societies. Work is also important for self-esteem and for everyday life to be as similar as possible to that of much of the population. Not least, work is crucial to be able to become financially self-sufficient.

In 2019, Andri Georgiadou, Maria Alejandra Gonzalez-Perez and Miguel R. Olivas-Luja published an extensive piece of work bringing together over 35 diversity scholars from around the world presenting different country perspectives on diversity within diversity management. An important aspect of this publication is how it presents new insights into how national and macrosocial environments impact the institutional approaches to diversity management across the world. This extensive collection of research indicates that there is a need for organisations to focus on deep level diversity, rather than choosing a tick-box policy on surface-level diversity. They need to adopt a diversity-friendly approach that best fits the structure, culture and the mentality of their top management team (Georgiadou et al., 2019).

Statistics show that the unemployment rates among non-European immigrants in Norway is substantially higher than the rest of the population. Exclusion from work life has such detrimental effects on one's self esteem and mental health, which is a cost to the society one way or another. We have met several in our research who seem to have given up hope of ever getting into employment or improving their lives.

Employers need to wake up to the realisation of the profitability of diversity utilizing the capabilities of this section of the untapped population. Through awareness training and coaching, those who have fallen outside the A4 norm must have access to the opportunities out there for them. It will require some adjustments; the point is to get employers to see the positive in all the negative and to see the possibilities beneath the barriers.

# Types of Immigrant Workers

There is no one size fits all in the description of immigrant workers. They come with all the internal and external diversity characteristics and have significant differences in goals, integration level and success. In order to somewhat categorize immigrant workers, and how best to integrate and include them in the workplace, one needs some knowledge of their situation in their homelands prior to emigration. These factors include, but are not limited to, their social standing back home, educational levels, occupational skills, and previous exposure to urban and Western cultures (Gibson, 2001).

Using the parameters related to their reason for their departure from their home country, immigrant workers are categorized into four types: Labour Immigrants, Professional Immigrants, Entrepreneurial Immigrants, and Refugees and Asylees (Georgiadou et al., 2019).

## Labour immigrants

The most common, and often most visible category of labour immigrants are the unskilled labourers. They form the bulk of contemporary immigrants. With free labour mobility across most of Europe, there is an influx from countries with low wages and high unemployment to countries with lower unemployment and high wages for the unskilled workforce.

There is a high demand for unskilled workers, and they are often appreciated for their diligence, reliability, and willingness to work hard for lower pay than the native workers. In Norway we can identify carpenters, builders, and painters mostly from Eastern Europe as the most likely workers on construction sites. In farms picking berries and vegetables one is most likely to find only foreign pickers. The native workers are perhaps not necessarily unavailable, based on unemployment figures, however, they are unwilling to perform hard menial jobs for low money.

To employers, this category of workers offers higher profitability. The recruitment process to get in such workers is very low, their wages are lower than average, and they are focussed on their tasks. Because getting the next job depends on a job well done, they often outperform native workers even under the most difficult conditions. They are profitable to the state as well, as upon completion of financial saving goals, most of them will return to their home countries.

However, because of the short-stay perspective, there is little inclination to integrate into the workplace or organisation. This short-stay perspective also means they do not burden the social security system of the host country with retirement benefits and the related costs of taking care of them towards the end of their lives.

## Professional immigrants

Professional immigrants are significantly higher educated, well experienced individuals who, based on their expertise can travel and work in different countries. They may leave their country of origin because of unemployment seeking greener pastures abroad, or they may be recruited to jobs abroad based on their expertise.

Professional immigrants, though well qualified still often receive lower salaries than the native workers doing the same job. One can see the injustice in that. In Norway, one can acknowledge the positive contribution of healthcare professionals from Sweden and Finland who for the most part do not receive equal pay with their Norwegian counterparts.

An example of this kind of labour contracting can be found in the airline industry which has in recent years recruited professionals from low-income countries to work in high income countries but with contracting mechanisms and frameworks in low tax countries. These professionals are then hired out as consultants from the contracting daughter companies registered in low-income countries to the mother company cheaply without legally having to abide by the high salary levels. In this way, the airlines were legally able to pay low wages to their professional foreign workers working in high income countries. While this is profitable to the airlines, it poses moral challenges and conflicts with national trade unions.

The airline company Norwegian ran into several scuffles with trade unions over contracting foreign professionals through a subsidiary in Ireland.

Professional immigrants are profitable not just for their organisations, but for the society they migrate to. They arrive fully educated and ready to contribute to the society which has spent no resources on their welfare or education. In most cases, they retire to their home countries, again without adding the burden of their healthcare, and general cost of care at the end of their lives on their host country.

## Entrepreneurial immigrants

In Entrepreneurial hubs such as Silicon Valley, there is a concentration of entrepreneurial immigration. This is a case of like minds attracting each other with a common goal of developing new technology, or industry. The development of such hubs and how well they attract the right minds is dependent on the availability of substantial business opportunities, access to capital, and access to the right 'human resources'; that is to say, the individuals with the right qualifications, grit and passion.

Because such a hub is likely to attract the 'right minds' from all over the place, we are bound to find it very diverse. It is in such a setting that diversity management is crucial for bringing out the best of the sum of already very talented individuals.

## Refugees and asylees

The diversity in refugees and asylum seekers is as wide as the human diversity. There are many reasons why people leave their countries, with different reasons for seeking protection. They are less driven by economic and job aspirations and depending on how long they expect to stay in exile, they may choose to adopt or not adopt the ways of the new country.

Refugees come in all social classes, capabilities, and skills. However, they remain a group that is least integrated into the workplaces. Often, they settle for low paying jobs, way below their capabilities. Many refugees have gone through devastating and traumatic experiences which take time to process.

There is a saying that Stockholm has the most educated taxi drivers, many are PhD holders who failed to get relevant jobs and settled for what they could get. While professional immigrants often get their capabilities recognised by employees, refugees seem to struggle to get the same recognition. Often their education is not recognised or valid in the host country, and they lack the knowledge of how to get their qualifications ratified.

*My mother is a geriatric nurse, her colleague, a fully qualified and experienced doctor by profession works as a nurse. Her medical degree from outside of Norway was not recognized by the accrediting body, and she did not have the money and time to retake part of the education in Norway in order to get that recognition. She settled for a job as an unqualified geriatric nursing aid and has now progressed to a nurse. There are many such stories in Scandinavia.*

By recognizing a talent pool that exists, instead of setting barriers, it would be more profitable for the state to have clearer mechanisms for validating expertise and the vast wealth of knowledge that resides in refugees and getting them into jobs they are passionate about. Instead, isolation and hopelessness drives many into depression and other mental health related ailments that instead cost the state.

# Accepting Cultural Diversity as the Norm

In addition to greater cooperation across geographies, there is an ever-increasing degree of people settling in a 'foreign country' (migration). Multicultural societies where the existence of several different cultures living side by side are, today, the most common in modern western societies.

Diversity is also an appropriate word to describe all the reasons why people cross foreign borders. It can be love, family, work, conflicts, war, poverty, adoption, education – to name but a few. In a globalised world, there are increasing opportunities and needs for relocation.

Speaking to Kurt Mosvold, the driving force behind the International Festival of Culture in the city of Kristiansand, I was humbled and impressed by the simple yet powerful concept of integration.

*We must celebrate each other and acknowledge each other's contribution to the society.*

The city of Kristiansand has a population of approximately 114,000 people and is home to foreigners from almost 170 countries.

During the international festival, the different nationalities and cultures showcase their cultures, foods and dances in the prominent city centre. What started out as a small event 10 years ago is now a vibrant city festival bringing together people from all walks of life and arenas. From sportsmen to politicians, young and old alike all celebrating each other.

The powerful concept behind this festival as an arena and platform for diversity and inclusion is through positive visualization of a diversity. Positive visualization creates affection, trust, through the lived positive experience. Artistic expressions, music, dance, drama, and foods are all uniting and fundamentally inclusive.

There are many such festivals in Scandinavia, but few are at the level of the Kristiansand festival. In my opinion, we need to find reasons to celebrate each other in the daily little things. This morning, I am personally grateful for a mango from Pakistan, and for the migration and diversity that enriched the start of my day.

Modern societies are culturally complex, but there are smooth transitions in the various cultural forms of mixing. Some immigrants are almost fully integrated into new societies, whilst others have made cultural adjustments to a lesser extent. If you are not willing to take root in your new country, you will live in a transit-like state. The roots do not get the necessary nutrients to grow and develop further without removing the plastic.

The danger of developing parallel societies is greater if we are not able to unite cultures better. In such societies, ethnic or religious minorities have organised themselves in such a way that social and cultural contact with the majority society is reduced to a minimum. This results in reduced opportunities for integration with, amongst other things, unemployment, and increased crime as some of the unfortunate consequences. Criminal activity amongst immigrants and immigrant youth can be largely explained by the same patterns used to observe other crimes which is a lack of participation in school, poor financial and living conditions, parents' low level of education and little participation in working life to name but a few.

## Polarisation and Society

Most people have realised that the homogeneous nation-state belongs to a bygone age. The National Conservatives' expressed longing to return to it is pure illusion. The large-scale immigration from the third world in Europe has created ethnic tensions and greater political polarisation in recent years. Europe and the United States stand at a crossroads where strong opposing forces are moving towards the outer wings of the political axis.

Among other things, the researchers write that the internet functions as a kind of echo chamber where people with equal views exchange and reinforce their opinions, which thus become more extreme. It often seems that debaters lie in their own trenches and pepper each other with allegations and arguments from each end of the scale. Especially on social media, one finds strong opinions far from the norm. Many people think this looks gloomy.

Many European political leaders do not have good enough control over the situation in Europe. Loss of control has taken hold in large parts of the population, who are full of distrust of politicians, and for the first time ever it is possible to imagine the EU crumbling. Uncertainty surrounds immigration at too high a pace, especially from immigrants who have a cultural background far removed from what they perceive as European values and culture. There is little doubt that immigration and especially Islam is the real epicentre of the national conservative wave of revival.

The far right and the far left are two sides of the same coin. They both operate in a world Where the individual must give way to the collective, and where violence against opponents of opinion seems to be okay. People live in ideological media bubbles where one would rather avoid being contradicted, and social media has provided forums for exaggeration and lies. While the National Conservatives long for a nation-state illusion, where the white majority population is portrayed as an endangered and cowed entity, the left and some liberals cultivate an exclusive identity policy, where the racism card is handed out with impeccable generosity and society is divided according to group affiliation. Racism is an obvious problem in our societies, but when you hear that it is racist to ask where someone comes from, many are shuffled into a booth they do not recognise themselves in. When new people with a quite different culture and language move into an area and in a relatively short time relocate the population composition, it is understandable that some feel under pressure. That fear cannot simply be dismissed with bad attitudes. In many ways, we have a society where many people do what they can to avoid having their attitudes confronted by someone who thinks otherwise. In the wake of this, 'fake news' and 'fake science' arise.

*❛ We build too many walls and too few bridges. ❜*

*Albert Einstein – 1951*

# Black Lives Matter: A Movement for Inclusion

Black Lives Matter is a decentralized political and social movement advocating non-violent civil disobedience in protest against incidents of police brutality and other racially motivated violence against black people. The broader movement and its related organisations typically advocate against police violence towards black people as well as pushing for various other policy changes considered to be related to black liberation. The overall Black Lives Matter movement is a decentralized network of activists with no formal hierarchy.

In July 2013, the movement began with the use of the hashtag #BlackLivesMatter on social media after the acquittal of George Zimmerman in the shooting dead of African-American teen Trayvon Martin seventeen months earlier in February 2012. The movement became nationally recognised for street demonstrations following the 2014 deaths of two African Americans, that of Michael Brown—resulting in protests and unrest in Ferguson, Missouri, a city near St. Louis—and Eric Garner in New York City. Since the Ferguson protests, participants in the movement have demonstrated against the deaths of numerous other African Americans by police action or while in police custody.

The movement returned to national headlines and gained further international attention during the global George Floyd protests in 2020 following the killing of George Floyd by Minneapolis police officer Derek Chauvin. An estimated 15 – 26 million people participated in the 2020 Black Lives Matter protests in the United States, making it one of the largest movements in the country's history.

## The defining power

The defining power of the term racism belongs to those who are exposed to such discrimination. It does not belong to society, and certainly not to those who discriminate and who act out of prejudice about race or exercise their white privilege – so that it goes beyond we melanin-rich.

*It is dangerous to be indigenous peoples either African Americans, or other types of minorities in the United States. You feel vulnerable and insecure when you do completely 'ordinary' activities, such as jogging, bird watching, grilling, shopping, or playing.*

*Recently, my 20-year-old son travelled to Los Angeles, his first holiday alone, without the rest of the family. Being a biracial well-built man, he would easily pass for an African American. He was born and raised in the relative safety of Scandinavia and perhaps naïve and innocent to the world.*

*While I wished him the experience of travelling and having fun with his friends, I was petrified that he was travelling alone to the USA. There were so many 'what ifs' in my head, all coloured by tragic events and experiences of African American men. For the duration of his holiday, I possibly did more praying than I have ever done. Thankfully he had the time of his life, while his mother lost weight worrying.*

## Self-empowerment

Blaming society and defining yourself as a victim will never solve any challenges, despite the fact that they are to blame. Even though authorities, private actors and societies can contribute with tools to help better integrations, the individual bears the greatest responsibility.

This is basically the case for all people, regardless of where they come from and what background they have. It is in one's best interest to see oneself as responsible for your own progress in life. You must not place the responsibility for your own situation as being not in your control. Unfortunately, some easily end up in a so-called 'victim' role where self-pity and focus on matters beyond your own responsibility are key characteristics.

> ❝ *It is a pity for me, and it is the fault of others.* ❞

For groups, it can be a collective way of thinking and talking. You expect others to solve your problems, and you become comfortable with dissatisfaction and with the lack of help from others. This attitude stops you trying to do something about your own situation. If you can't see the connection between what you do and how you feel, you have put yourself into a hopeless situation.

Fortunately, this is not the most common attitude among people with a minority background. Most want to be part of the community and want work participation. The majority strive, despite the odds. It is not sad to read about graduates applying for hundreds of jobs and never being called to interviews because of their names but rather could be seen as inspirational as despite each rejection they still pick themselves up and send one more application after the other.

*When I was finishing my masters, I dreaded having to apply for jobs. I knew that my ethnicity would play a role in the selection process. I knew I was likely to not be called in for interviews, I had already experienced that during previous summers looking for a summer job.*

*I decided I was my own captain and commander, and creator of my own narrative.*

*In my standard application letter template, I wrote:*

> *I am a Norwegian citizen of Ugandan/African decent and I am proud of my cultural heritage. If this is a problem for your company, then I do not want to work for you either.*

*I had some rather interesting interviews I must say. In one interview, the interviewer spent the better part of an hour trying to sell me their policy on inclusion and diversity to convince me that the company was indeed not racist. In taking charge of my narrative, it was my choice who to work for, I had taken back my power.*

# Class Diversity

Class diversity is about including those from the lower social class into the organisation. Unlike in Scandinavia where universal education is free, in most countries, education is a privilege which those born into the lower classes may not be able to access. Without access to money and education, mobility up the socio-economic ladder is difficult.

This means that a large portion of highly capable people are otherwise excluded from managerial roles and may end up in low paying blue collar roles or no job at all simply because of the class they were born into.

Class diversity is important to organisations for many reasons. People from lower social classes have been found to be less egocentric and more caring and giving, all which are important traits for inclusion and leadership.

If a marginalised population is included in the leadership, it has been observed that there is more effective advocacy for the marginalised. In addition, as discussed in the section on diversity and customer service, representation of a marginalised group in a company's leadership has similar effects on its ability to reach, understand, and retain clients of that group.

Therefore, it follows that discrimination of a certain social class is actually a loss of services and a lack of access to a workforce with traits needed despite the lack of formal education.

The opposite applies to favouritism and elitism. Hiring someone simply because of an inherited name/status or qualification which was a result of generational wealth may be detrimental to the organisation. They may not necessarily have the skillsets, drive, or motivation to do a good job. They may also feel untouchable, hence uninterested in delivering results because they know they will not face any consequences.

## Social inclusion and poverty

According to the World Bank, social inclusion is about improving the terms on which individuals and groups take part in society. Poverty and social identity cut across all the dimensions of diversity. Irrespective of race, age, gender, religion, disability, ethnicity, gender identification, the poor are marginalised and are not able to access the same opportunities as the rich despite having talent, drive and putting in the effort in many cases. It is common knowledge that the gap between the 'haves' and the 'have nots' is growing with the chasm between the two camps getting deeper.

Social inclusion is not only the right thing to do in order to achieve a fairer society but is also the most profitable thing to do. From a societal perspective, social exclusion has an impact on stability, crime and violence which are not only reflected in the national spending but also on the GDP as a loss. A study by the World Bank found that in Romania, the exclusion of the ethnic minority the Roma cost Romania 887 million Euros in terms of productivity in 2018. Working individuals not only pay taxes but they contribute to the welfare of the state.

Fighting poverty does not prevent anyone from getting rich. Wealth is then not a problem either. It is, in fact, a prerequisite for welfare. Poverty is the starting point - welfare must be created. Therefore, everyone should cheer on those who succeed in business in the same way as we cheer on our sports heroes. The greater the income one manages to generate, the greater the income for the common good in the form of taxes, fees and more and more jobs which will be created. The vast majority, regardless of political point of view, however, want a fairer distribution of the world's benefits, but we differ in our views on how to achieve this in practice.

While there is a trend in the business community today that social responsibility is proven by the fact that profits in companies to a greater extent go to various charitable causes, charity itself has not been able to permanently solve the world's problems. Most people experiencing social exclusion and poverty would rather be given the opportunity to participate in society than be given handouts.

Some of the richest people on the planet, such as Bill Gates, Warren Buffett, George Soros, Steve Case, David Rubenstein, and Leon Black, have given away hundreds of billions of dollars of their personal wealth in recent years.

Their behaviour and stories of the joy of giving back to society which has helped to make them rich also seem to have found a sounding board here at home in Norway, with examples like Olav Thon, Kjell Inger Røkke, the Kavli foundation, to mention but a few. This is despite our well-developed welfare state taking care of much of the distribution.

# 2.6: (DIS)ABILITY DIVERSITY

Disability means permanent health problems that can lead to limitations in daily life. There may be impaired vision, hearing, or mobility, reading and writing difficulties, heart or lung problems and mental disorders. Nearly 17% of the population aged 15-66, that is 585,000 people, stated that they had a disability in 2015 (Statistics Norway).

People with disabilities face many barriers and challenges when accessing workplaces and being included in employment opportunities. Despite the discrimination towards people with 'visible' and sometimes 'invisible' disabilities, they are rarely included in the debates around diversity and inclusion in organisations.

In general, and across geographies, people with disabilities are less represented in work life compared to the able bodied despite having equal competencies. When organisations do not include employees with disabilities, they do not capitalise on the profitability of this group of people.

In 2015, 74% of the population aged 15-66 were employed. The same was true for 43% of people with disabilities. Since 2002, the proportion has fallen by almost three percentage points for the disabled, compared with two percentage points for the entire population. More than half of the disabled who have been employed have had their work situation adapted to their disability. This is a clear increase from 2002.

Occupational activity increases with rising levels of education among the disabled, as it does in the general population. While 44%of the disabled with upper secondary level education are in work, this applies to 64% of those with a college or university education of up to four years and 77% of those with higher education than this. The difference between the disabled and the general population is least among those with higher education (SSB: 2017)

Of the 325,000 disabled people who were not employed in the second quarter of 2015, 87,000, or 27%, wanted a job. This proportion has largely remained at the same level since these surveys started in 2002. There are some surveys which show that in most cases disabled people do not even get a chance in the job market.

The MMI survey, which was commissioned by the Documentation Center, shows that only every tenth leader in the private business sector will call in a blind jobseeker with a guide dog for an interview, even if he or she is very professionally qualified for the job. And two out of three employers will reject a wheelchair user even with particularly good qualifications (Britta Nilsson 2015). Lack of infrastructure to enable them easy access and mobility is one reason, but mostly, ignorance and fear of not knowing what to do with a disabled person are the barriers.

## Technology as an enabler for the disabled

With the right help, not all disabilities are a disability anymore. Technological innovations for the blind, partially sighted, hard of hearing and support for people with mental challenges can counteract and in certain cases neutralise the disability. Many managers do not know that there are good aids, not least in connection with computer technology, which will enable, for example, the blind and deaf to function much like any other workers. In Norway, expenses for such aids are covered by the public sector, but the information about the aids can be confusing and inaccessible to employers.

If you are aware that these people are a resource, which is something we previously, and perhaps still, overlook in hiring processes, then you increase the opportunities to recruit the best. Disabled people are often strong-willed people who have worked hard to show what they can do, and they can have attitudes which our companies can benefit from.

*Photograph 2: Then Prime Minister Erna Solberg in conversation with Michael Moore, an Energy Broker with severe visual impediment*

Michael Moore, who has severely impaired vision, was visited by former Prime Minister Erna Solberg at his workplace, Icap energy. She wanted to hear his story. NAV initially wanted to provide him with disability benefits, but with the employer's help, the Norwegian Association of the Blind's rehabilitation course and his own willingness, he still works as an energy broker despite minimal vision. This was a happy story, said Erna, who met the Association of the Blind afterwards and heard about the general lack of follow-up of the visually impaired in the health care system.

Every single year, 14,000 Norwegians lose their sight completely or partially. Fortunately, many can live well without sight. They have, thanks to technology become active again and been given back their dignity.

Training in 'living without sight' is the key to people regaining faith in their own abilities, and learning that life can still be good as a blind or partially sighted person. Of particular importance are the courses that the Association of the Blind offers at the vision and mastery centres.

Many have been through exceedingly difficult periods after they completely or partially lost their sight. Some were close to ending everything. Severely visually impaired Michael Moore was in a situation where he envisioned being insured by NAV for the rest of his life, but he refused to let that happen. Today he is one of the best energy brokers in Norway.

# Mental Health

## Psychological safety

According to Wikipedia, Psychological safety is the ability to show and employ oneself without fear of negative consequences of self-image, status, or career. It is the shared belief, or rather the built trust that one is accepted and respected even when they make mistakes or have different opinions from other team members.

For an organization to benefit from diversity, honest communication is vital. When employees are afraid to speak up or share their concerns, management loses the opportunity to have clear situational awareness of the internal environment of the company. Fear of speaking up also means that many innovative ideas remain unshared.

> *One of the most important forms of antidepressants is having the opportunity to work and feel valuable by contributing to the company and society*
> *(Lars Erik Lund 2022)*

Unfortunately, many people do not feel safe in their workplaces and do not feel comfortable being themselves. Without psychological safety, there is no passion. While this lack of passion may create a 'peaceful' working environment without much conflict, more is lost in the so-called fearful peace. When people cannot voice half-baked thoughts or ask questions, the organization will lose the opportunity to build an innovative culture.

Psychological safety in the workplace is not an issue that should be sitting with HR or leadership alone. Everyone in the workspace is responsible for creating and fostering a trusting and safe workspace. A team may have the most brilliant and qualified members but if there is no sense of trust and safety, their performance will not be as good as it could otherwise be.

In her 2018 book The Fearless Organization: Creating Psychological Safety in the Workplace for Learning, Innovation and Growth, Amy C. Edmondson presents her findings from more than 20 years of research on psychological safety.

She defined a safe working climate as one where employees feel:

- Comfortable being themselves and expressing their views
- Able to share concerns and mistakes without fear of retribution or fear
- Confident to speak up without the fear of humiliation, or blame
- Can ask questions when they are unsure about something
- Trusted and respected by their colleagues and can trust and respect their colleagues in return
- Confident in reporting mistakes made quickly without fear of retribution
- Confident that mistakes are welcomed, rather than sanctions or shamed
- Courageous enough to share innovative ideas even then raw ideas
- Their opinion matters
- Confident that they won't be suppressed, silenced, ridiculed, or intimidated for expressing an original thought
- Confident that they can speak their truth even when it is a difficult truth
- Confident in the knowledge that their performance will still be valued and managed even when expectations are not met.

Figure 17: Maslow's Hierarchy of Needs

As can be seen in Maslow's pyramid of needs, psychological safety is a fundamental need that must be met before the inclusion and belonging needs can.

## Skillsets beyond physical disability

By excluding people with disabilities, organisations are missing out on a variety of the skills available in this group. They can provide a wide range of skillsets that may well go beyond the skillsets of any individual otherwise seen as able.

People with disabilities have often faced many hurdles during their lives and thus have good cognitive skills with as a high dose of resilience, coupled with creative problem-solving skills, which means they can be innovative, and are generally far kinder and more accepting of others.

Stephen Hawking was an incredible man who, although severely handicapped did not let it hold him back. He is perhaps one of the greatest authorities in recent years amongst scientists. He broke through with his dissertations on black holes and created a connection between the general theory of relativity and quantum mechanics.

Hawking suffered from a motor neuron disease related to amyotrophic lateral sclerosis (ALS), a disorder that confined him to the wheelchair and deprived him of all opportunities to communicate directly with the outside world. He therefore worked with a special language computer that was controlled by his eyes and some muscles in his face. This enabled him to hold lectures, have conversations and so much more. If such a severely disabled person could reach this far, this should be an inspiration to others with disabilities, as well as an eyeopener to the rest of us of the potential that lies within the human spirit.

Stephen Hawking died on March 14, 2018. Despite his enormous disability he became one of the world's most influential scientists of our time.

# 2.7: AGE DIVERSITY

Today's older generation have had a better education, are healthier and live longer, and as many as 50% of employees over the age of 67 can imagine working for a long time (Center for Senior Policy: 2015). This shows that there is obviously a significant potential for Norwegian working life to facilitate that for those who want it.

Elderly people at work are an important key to competitiveness in companies and to the welfare of the future. Unfortunately, the potential of older workers is really not used well enough and is often overlooked. A large part of this is due to stereotypes about age. Stereotypes range from saying about older people:

- Skills have gone out of date.
- Won't fit in as we need a young and dynamic environment here.
- Have less to contribute to society.
- Do not have as much energy anymore.
- Are to be pitied because of their age and more.

However, most older people are in good health, have lots of experience and represent a wide range of resources, knowledge, culture and so on. Getting older is not the same as it was a few decades ago. You are no longer past it just because you are 60 or 70.

The biggest mistake made about age is the same as with gender and geography, which is to generalise. Older workers are not a group of people with clear common denominators. They are extremely different individuals with different energy levels, a variety of skills, and many qualifications.

Even though in some countries there is legislation that is intended to counteract age discrimination, it still happens a lot for a variety of reasons. As a result, far too many older workers become an untapped resource. A combination of long experience and continuity combined with young curiosity and innovation can often be an excellent combination in a team. However, many managers are unaware of this.

Age is currently no limit for Warren Buffet who remains actively involved in business despite his age which is in the 90's.

# Age Discrimination

Healthy able-bodied people over the age of 50 are systematically put on the scrap heap, but few will talk about it. The problem is that there is a widespread acceptance that differential treatment of older workers is completely legitimate - while there is discrimination in line with gender, ethnicity, and disability and more according to Norwegian law. There is a definite trend towards employers wanting younger workers, with the elderly being encouraged to downsize.

The reason why people over 50 end up on the scrap heap can be simpler than you think. Imagine that after a few years you have managed to get to a level of managerial responsibility in a company. Then you get a new employee who is not only older than you, but who also knows your job better. Now you have managerial responsibility for this person. For some, that can be really hard as they will feel threatened by the new employee.

In fact, as an employer you should be looking widely for employees who think it is okay to manage someone who is more competent or experienced than themselves. It is a very different type of management, and most managers will do anything to avoid being in that situation, so recruiters therefore act accordingly.

The consequence is that an older person's chance of being hired for a new job when they have passed 50 becomes smaller the more competent they are on the grounds that 'we do not need that much experience in this job' or 'you are overqualified'. Think of the skills and experience you are missing out on. You just need the right manager in place to manage that experience.

Many countries have Working Environment Acts in their legislation which prohibit an employer from discriminating against anyone on the grounds of age in working life. The prohibitions against age discrimination normally apply to all aspects of the employment relationship, including selection for an interview, regardless of whether they would have been offered the position. When hiring, the employer should hire the one who is best qualified, and in principle should not emphasise the age of the applicants who can apply. In Norway, we have a flexible age limit of up to 72 years in most areas of working life. If you are 58 years old, you can still work for another 14 years.

Differential treatment due to age can sometimes be permitted after a closer assessment. In certain cases, the employer may emphasise the age composition when hiring, but this must be justified by something more than just a general desire for age distribution. An example where this may be permitted is where several employees in a team will retire shortly and the employer may lose too much important experience all at once.

## Why Older Workers Should Stay Longer in Service

Everyone knows the value of knowing that '*I can achieve something; I can do something*' - from the time you are little until you retire. This is also most likely why the elderly want to work for longer. The best way to maintain health is physical and mental activity, which working supplies for the older workers. Most importantly work can also give dignity.

The elderly can contribute well to companies. The Center for Senior Policy has reviewed research on this, and there is no basis for claiming that older workers are less motivated, less willing to change, less loyal, have poorer health or are more vulnerable to the balance between work and leisure. In fact, it was found that older people can be better than their younger colleagues on corporate internal responsibility, including loyalty and helpfulness towards other colleagues and especially new employees. Older people are a good thing, and the working environment needs to accept them and all they have to offer.

Having elderly people at work is sensible and good policy. Those who look to the future agree that our financial sustainability will be significantly better if older workers work for longer. The elderly make up around 20% of all people of working age in western societies. That is about the same as in 1970, but it is likely that this will double by 2060. At the same time, we know that if people work two years longer than they do today, public budgets will be strengthened by five%. Imagine if they worked for another 10 - 15 years just how productive that could be.

## Performance-enhancing age composition

Age diversity in the workplace enhances productivity and the working environment, says senior researcher Bjørg Åse Sørensen at the Institute of Labour Research. She has worked for several years on research on working life and the working environment, and the common denominator for the research she has done, shows that an even age distribution creates better job satisfaction and increased productivity throughout.

From a professional point of view, it is a good combination to match the young, recent graduates who have the updated knowledge with the older employees' network and experience. Seeing the company and the opportunities with fresh new eyes in combination with continuity and experience provides a performance-enhancing diversity. Sørensen points out that an even age distribution, where one third is young, one third adults and one third older, has greater productivity and it is easier to solve problems. Jobs with only young people or only the elderly have lower productivity.

# PART 3
# INVISIBLE
# DIVERSITY

# 3.1: PERSONALITY DIVERSITY

Personality consists of the qualities that give a person their individual character. It encompasses the more enduring qualities of being human, such as needs, temperament, abilities, habits, attitudes, values, interests, and self-perception. In other words, one can say that a personality is...

*the behavioural and mental characteristics by which an individual is recognised as being unique.*

Different personality traits provide the prerequisites for success with different types of tasks. Personality diversity is one of those diversity categories which cuts across the whole human diversity spectrum. Needless to say, every individual exhibits a personality, irrespective of age, gender, race, faith and any other 'category' one may box them into. For a well-functioning society and organisations, we need a mix of personalities.

From the dawn of time, attempts have been made to categorise people in different ways. From the four temperaments of antiquity - the sanguine, choleric, melancholic, and phlegmatic to today's more holistic and well-defined models. The systems today cover most of our personality types and can often, with a high degree of accuracy, predict how we will behave in different situations. I have personally worked extensively with the MAP Technical Manual for Measuring and Assessing Individual Potential (Sjöberg et al., 2012). This manual is based on extensive research and widely used in Scandinavia.

It is common to categorise different personality traits using different test tools that address different variants of the five-factor model popularly called 'The big five'. The five-factor model is a hierarchical model with five major features at the top which are also called domains and several smaller features below which are called facets. The five-factor model has clear relevance for various situations in working life. In several meta-studies, it has been found that the five main features have implications for creativity, academic achievement, and job performance in various positions.

## 1. Extroversion

Extroversion measures the degree of energy with which a person encounters life and thus describes the social position he or she takes in different situations. The scale captures the person's need and interest in being social and interacting with other people. Through this scale, a picture is generated of how the person presents him or herself and how he or she is experienced by others.

This applies to whether you need to take a seat and think, as well as whether you feel comfortable being the focus of others' attention and expectations. The scale also reflects the degree to which one feels comfortable moving freely amongst other people, even amongst strangers. The search for experiences which provide excitement and stimulation, together with the person's pace of life is the core of this scale.

Our experience of leaders who score highly on the extroversion scale is that they seek out and get energy from social situations. They like to have people around them and prefer to develop ideas through discussion in their working life. They may tend to be a little impatient and may at times act quickly without thinking things through properly. Those who score lower on the extroversion scale are more attracted to their own reflections and prefer to act more privately and in a more controlled manner. They like peace and calm in order to concentrate and do not like to be interrupted. People with low scores like to work long-term and preferably alone for long periods. A good example of an introverted person is the chess genius Magnus Carlsen.

There are more extroverts than introverts in leadership roles, and extrovert leaders seem to be more effective in some areas than introverts. However, it is even more clear that introverts and extroverts can contribute complementary skills within a group or team. We need the long-term and 'tolerant' thinkers as well as those who can control, and quality assure their work. Several researchers and scholars have recently spoken out because it has been easy to underestimate the leadership qualities of introverts. Several of them claim that, on average, organisations may, in fact, be better served by leaders who are introverts.

In many contexts, it is extremely important that managers have good listening skills, and that they reflect well before decisions are made. It is not always those who speak first and loudest who have the best solutions. Jim Collins' research from the book 'Good to Great' was based on eleven successful companies which had bosses who were low-key, not exposed, but very hard-working and who really brought their companies to great new heights (Collins, 2001).

There are good and bad leaders who are both introverted and extroverted and one is on average no better than the other. It will ultimately be just a different style - where some prefer one type of leadership style, while others prefer something else.

It is hardly a coincidence that hotel founder Petter Stordalen tweets his way, while Statoil boss Eldar Sætre excels with his absence on social media.

Charismatic and socially outgoing leadership has its advantages as well as its disadvantages, just as a more introverted case- and task-oriented style - has. What can be considered, however, is which style is suitable for the various phases a company is in. In a large 'turnaround' process, one might prefer a strong and clear leader with good communication skills. In a more long-term strategic situation where you must build stone by stone, you might be just as well served by an introverted leader, but here too, the picture can be ambiguous.

In a technology company where the requirement for innovation is high, it is extremely important to be able to listen well to all specialists. Here, introverted leaders are preferred as they often possess better listening skills. In a retail company where the purpose is to motivate large masses for increased sales, you can see why a charismatic leader with the ability to inspire will be preferable. But there are no documented final answers here.

## 2. Openness

The scale of openness reflects a tendency to be open to, and in need of, inner experiences - that is, emotional and cognitive experiences that take place inside a person. These inner experiences are usually stimulated by external events or activities, but can also come from within the individuals themselves, for example with the help of their own imagination.

Openness includes the tendency to have a vivid imagination, an aesthetic sense, a responsiveness to inner emotional life, a love of variety, an intellectual curiosity and to be independent of the views and opinions of others. It also reflects whether a person prefers variety, complexity, and creativity, or whether one is increasingly interested in specific knowledge and is happy to choose the known and traditional over the unknown and unconventional. Openness corresponds positively with efficiency in the leadership role.

In general, those leaders who score highly on the openness scale are happy to seek new ways of doing things, and often have a liberal view of life. On average, they are probably also better in terms of change-oriented management. At the other end of the scale, we find a tendency to prefer the down-to-earth, practical rules, systems, and a greater degree of being closed off. In a team or group, you also need both the visionary and creative, but also the more down-to-earth and practical who are on average better in practice at carrying out the jobs.

Where changes are required, it is good to have an advocate of change as leader, but there are leaders who want to change too many things, and maybe change too much at the same time This can lead to huge wear and tear inside the organisation. which almost gets to the point of reform fatigue, and eventually they will struggle to get the employees involved, especially those who were less open to change in the first place.

However, the whole world is facing major changes right now, and Norway is no exception in that respect, in fact, quite the contrary. Openness to change and adaptability will be even more important resources in the future. The challenges the world faces require collaboration beyond borders and boundaries with an openness to new ideas. We are heading for a world where 'survival of the fittest' principle is more 'survival of the most adaptive to change'.

## 3.  Agreeableness

The agreeableness or sociability scale reflects how a person interacts with others. This shows in the degree of trust in others, the belief in other people as basically good, the ability to empathise and the tendency to help and support others. Central to this scale is the emotional quality that characterises a person's relationships, as well as the ability to express love and compassion for others and in the presence of others. This scale reflects a genuinely sympathetic attitude - in the sense that one is direct or sincere towards others even if it means that you appear less flexible.

Managers' sociability correlates positively with job satisfaction in the organisation. It is important to note that sociability is as diverse and varied between individuals as societies. It is important to remember that the expression of emotion varies between cultures. Within some cultures, it is encouraged to be vocal while others promote silent acceptance of situations. One can talk about the Latin temper, or the Scandinavian 'Sweep things under the rug' ways. In leading a diverse group, it is vital to take that into consideration and in that case be aware that some people express their frustrations better than others.  A leader may be mistaken in assuming that a team is well functioning purely due to the absence of feedback when it may even be the very opposite.

Leaders who score highly on sociability seem loving and sympathetic by nature. They are kind-hearted and willing to cooperate, are more forgiving, flexible, and polite, but they can tend to be gullible at times. Then again, you will also find those who are more concerned with their own needs. They are tougher, more competitive people who are concerned with getting things done their way. In a team or in a group, you need the caring and relationship-oriented, but also those who can separate feelings and facts and make the tough business decisions which may be at the expense of individuals' needs and desires.

Many of us will probably like the leaders and colleagues who are sympathetic by nature and who show care and understanding of different people's needs.

They are nice to be with, are often socially competent and are usually good team players. The problem is that they can often be the conflict-shy type who will avoid confrontation at all costs and who promise more than they can deliver. Sympathetic people may have some difficulty separating emotions and facts and may be too preoccupied with keeping everyone happy.

Good leadership is not always about winning popularity contests. Goals must be delivered in accordance with the board and the owners' requirements, so it is often the slightly tougher type of leadership with learned sociability which will be what is required.

## 4. Emotional Stability

The emotional stability or emotional balance scale reflects a person's general emotional state. By this is meant the intensity and frequency with which the person experiences mostly negative emotions such as anger, restlessness, guilt, and depression. Intensity and frequency are crucial factors as they form the basis of the emotional state which influences behaviour in everyday life. This will include whether that person has a steady mood and good self-confidence, as well as how effectively they handle their own impulses.

Of vital importance is how constructive they are when it comes to dealing with adversity and other stressful situations they encounter in life. The scale also reflects what emotional resources a person must use to solve problems and conflicts which arise every day. The dimension corresponds positively with effective leadership whereas neuroticism often correlates negatively with leadership efficiency and well-being in the workplace.

Emotionally stable leaders can withstand stress and insecurity without spending a lot of energy worrying or feeling anxious while emotionally unstable and anxious leaders tend to experience negative emotions, and more often than not, show them repeatedly. Even though emotional stability in most situations will be preferable, perhaps too much emotional stability can lead to underestimating the dangers, threats, or unexpected competition. A little worry in a group can always help to balance a somewhat uncritically positive image.

## 5. Conscientiousness

This scale describes the person's attitude to tasks and obligations, is associated with performance and describes how one prefers to work, whether it is systematic, methodical, and purposeful or spontaneous, flexible, and unplanned. The scale represents whether there is an underlying driving force to achieve the goals required. It also measures further characteristics that are necessary to be able to follow this driving force, such as the tendency to be organised, systematic, conscientious, efficient, and energetic. The dimension corresponds positively with job performance.

Leaders who score highly on the planning scale seem more conscientious, thorough, thoughtful, responsible, and careful. At the other end of the spectrum, we find those who are more laid-back and less organised, but somewhat less risk-averse, flexible, and spontaneous. Controlling impulses, being able to control oneself, being able to postpone satisfaction in the short term in order to achieve more long-term goals is a key element in the adult, modern personality. A conscious and active self-control is necessary to achieve goals in education, profession, and career. Planning is about making realistic plans and persevering in efforts to realise those plans. Anyone who makes new plans every day will find it difficult to get anywhere. Planned personality is the only personality trait associated with efficiency and success across most professions.

In a high-performing team, you are nevertheless served by the thorough, conscientious, long-term, and strategic leaders as well as the more flexible and more spontaneous. It creates a better dynamic in the management team and means that it is easier to make the necessary adjustments along the way, so if a 'Fat pig appears during the year' which you had not planned or budgeted for - then you take it and run with it anyway.

## 6. Arrogance and insecurity

You might think that arrogance is simply a result of a good overdose of self-esteem. This is not always the case, although there are many of them with good self-esteem who often, or at times, also succumb to an arrogant demeanour. Pride is a behaviour which compensates for an inner helplessness and uncertainty. In many ways, you build up a big ego as a compensation for lack of self-confidence, and for that reason you become more self-absorbed. Whether the leader in question has an excess of self-confidence or has built up a big ego to bolster a lack of self-confidence is not always easy to spot at first glance, but you will discover this after a while if you are a little observant.

Those who are arrogant, with a big ego, can appear as if they are independent, confident, and controlled. Self-righteousness keeps others at arm's length and prevents people seeing the actual situation. Arrogance then acts as a cool and protective wrap around the insecure and hurt ego. Such a protection strategy can be effective in the short term, but in the long run it simply generates additional problems. One of these is isolation and loneliness.

A leader who compensates for their internal insecurity with arrogance will quickly impact on their own judgement and alertness and help to create a distance between themselves and those they lead. Being able to humbly listen to employees' assessments is the key to good leadership. The problem is that the arrogant often have a challenge doing this. This inability to actively listen, slowly but surely undermines the leader's own power base. The fear of being exposed as confused and insecure means they constantly focus on themselves and prop up their own private defences. In this process they become blind to the needs and contributions of others, and in thinking, judging, and acting they become one-sided and narrow-minded.

An arrogant leader wants to control everyone else but struggles to control himself. The nature of arrogance is to surround themselves with employees who support their type of control by promoting colleagues who support them. In this way, critical and honest voices which could have helped to adjust the course in a constructive way are silenced. All constructive course adjustments are lacking, and the results are not based on what benefits the community and the organisation but are based on what benefits the arrogant leader. The leader's vulnerability becomes more important to protect than the community's best interests.

It is not uncommon to build a big ego as compensation for a lack of self-confidence. It can then be difficult to distinguish extremely high self-esteem and a big ego. Arrogance is not a personality that builds trust and honest communication, components which we have said repeatedly are vital for a well-functioning diverse team.

Many of us are not aware of our dominating personality traits and how they affect our choices, lives and decisions. Taking a personality test for fun or for identifying fit to an organisation is something I recommend. We are a combination of all the personality traits, sometimes, depending on the situation we find ourselves in. Becoming aware of why we act and react the way we do is a first step to monitoring and altering our undesired responses and behaviour that arises from our personality. It is about taking charge and not being on autopilot.

# 3.2: NEURODIVERSITY

In her recently published article in the Financial Times, Dr Anna Doyle delivers a powerful piece on why the world needs the neurodivergent right now in the Covid-19/post-Covid times. She puts forward the different 'superpowers' that different neurodiversity carries with it and just how badly we need those powers right now. The ability to think outside the proverbial box and produce new ways of working and socialising has been crucial during the pandemic (Doyle, 2020). We have all used Zoom and Teams far more than we knew we could. From virtual meetings to lunches, concerts, funerals, and more. The virtual world that once was the domain of nerds and geeks became everyone's common survival platform.

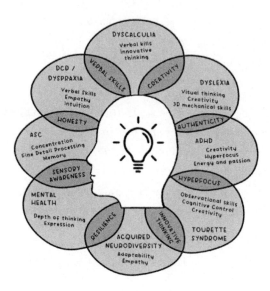

(Dr Nancy Doyle, based on the work of Mary Colley)

*Figure 18 : The Overlapping Strengths of Neurodiversity (Doyle, 2020)*

# Genius Arises on the Verge of 'Madness'?

It is reasonable to assume that you must be a little special yourself to achieve something incredibly special. Behind extraordinary achievements, there is naturally also a completely extraordinary effort. Those who succeed with superior results have almost infinite energy, they are risk-averse, persistent, and often think outside the box.

Many have argued that one needs a form of 'obsession' as a driving force to achieve excellent and world-class results, and that this extra energy arises in the 'borderland of madness'. Regardless of such a perspective, there is little or no doubt that difference is a prerequisite. Medium effort and completely normal behaviour usually achieve normal results.

If you look historically at the people who have achieved something extraordinary in life, they are often characterized by being special, distinctive, and different. You simply must be 'a little crazy' to achieve world-class results. This view is shared by many psychologists. Among other things, there seems to be an inability to filter impressions which create everything from ingenious ideas at one end with a potential for deep psychosis at the other. It is even claimed by some that geniuses get madness as part of the deal.

American John Nash was one of the world's most brilliant mathematicians of the 1950s. Like many other geniuses, he had mental disorders (in his case, the diagnosis was paranoid schizophrenia). In 1994, the mathematics genius was awarded the Nobel Prize in Economics. His theories have been used in economics, computing, evolutionary biology, artificial intelligence, accounting, computer science, knowledge games, politics, and military theory.

Examples of other geniuses on the verge of madness are the painters Vincent van Gogh, Edvard Munch, and the author Janet Frame to name but a few.

## Neurodiversity Explained

According to the Autistic Self Advocacy Network, neurodiversity covers Neurocognitive differences such as autism, attention deficit hyperactivity (ADHD), dyslexia, Tourette's syndrome, anxiety, obsessive compulsive disorders, depression, intellectual disability, and schizophrenia as well as normal neurocognitive functioning or neurotypicality.

It refers to variations in the human brain regarding sociability, learning, attention, mood, and other mental functions in a non-pathological sense.

The neurodiversity paradigm was taken up first by individuals on the autism spectrum. Subsequently, it was applied to other neurodevelopmental conditions such as attention deficit hyperactivity disorder (ADHD), developmental speech disorders, dyslexia, dysgraphia, dyspraxia, dyscalculia, dysnomia, intellectual disability and Tourette syndrome, as well as schizophrenia, bipolar disorder and some mental health conditions such as schizoaffective disorder, antisocial personality disorder dissociative disorders, and obsessive–compulsive disorder.

The major question for debate is whether neurodiversity is a disorder or not. John Elder Robinson and many others argue that neurodiversity 'is a result of normal natural variations in the human genome' (ref). Hence, rather than seek a cure, we must seek to accommodate and harness the incredible potential that lies in the diversity of the human gene pool that has allowed such progress in humankind.

The basic principle of neurodiversity is that differences don't have to only be looked at as weaknesses. They're not problems that need to be fixed or cured. They're simply variations of the human brain. Neuro-differences should be recognised and appreciated as a social category on a par with ethnicity, sexual orientation, gender, or disability status. Unlike physical disabilities and challenges, neurodiversity remains invisible. Many people with neurodiversity, because of the social stigma or taboos, become silent about their conditions.

The neurodiversity view is personal; it is to openly accept that we are all different, and to acknowledge that there are positive and negative traits with all of us and we must work towards a working environment that is inclusive and conducive to bringing out the best in all of us. Without openness, it is difficult to tackle an invisible obstacle or challenge. The first step is to accept and embrace neurodiversity in order to profit from it.

Being neurodivergent can help shape identity and how people see themselves and their value in the world. Neurodiverse people experience, interact with, and interpret the world in unique ways. That can sometimes create challenges, but it can also lead to creative problem-solving and new ideas — things that will benefit everyone.

Many people with neurological conditions such as autism spectrum disorder, and dyslexia have extraordinary skills, including pattern recognition, memory, and mathematics. Yet they often struggle to fit the profiles sought out by employers. A growing number of companies, including SAP, Hewlett-Packard Enterprise, and Microsoft, have reformed their HR processes to access neurodiverse talent—and are seeing productivity gains, quality improvement, boosts in innovative capabilities, and increased employee engagement as a result (Robert D. Austin and Gary P. Pisano – 2017).

## Accessing Neurodiverse Talents

As already mentioned, a growing number of prominent companies have reformed their HR processes to access neurodiverse talent; among them are SAP, Hewlett Packard Enterprise (HPE), Microsoft, Willis Towers Watson, Ford, and EY. Many others, including Caterpillar, Dell Technologies, Deloitte, IBM, JPMorgan Chase, and UBS, have start-up or exploratory efforts under way. They have had extensive access to the neurodiversity programmes at SAP, HPE, and Specialisterne (the Danish consulting company that originated them) and have also interacted with people at Microsoft, Willis Towers Watson, and EY.

Although these are still in early development, SAP's, the longest running among major companies, is just four years old. Managers say they are already paying off in ways far beyond reputational enhancement. These include productivity gains, quality improvement, boosts in innovative capabilities, and broad increases in employee engagement. SAP has announced an intention to make 1% of its workforce neurodiverse by 2020—a number chosen because it roughly corresponds to the percentage of autistic people in the general population (Robert D. Austin and Gary P. Pisano – 2017).

Nevertheless, the neurodiverse population remains a largely untapped talent pool. Unemployment runs as high as 80% as this figure includes people with more-severe disorders, who are not candidates for neurodiversity programmes. Even highly capable neurodiverse people are often underemployed. Not surprisingly, when autistic people do manage to get hired, many turn out to be capable, and some are great.

Over the past two years HPE's programme has placed more than thirty participants in software-testing roles at Australia's Department of Human Services (DHS). Preliminary results suggest that the organisation's neurodiverse testing teams are 30% more productive than the others.

The case for neurodiverse hiring is especially compelling given the skills shortages that increasingly afflicts technology and other industries. For example, the European Union faces a shortage of 800,000 IT workers by 2020, according to a European Commission study. The biggest deficits are expected to be in strategically important and rapidly expanding areas such as data analytics and IT services implementation, where tasks are a good match with the abilities of some neurodiverse people (Robert D. Austin and Gary P. Pisano 2017).

# Neurodiversity Hurdles in Accessing Employment

But two big problems cause neurodiverse talent to be missed. The first involves a practice that is almost universal under the traditional approach: interviewing. Although neurodiverse people may excel in important areas, many don't interview well. For example, autistic people often don't make good eye contact, are prone to conversational tangents, and can be overly honest about their weaknesses. Some have confidence problems arising from difficulties they experienced in previous interview situations. Neurodiverse people more broadly will perform poorly in interviews as against the less talented neurotypical candidates.

The second problem, especially common in large companies, derives from the assumption that scalable processes require absolute conformity to standardized approaches. As mentioned, employees in neurodiversity programmes typically need to be allowed to deviate from established practices. This shifts a manager's focus from assuring compliance through standardization to accommodating individual work contexts. Most accommodations, such as installing different lighting and providing noise-cancelling headphones, are not very expensive but do require managers to tailor individual work settings more than they otherwise might.

# 3.3: ADHD

## Entrepreneurship and ADHD

Attention Deficit Hyperactivity Disorder (ADHD) is a neurodevelopmental disorder, presenting with its own strengths and challenges. The three types of ADHD diagnoses are:

1) predominantly inattentive
2) predominantly hyperactive
3) a combination of inattentiveness and hyperactivity.

ADHD is characterized by symptoms of inattentiveness, impulsivity and hyperactivity displayed across multiple environments such as work, school and/or home life, and these traits can cause issues within these environments.

ADHD is overrepresented among entrepreneurs. Being hyperactive, wanting to do many things at once, getting things done, breaking boundaries and more are important in entrepreneurship. Many are also willing to take risks and are far more industrious in achieving goals. An entrepreneur who is completely engrossed in a task and works hour after hour can perform miracles. They do not give up until they succeed.

Many of the world's most successful entrepreneurs diagnosed with ADHD often attribute a large part of their success to their ADHD symptoms. This includes Sir Richard Branson (Virgin), Ingvar Kamprad (IKEA) and David Neeleman (JetBlue).

Recent research (Yu W & A., 2021) has shown that certain entrepreneurial characteristics are linked to ADHD symptoms. The research suggests that the performance advantages of entrepreneurs ADHD symptoms can be derived from greater focus on innovation, proactiveness, and risk-taking. Such traits enhance opportunity recognition, innovative achievement, risk taking, action orientation, entrepreneurial intentions, entrepreneurial alertness and may even be linked on a genetic level. This demonstrates the entrepreneurial orientation of individuals with ADHD symptoms.

Entrepreneurial orientation is a crucial factor in the success and growth of a business and refers to the strategic policies and practices businesses use when launching new ventures and identifying opportunities. These practices are influenced by the personality and behaviour of the founder or owner which are three dimensional — risk taking, innovation and proactiveness.

The ADHD Norway organisation sums up the following typical traits of people with ADHD which are great for business:
- Enterprising
- Driven
- Energetic
- Creative and thinking outside the box
- Fearless and daring to invest in new ideas
- Curious, intuitive and asks questions.
- Good at hyper-focusing
- Resilient
- Good at thinking laterally - able to see things from new angles
- Good at shaking off adversity and not dwelling on past mistakes.

# The Challenges with ADHD

ADHD is used in most contexts as a negative, stigmatizing term. Among other things, it is portrayed to little advantage in the media in the form of unfortunate headlines such as 'people who are involved in criminal acts have ADHD'. This negative impression is further reinforced by the challenges children with ADHD diagnoses have with concentrating and being impulsive in school; often branded as the troublemakers in the class based on the following challenges:

Concentration problems:
* Difficulty completing tasks
* Often changes from one activity to another without completing the first
* Problems following instructions

* Difficulty organizing activities
* Easily distracted

<u>Hyperactivity:</u>
* Difficulty sitting still
* Restlessness in hands and feet
* Restlessness, inner turmoil
* As if driven by an internal motor

<u>Impulsivity:</u>
* Impatience
* Interrupts or disturbs others
* Acts without thinking about the consequences

Children with ADHD are more susceptible to new impressions. They usually have a greater range of thought, are more easily distracted, are impulsive and struggle with concentration. Thus, it becomes difficult to sit in a classroom for a whole day. It is however important to remember that today's compulsory school has only existed for a little over 200 years. Before that, being open to new impressions, being inventive and constantly on the move was not seen as a handicap. In our society, it is beneficial to systematically plan for tomorrow, and consequently it is a disadvantage to be impulsive, hyperactive, and easily distracted.

# The Magic of ADHD

## ADHD and creativity

Most people with ADHD are usually more creative than others especially when it comes to coming up with innovative ideas. It is often easier to think outside the box, see problems from new angles and to see the solutions that others have missed. People with ADHD perform better on average than others in creativity tests (White and Shah 2011). They usually have a brain that is more receptive to new impressions, and thus also becomes more flexible. This is how they absorb more information, and the more they acquire, the better they can connect information and impressions in an unexpected and different way. It is probably no coincidence that many artists and creative people have a touch of or have ADHD.

## Hyperactivity and hyperfocus

While having ADHD is strongly associated with having difficulty concentrating, the fact is that there are few who are as good at hyperfocusing as those with ADHD. One is therefore either distracted or hyperfocused. Hyperfocusing can be a disadvantage, for example playing video games or sitting in front of the PC for hours, so that it affects school and work, but it can also be an advantage.

In turn, entrepreneurship, and neurodiversity, particularly in terms of ADHD, have been topics of academic studies over recent years with increasing attention being paid to how ADHD symptoms can be strengths within the context of entrepreneurship, rather than the weakness it is too often perceived as.

How can one explain that people with ADHD may have difficulty concentrating and yet have the ability to hyperfocus? The key word is interest. When people with ADHD work on tasks and things of great interest, they can focus wholly on it. When they are focused, they can see solutions that others cannot normally see. For example, someone with ADHD may be a super salesperson, but not so good at making a sales report. Many with ADHD are highly creative and produce new ideas that, for example, can be useful in project and entrepreneurial contexts.

Inattentiveness can manifest through daydreaming; *'the desire to imagine and discover unexplored terrains'* which contributes to increased idea creation and can enhance creativity.

Whilst sustaining attention and persisting with tasks that are uninteresting to them is difficult, those with ADHD possess the ability to engage in a state known as hyperfocus; *'the ability to sustain rare levels of intensity and focus on activities and projects that capture their interest.'*

Impulsivity, urgency, and sensation seeking are all traits consistent with ADHD and entrepreneurship. ADHD individuals are driven by a sense of urgency, and often function highly when engaged in crisis mode, giving them the ability to assess and act quickly in situations where neurotypical individuals may panic and freeze.

These primary traits relate to entrepreneurship in numerous ways, and often intersect with each other. Whilst inattentiveness can impede proactiveness, it also encourages the conception of ideas; thereby enhancing creativity and problem solving — which is needed for innovation. Hyperactivity leads to elevated levels of proactiveness, culminating in initiating change when needed rather than engaging in reactionary behaviour. When combined with hyperactivity, inattentive ideation facilitates proactive innovation.

# Capitalizing on ADHD

## In what roles do individuals with ADHD thrive?

We must realise that all people are different, and that all types of people have a place in society. However, not everyone fits into the mould in today's conformist society. All rules, guidelines, routines, collective solutions, requirements, laws, paragraphs, and more are made by those who fit well into such a regime.

There is certainly good reason to focus on those with ADHD in working life. They have the potential to be work machines with almost infinite energy and courage. They can go deeper into various issues and matters and have a far higher work capacity. They are also imaginative and can produce new creative solutions. The challenge is accepting the difference in relation to other types of behaviour. They may be a little more temperamental and restless, and do not always get all the details in the information provided. This is nevertheless a 'cheap investment' in relation to the capacity one can capitalize on at the other end.

Summing up the overall strengths for ADHD in business:

### Hyperfocus

When interested, people with ADHD can be very focussed on, and committed to, specific projects and tasks, making them super-efficient.

### Creativity

The imaginative and busy minds of those with ADHD encourages original ideas and novel solutions to problems, time after time.

### Enthusiasm

Despite periods of low energy, people with ADHD also have bursts of speed, enthusiasm, and determination.

### Innovation

The fearless and sometimes irrational approach that those with ADHD can often exhibit leads to bold, innovative ideas.

Based on those strengths the following are a few examples of jobs that could be well served by those with ADHD:

### Graphic Designer

Creativity, innovation and enthusiasm combine to make people with ADHD fantastic graphic designers. The ability to explain the vast ideas that run through their heads in visual form offers a platform for them to embrace their neurodivergence and create amazing graphics.

### Teacher

The enthusiasm associated with ADHD also makes them brilliant teachers, encouraging and motivating students through their approach. Having the creativity to design interesting lessons also matches up well with a teacher role.

### Computer Technician

Hyperfocus is a unique skill for those with ADHD and is no better harnessed than when in an important technical role. IT technicians frequently require this level of attention, and creativity to solve problems, making it a key role for someone with ADHD to develop in.

### Chef

The creativity and innovation traits allow ADHD people to produce interesting ideas and concepts, making them ideal people to concoct new recipes and meals as a chef, and deal with the often-chaotic setting of a restaurant kitchen.

Jamie Oliver, the British food activist and celebrity chef was diagnosed with ADHD and dyslexia as a child. Despite having a learning disorder characterized by difficulty reading in his childhood, he is an author of cook books, an extremely creative chef, leader and passionate food activist.

# Famous People with ADHD

Many great personalities who have shaped the history of humankind have either been diagnosed with ADHD or shown signs that are easily recognizable as neurodiverse. Even today, some of the greatest minds and personalities shaping our common future are people with ADHD.

## Thomas Alva Edison (1847 – 1931)

Thomas Edison is considered one of the most talented inventors in history. He is behind more than 1,000 patents, including the light bulb and the phonograph. Edison started school when he was seven years old. But after 12 weeks at school, the teacher lost patience with the hyperactive and fussy Edison who constantly asked questions and, in the teacher's, opinion was rather self-centred. He was often so deep in his own thoughts that he did not listen to what was being said. One teacher said he was stupid and confused, which led his mother to take him out of school and home school him. He developed early hearing problems, which he perceived as an 'advantage' because then he was better able to focus without being disturbed.

## Albert Einstein (1879-1955)

Albert Einstein was a German-born theoretical physicist and Nobel Prize winner best known for formulating the theory of relativity and showing that mass and energy are equivalent in the Mass Energy Act, $E = mc2$. Through the special theory of relativity, he revolutionized mechanics and clarified the concept of time. He was central to the development of quantum mechanics and is the founder of modern cosmology. He is one of the most important scientists of the 20th century.

Albert Einstein was dyslexic, antisocial and did not go to school. He had speech problems until he was 9 years old, and his parents thought for a while that he was mentally behind. He began building mechanical models as a 6-year-old, and as a 12-year-old he had learned advanced geometry and mathematics. His maths teachers were dissatisfied with his way of solving problems because Einstein solved them differently.

Einstein disliked the school's authority, which prompted one principal to fire him. Another principal thought that he will never be anything. Albert applied for the ETH Zurich when he was 16 years old but failed one of the entrance exams. It is said that he had ADHD in combination with autistic traits.

## Leonardo da Vinci (1452-1519)

Leonardo di ser Piero da Vinci was one of the greatest and most versatile talents the world has ever fostered. He was, amongst other things, a painter, sculptor, architect, engineer, inventor, and scientist. He is considered the universal genius of all geniuses.

Primarily, it is as the painter that Leonardo is best known. Two of his works, 'Mona Lisa' and 'The Last Supper' are the best known and are the most often reproduced and parodied.

However, Leonardo was also an outstanding engineer and inventor with ideas far ahead of his time. On the drawing board he invented, amongst others, the helicopter, the tank, the use of concentrated solar energy, the calculator, the double hull, and a basic theory of plate tectonics. Few of his drawings were constructed and realised during his lifetime. As a scientist, he made discoveries in anatomy, astronomy, construction techniques, optics, and hydrodynamics.

The world's most creative person of all time showed all the signs of ADHD. He was dyslexic, unable to write or learn new languages. It is said that his brain worked like 100 wild horses at a gallop, and he was unable to focus on one thing at a time. He tried different subjects in school but could not keep his interest up other than for drawing as a young man.

## Wolfgang Amadeus Mozart (1756-1791)

Johannes Chrysostomus Wolfgangus Theophilus Mozart was an Austrian composer, pianist and violinist. Together with his contemporaries Joseph Haydn and Ludwig van Beethoven, Mozart is considered the foremost representative of Viennese classicism.

He composed over six hundred works in most genres, and his production in particular operas, solo concerts, symphonies, and chamber music is today the core repertoire in classical music life. Mozart is considered one of the greatest composers in world history.

Scholars dispute the exact diagnosis, but many traits may indicate ADHD and bipolar traits.

## Winston Churchill (1874- 1965)

Winston Churchill was an English politician, officer, and author, best known as the Prime Minister of Great Britain during World War II. Churchill is considered one of the most important leaders of modern times. An outstanding speaker, he had a career as an officer, writer, and politician. He received the Nobel Prize in Literature in 1953 for his books on British history and World War II.

Winston Churchill stammered and read, was perceived as boring, and did not have very many schoolmates. He was hyperactive as a child, once kicking the principal's hat to pieces, and was called by a teacher 'the worst boy in all of England'.

He refused to learn mathematics, Latin and Greek, but he was interested in war toys and war poems. It was his primary school nanny who taught him to read, write, and count. He was amongst the weakest students overall in the school, but he was above average in English, Shakespearean literature, and fencing. He had to sit exams three times before he scraped into university. As an adult, he described his school days as a 'waste and a miserable interlude'.

## Richard Branson (1950 – present day)

Richard Charles Nicholas Branson is an English businessman, best known for the company Virgin, which encompasses over 360 different companies. Among these are the record store chain Virgin Megastores, the record company Virgin Records and the airline Virgin Atlantic.

He is known as a very colourful character and has also played supporting roles in several TV series and films, including *Friends*, *Baywatch* and *Around the World in 60 Days*.

In 2000, Branson was made a knight for his efforts in entrepreneurship. He was thus elevated to the rank of knight and was given the right to carry the title Sir in front of his name. Richard Branson has been diagnosed with ADHD.

## Simone Biles (1997 – present day)

Simone Biles is an American gymnast and the most decorated American gymnast of all time. She has won 19 World Championship gold medals, 4 Olympic gold medals, and is the female gymnast with the most World all-around titles, five in total.

As a child, she was diagnosed with ADHD and has been taking medication for it ever since. She speaks out against ADHD stigma, encouraging young people with ADHD.

## Will-I-Am (1975 to present)

William James Adams is most known by his artist name Will.i.am. He is the performer, producer and award-winning founder of the hip-hop group the Black Eyed Peas. The eight times Grammy award winner is also an inventor of tech gadgets, as well as a philanthropist running a foundation that provides education and college scholarships to low-income kids.

He credits his energy and creativity to ADHD. In an interview with Understood, he said;

> *One thing I learned about ADHD is that it's hard to keep your attention, and you can't sit still and you're always moving and thinking about a whole bunch of things. Those traits work well for me in studios and creative times.*

He also credited music with helping him cope witn the ADHD. He has said:

> *It keeps my mind from wandering. I can stay in the music. Music brings control to my thoughts.*

## Solange Knowles (1986 to present day)

Solange Knowles is an impressive artist, a Soul Train Award recipient, an honoree at Glamour's Women of the Year 2017 Awards, and, a Grammy winner. Her impressive career spans music, art, dance, and acting.

In an interview for The Respect Ability Organization, Solange said;

> *I was diagnosed with ADHD twice.*
>
> *I didn't believe the first doctor who told me, and I had a whole theory that ADHD was just something they invented to make you pay for medicine, but then the second doctor told me I had it.*

Diagnosed as an adult, she recognizes the ADHD traits that she carries, but that has not prevented her from achieving her goals. She is open about her diagnosis to encourage others, especially African American girls who have few successful role models with ADHD.

## Emma Watson (1990 to present day)

Emma Watson is a brilliant, and beautiful actress, and women's rights activist. The brilliant Hermione Granger, to us Harry Potter fans, and former United Nations Goodwill Ambassador was diagnosed with predominantly inattentive ADHD. And while she does not speak about it, in a Facebook post, the ADHD Foundation wrote:

'Emma Watson has appeared in 15 films gained straight As at GCSE and A Level and has a degree in English Literature from Oxford University. She was diagnosed with ADHD as a young child and was medicated throughout the filming of Harry Potter.'

## Will Smith (1968 to present day)

Will Smith is a four times Grammy award winner, an Oscar winner, an accomplished rapper and actor.

While he does not talk much about ADHD and has not been formally diagnosed, in an interview with Rolling Stones Magazine, he had this to say about his ADHD:

> *I was the fun one who had trouble paying attention. Today they'd diagnose me as a child with ADHD. I was a B student who should've been getting A's, a classic underachiever. It was hard for me to read an entire book in two weeks. Today I buy a book and have someone read it for me on tape!*

While he struggled with reading, his creativity and energy were certainly outstanding. He has excelled in the performing arts beyond most Hollywood stars.

## Steve Jobs - The world's most influential person in computer technology (1955 – 2011)

**Steven Paul Jobs** was an American business magnate, industrial designer, investor, and media proprietor. He was the chairman, CEO, and co-founder of Apple Inc.; the chairman and majority shareholder of Pixar; a member of The Walt Disney Company's board of directors following its acquisition of Pixar; and the founder, chairman, and CEO of NeXT Jobs is widely acknowledged as the pioneer of the personal computer revolution of the 70's and 80's along with his early business partner and Apple co-founder Steve Wozniak (Wikipedia).

They co-founded Apple in 1976 in order to sell Wozniak's Apple 1 personal computer. Together the pair gained fame and fortune a year later with Apple 11 which was one of the first highly successful mass-produced microcomputers.

Jobs saw the commercial potential of the Xero Alto in 1979, which was mouse driven and had a graphical user interface (GUI). This then led to the development of the Apple Lisa in 1983 but this was not a success followed by the breakthrough Mackintosh in 1984 which was the first mass-produced computer with GUI.

Jobs was forced out of Apple in 1985 after a long power struggle with the company's board and its then CEO John Sculley.

That same year, Jobs took a few Apple members with him to found NeXT, a computer platform development company which specialized in computers for higher education and business markets. In addition, he helped to develop the visual effects industry when in 1986 he funded the computer graphics division of George Lucas's company LucasFilm. The new company was Pixar, which produced the first 3D computer animated feature film Toy Story (1995) and went on to become a major animation studio producing over 20m films since then.

Jobs became CEO of Apple in 1997 following his company's acquisition of NeXT. He was largely responsible for helping revive Apple which had been on the verge of bankruptcy. He worked very closely with designer Jony Ive to develop a lime of products that had larger cultural ramifications beginning in 1997 with the 'Think different' advertising campaign and leading to the iMac, iTunes, iTunes Store, Apple Store, iPod, iPhone, AppStore and the iPad.

In 2001 the original MacOS was replaced by the MacOS X (now known as MacOs) based on Next's NeXTSTEP platform giving the MacOS a modern Unix-based foundation for the first time. Jobs was diagnosed with pancreatic neuroendocrine tumour in 2003. He died of respiratory arrest related to the tumour at the age of 56 on October 5th 2011.

## Did Steve Jobs have ADHD?

The only way to prove that anyone has ADHD is through diagnosis. Steve Jobs has not been diagnosed as ADHD – nevertheless there are so many things about him that indicate so and I guess that no one would disagree that he was a neurodivergent individual with strong characteristic in his personality. This is not an ordinary person who just happened to work a little harder. A statement he made when he came back to Apple in 1997 is quite interesting in this regard.

> Here's to the crazy ones, the misfits, the rebels,
> the troublemakers, the round pegs in the square holes.....
> the ones who see things differently – they're not fond of rules....
> You can quote them, disagree with them, glorify or vilify them,
> but the only thing you can't do is ignore them
> because they can change things....
> They push the human race forward,
> and while some may see them as the crazy ones, we see genius,
> because the ones who are crazy enough to think
> that they can change the world,
> are the ones who do.

*(Steve Jobs, 1997)*

Although Steve Jobs has not been diagnosed ADHD – there are so many things about him that indicates he had ADHD. Many would say he is the prototype of a successful business leader and entrepreneur with ADHD.

Steve was close to the edge between genius and madness. His personality is described by several as:

**Innovative and long-term:** Steve Jobs saw images of products that could change the world before he even decided to bring the ideas to life.

**Fearless:** He was willing to take enormous risks.

**Rebel:** He refused to conform to the rules of others.

**Extreme Passion:** It gave him a completely insane energy.

**Extreme self-esteem:** He believed in himself and his ideas even when things went badly.

**Extreme ambitions:** He was ready for his mission from day one. He wanted to change the world and make a big difference which he did.

# 3.4: DYSLEXIA

## Dyslexia and Creativity

The word creative is an overarching umbrella term, with multiple meanings and associations. Artistic, inventive, innovative, imaginative, identifying hidden or undiscovered patterns and 'thinking outside the box' are many attributes that may come to mind when one considers creativity. It is a fascinating and versatile trait to both possess and explore within our lives.

Within literature discussing neurodiversity there have long been links and connections between dyslexia and creativity/artistic flair where dyslexics are seen as particularly creative and imaginative thinkers. One such study by Cancer, Manzoli and Antonietti (2016) has shown that junior high school students who were diagnosed with dyslexia performed significantly better in a creativity test than their non-dyslexic counterparts. They concluded that despite the often negatively perceived peculiarities of dyslexia, it does involve very useful and productive traits.

## The Magic of Dyslexia

Research and literature (Cancer et al., 2016) strongly suggest that dyslexics strive to find creative solutions and coping strategies for tasks and situations they find difficult and strenuous. This can include expressing their thoughts and ideas verbally or through pictures and images rather than via written words. In addition, individuals may develop spelling hacks and unique ways of learning difficult words to spell, such as breaking words into smaller more memorable words, using mnemonics, and even rhymes. Moreover, many dyslexics are excellent visual and/or spatial thinkers. This means they often learn, process information, and work best using pictures, images, and demonstrations, compared with reading, and memorizing substantial amounts of written text.

Furthermore, there are some who think that the connection has nothing to do with the difficulties, it is just that if someone has great talents in artistic subjects, and it differs greatly from results in theoretical subjects, one becomes extra aware of it. In addition, one could imagine that the 'weak in theory' are to a greater extent forced in creative directions, because their opportunities are reduced.

Regardless of whether it is true that there is a connection, and regardless of what the possible cause is, it has been proven through several studies that amongst people who are particularly creative, dyslexics are overrepresented (Wolff and Lundberg 2002). Dyslexics are also strongly overrepresented amongst founders (Winner et al 2000).

There definitely seems to be a link between creativity and dyslexia. Looking at the long list of famous artists and entrepreneurs with dyslexia, including Pablo Picasso, Steven Spielberg, Richard Branson, to name but a few who, in their line of work have been and continue to be exceptionally successful and innovative, being dyslexic should not be seen as a negative diagnosis. And while there still is a long way to go, despite the rigid educational system, there are a lot of success stories, which will increasingly shape society's perceptions and make us more open to neurodiversity.

For all those belonging to the neurodiverse community, identifying, and focusing on individuals' strengths is vital. If an individual excels in creativity, this should be encouraged and praised to allow the person to further explore their creative potential and energy.

## Erna Solberg

Erna Solberg, in figure 19 the former Prime Minister from 2013-2021 has dyslexia. She struggles to write words correctly like everyone else. When she received assignments back from her teacher, they were full of red lines where she had written incorrectly and was told to read more. Fortunately, Erna was exceptionally good at talking which helped her through her subjects. Reading was not a problem either. Solberg felt she could not bring out everything she could, and it was tough at times. Maybe this became a driving force to show the world that she still could succeed?

# Capitalizing on Dyslexia

## In what roles do individuals with Dyslexia thrive?

Dyslexia enhances skills in several different areas, meaning these individuals are often the ideal candidate for several jobs. These particular jobs may require creativity, problem solving or seeing the bigger picture, all which dyslexics are often found to excel at.

### Creativity

Dyslexics are often very creative individuals. This is because they are often trying to find other ways to solve problems, learn things differently, or make things easier, giving them the capability to think outside the box.

### Design

Strengths in spatial awareness and pattern recognition means that dyslexics tend to be able to design graphics, structures, even buildings, in ways which others haven't considered. This makes them ground-breaking innovators.

### Communication

A common misconception is that dyslexic people are poor communicators, but in fact it is usually a strength for them. Having to explain how you live with dyslexia, in a way that is easy for others to grasp, requires strong communication skills.

### Big Picture

Another common strength is being able to consider the bigger picture. Dyslexics are good entrepreneurs and managers, as they can look past the detail and focus on what really matters – and they've been doing it their entire lives!

## Lisa Nichols: The unstoppable Dyslexic

Lisa Nichols is the Founder and CEO of Motivating the Masses, Inc. Despite being severely dyslexic, Lisa is a very successful entrepreneur, author and motivational speaker. She speaks of failing an English test at school as a child, and her English teacher was, well, shall we say horribly unkind enough to tell her in front of her entire class:

*'You have to be the weakest writer I have ever met in my entire life'.*

The same year, following a D in Speech, her teacher continued:

*'Miss Nichols, I recommend you never speak in public…and I recommend You get a desk job'.*

Growing up with dyslexia was tough, it still is. Lisa was kicked out of school and got fired from her job 5 times. Yet, she embodies the creativity, empathy, drive, and the ability to see the bigger picture that so many dyslexics have. Having been through so much, her empathy and drive to help others shines through her life's work.

I do hope her teachers were alive to see her succeed, and that her story is a lesson to other teachers on building, not breaking the child.

Based on those strengths the following are a few examples of jobs that could be well served by those with Dyslexia:

## Graphic Designer

Because of the visual way in which dyslexic people think, it makes them brilliant for coming up with creative ideas that others haven't thought of. Graphic design is a perfect job for dyslexics because it allows them the safe space to be as creative as they want and contribute hugely.

## Journalist

Similarly, there are lots of roles in journalism for people that think visually and are creative. Broadcast and radio journalism are perfect jobs for dyslexics, allowing visual and sound elements to engage an audience, rather than just words.

## Website Developer

Dyslexics are ideal as web developers. They can use their problem solving skills to solve technical problems and deal with tough situations every day. They need constantly to face challenges and be adaptive and to dyslexics this can be second nature.

## Entrepreneurship

Dyslexics make fantastic business founders. It's a fact – just look at Richard Branson, he's dyslexic. The ability that many dyslexics have to see the bigger picture, and their creativity, means they can do incredible things!

# 3.5: DYSPRAXIA

According to the NHS, Dyspraxia is a Developmental Co-ordination Disorder (DCD). Dyspraxia is a motor learning disability that can impact on gross and fine motor skills, coordination, and planning ability. It causes a child to perform less well than expected in daily activities for their age and appear to move clumsily. In certain cases, processing speed, attention and memory may also be affected. Because no two people will present with the same set or severity of symptoms, every dyspraxia individual has different needs. For example, it can be helpful for some students to have task instructions broken down into individual steps and lesson material chunked into more manageable sets.

Employees with dyspraxia are often extremely motivated as they've had to persevere in the face of adversity all their lives. They are often strategic thinkers who have had to approach old concepts and problems with new innovative ideas. The organisation: Dyspraxia Doctor has highlighted the following adult strengths based on research.

Dyspraxias are:

- Determined and resilient
- Enthusiastic and passionate about interests
- Thinking differently – outside the box
- Good with long-term memory
- Good at noticing details other people don't
- Appreciative of things other people take for granted
- Quirky and unique
- Sensitive and empathetic to others, particularly those who are struggling.

# Capitalizing on Dyspraxia

## In what roles do individuals with Dyspraxia thrive?

This neurodiversity can lead to difficulty in several areas: movement, coordination, processing, judgement, and memory. These can show themselves through symptoms such as appearing clumsy, having unclear speech or difficulty planning, or organizing thoughts and tasks. However, as with all neurodiversity, people with dyspraxia have a great deal of strengths too.

Daniel Radcliffe, for most of us is Harry Potter. The actor was diagnosed with Dyspraxia as a child. Because he struggled at school, his mother encouraged him to audition for a play at the age of 9. She thought acting would boost his self-confidence. As Harry Potter fans, we are thankful for his incredible talent and abilities.

## Leadership

Dyspraxias often learn to develop soft skills such as active listening, empathy, and when to delegate tasks to others. Their desire for people to understand what they deal with ensures that they communicate clearly too. All these result in dyspraxias making good leaders.

## Empathy

People with dyspraxia tend to have an innate ability to understand and respect what others are thinking or feeling. Their experience in struggling with things like coordination can mean they are empathetic when they see others in a tough situation.

## Strategy

Dyspraxia does not affect a person's IQ, but they may often have to navigate a mind which can be disorganised, meaning they are usually very intelligent people. Navigating around these barriers results in creating strategies to overcome problems well.

### Creative problem solving

People with dyspraxia are great at producing different approaches to situations. Throughout school, dyspraxias find innovative ways to help themselves learn topics better, and this translates into working life, with them being able to see alternative routes to others.

### Project management

The ability to lead a team well and deal with situations strategically make dyspraxias perfect for a role as a project manager. Although they may struggle with organisation at times, with effective support, they can make brilliant commanders of teams!

### Customer service

With the ability to empathize and overcome problems in innovative ways, people with dyspraxia can be effective at dealing with customer complaints. A role in customer service would allow someone with dyspraxia to help people, something they are often passionate about.

### IT support

Problem solving also proves useful for roles in IT, where dyspraxias can use their skills to solve difficult problems. Having a strong strategic ability also allows them to make decisions taking into account the future of an IT system, not just the immediate problem.

### Job advisor

Often what a lot of people looking for work or looking to develop their skills require is more self-confidence. The leadership qualities, partnered with empathy and problem solving skills, make dyspraxias some of the best job advisors and development coaches.

# The Superpowers of Dyscalculia

Dyscalculia is a learning difficulty that affects a person's mathematical abilities and can make it much harder for students to understand maths in school. Many countries have only recently started diagnosing students with dyscalculia. Although it remains an under researched condition, there are some clear strengths in a dyscalculic profile.

Like dyslexia, the dyscalculic brain is wired differently but this is what makes having dyscalculia a positive attribute, like a superpower. Here are some common super traits:

## Creativity

A lot of people with dyscalculia are very artistic and have above average imaginative skills, which is reflected in their learning style.

## Strategic thinking

People with dyscalculia see situations holistically, enabling them to identify the crucial elements and not just focus on one element or the minor details.

## Practical ability

People with dyscalculia are very hands on and practical, which is a great skill to have both inside and outside of education and can lead to some very exciting careers.

## Problem solving

People with dyscalculia are fast problem solvers, can think outside of the box and can reflect on past experiences. This provides unique insight and methods for solving problems.

## Love of words

People with dyscalculia are often exceptional at reading, writing, and spelling.

## Intuitive thinking

People with dyscalculia are good at interpreting reality and processing knowledge, experiences, and signs around them. Albert Einstein, who had learning difficulties, said that his studies relied a lot on intuition.

# Celebrities with Dyscalculia

Although dyscalculia is a newly diagnosed condition, it is not just school students who are identified as dyscalculic. All the great superpowers identified above can be seen in a range of well-known people who have dyscalculia. For example, singers and actors with creative talent. Celebrities with dyscalculia include:

- Robbie Williams, Singer
- Cher, Singer
- Mike Hucknall (Simply Red), Singer
- Bill Gates, Philanthropist and founder of Microsoft
- Benjamin Frankllin Founding Father of the USA
- Mary Tyler Moore, Actress

# 3.6 AUTISM SPECTRUM DISORDER

## Autism

Autism, or autism spectrum disorder (ASD), refers to a broad range of conditions characterised by challenges with social skills, repetitive behaviours, speech, and nonverbal communication. Autism is widely spread across the globe and in the USA, according to the Centers for Disease Control, autism affects an estimated 1 in 44 children.

## Common Challenges of Autism

- Hard time getting motivated
- Difficulty focusing on something other than what interests them
- Following unwritten social rules; these rules can be learned through instructions
- Getting the big picture
- Unbalanced set of skills
- Difficulty with generalization concepts
- Trouble expressing feelings in a way that other people would understand or expect
- Trouble with functioning, hence difficulties in planning long-term activities
- Perceiving emotions of other people
- Trouble with summarizing information to include in speech.

Apart from the challenges they face due to autism, there are also some other aspects that can be listed as strengths or skills in people that have been diagnosed. As an employer, one must know that each employee is a unique being. Even the autism he or she has is unique.

A child with autism may not be clumsy, although it is a very common challenge. Furthermore, he/she may not be very good at maths even though it is a common ability among individuals with autism. Determining what people with autism are good at may come in handy in terms of providing them with the sense of achievement. These abilities can blend into their everyday activities. They will get joy and satisfaction while learning more. The more they practice their skills or build upon their strengths, the happier and more successful they will become in their future life.

People with autism can solve some problems faster than others even though they may have the same intelligence. It is first and foremost the requirements for social interaction that make it difficult to live with autism. Therefore, people with the diagnosis need special adaptations in their workplace to get the full benefit of the abilities.

## Common strengths of Autism

- Strong long-term memory skills
- Direct communication
- Maths, computer, musical, artistic skills
- Thinking visually
- Hyperlexia, which is decoding written language at an early age; some children with autism can decode written language before they can comprehend it
- Punctuality
- Honesty
- Detail oriented
- Average to above average intelligence
- Independent thinking, which is being less concerned about what others may think of them
- Loyalty
- Non-judgemental listening
- Extensive knowledge resulting from deep study in favourite topics
- Understanding rules and sequences
- Logical thinking that is helpful in decision-making process
- Intensive focus when working on a favourite activity

Note: Some of these strengths can be seen among children with high functioning autism and Asperger syndrome.) Sources: Adapted from Sally Ozonoff, Geraldine Dawson and James McPartland's A Parent's Guide to Asperger's Syndrome and High-Functioning Autism post at _Autism Speaks 100 Day Kit_ and from Stephen Shore's own list featured at _Autism Speaks 100 Day Kit_

# In search of Autistics

Microsoft has its own recruitment programme to get more autistics on the staff with 100% job satisfaction and claims that Microsoft as a company is stronger when you expand the opportunities and get a work environment as diverse as its customers. Everyone is unique, and some have an astonishing ability to absorb knowledge, think in detail and depth, or excel in maths or coding, says Microsoft's Global Vice President Mary Ellen Smith.

> ❜ We built the Microsoft Neurodiversity Hiring Program on the belief that traditional recruiting does not allow individuals who are neurodiverse to demonstrate their strengths and qualifications. Through this program, applicants engage in an extended interview process that focuses on workability, team projects, and skill assessment. Our process gives candidates the opportunity to showcase their unique talents while learning about Microsoft as an employer of choice. ❜

(Mary Ellen Smith)

# The Magic of Aspergers

Climate change activist Greta Thunberg in figure 20 has often declared that having Asperger's syndrome — a form of autism — has helped power her environmental campaigning.

Figure 20: Gretha Thunberg

> ❜ It makes me different, and being different is a gift, I would say. It also makes me see things from outside the box. ❜

195

Those with Asperger's have challenges with social interaction, repetitive behaviours, and narrow interests, but they do not want to isolate themselves from others, which sets them apart from others within the autism spectrum. They like to relate to other people, but in an awkward way. It is a pity is that they are often isolated due to lack of communication skills. They experience bullying and often fall outside the support system, both because they are misinterpreted and because there is little understanding in this area.

There are things they are particularly good at, which often involves data. The ability to concentrate and be totally focussed is highly developed, in addition to being very conscientious and loyal. If you get the right person in the right workplace, you have made a huge difference. If you go for it, you will get very loyal and honest employees who will more than do the job you give them. Most of them are always focussed on the detail, are very meticulous and rarely sloppy.

## Autism and unemployment

Figures from England show that 80-90% of those with Asperger's are out of work and end up with disability pensions and early retirement due to the social requirements. Had employers chosen to look at their strengths, they would have won the battle for many of them to achieve far more.

The ability to see details and patterns which are often overlooked by others is an important trait and is what gives people with Asperger's an advantage in certain jobs. The inspiration to start a social enterprise was credited to the Unicus manager from a company in Denmark, called *The Specialists*. Thorkil Sonne had a son with Asperger's and wanted to do something positive to help him and others like him. He liked the idea of a social enterprise and wanted to do something new and something that could make a difference to the life of his son and others like him, *The Specialists*. Today he has a contract with the Danish company to transfer experience and knowledge from people with Asperger's. *The Specialists* aim to create one million jobs for people with Asperger's worldwide.

Johansson-Kjellerød founder and CEO of Unicus emphasises that what he does is not charity or rehabilitation and that Unicus in no way shields them within the company. They must survive on business terms and are basically operating like any other limited liability company. In addition to hiring people with Asperger's and seeing them as a unique resource, the company is committed to donating 20%of its profits to support measures for autistic people and people with Asperger's who cannot function in a regular job.

# Famous people who have disorders within the autism spectrum

There are several famous people who have disorders within the autism spectrum. Nobel laureate in economics, Vernon Smith has Asperger's syndrome as does Bram Cohen, who developed the file-sharing program Torrent.

## Elon Musk

Elon Musk, the wealthiest person in the world has Aspergers.

Elon Reeve Musk is an entrepreneur and business magnate. He is the founder, CEO and Chief Engineer at SpaceX; early-stage investor, CEO and Product Architect of Tesla, Inc.; founder of The Boring Company; and co-founder of Neuralink and Open AI. With an estimated net worth of around US$255 billion as of December 2021, Musk is the wealthiest person in the world (Wikipedia 2021).

Musk was born to a Canadian mother and South African father and raised in Pretoria, South Africa. Musk has founded several companies successfully and becoming the Tesla CEO in 2008 catapulted him even further.

*'It's an honour to be hosting Saturday Night Live. I mean that,'* he began.

*'Sometimes when I say something, I have to say that I mean it so that people really know that I do. That's because I don't always have a lot of intonational variation in how I speak … which I'm told makes for great comedy.'*

He went on to say that he has Asperger's.

*'So, I won't make a lot of eye contact with the cast tonight. But don't worry, I'm pretty good at running human in emulation mode.'*

There are plenty of other Asperger's characteristics that he didn't mention but has clearly displayed:

- People with Asperger's are known to have interests that become obsessions (check).
- They are often fascinated by machines (triple check).
- They often are socially awkward (check).
- They lack empathy and may not understand conventional social rules, which might explain Musk's bizarre decision to call a leader of the Thai cave rescue '[paedo guy]' in a tweet, which got him sued (check).
- And according to the Autism Society, most people with Asperger's have average-to-above-average intelligence (check).

## Magnus Carlsen

Magnus Carlsen became the world chess champion on 22 November 2013 and defended the championship title in November 2014 and November 2016. He won the World Championships in lightning chess in 2009, 2014 and 2017, and the World Championships in fast chess in 2014 and 2015. In January 2013 he achieved the highest FIDE -rating among all chess players through the ages with 2861, later increased. Carlsen became Grand Master (GM) in chess in 2004 at the age of 13 years and 148 days.

Magnus showed interest in intellectual challenges at an early age. As a 2-year-old he could put together puzzles consisting of 50 pieces and as a 4-year-old he sat for hours and studied the population in a book about countries and municipalities. In parties with the family, he often sat by himself and investigated the air. He would rather do his own thing. In many ways, chess became a refuge where he could hold on without too much social interaction. He had his own dining table when he was little where he sat and read chess books. When he was on a stage with some of the world's greatest chess players in his early teens, he ended up hiding behind a poster.

Magnus Carlsen is introverted, and society is in many ways not adapted to those who are very introverted. We do not value concentration and thinking in the same way. The ideal person is livelier and more outgoing.

As the world's best chess player, however, he does not escape attention and social interaction. In some situations, he may look socially awkward because he is very introverted but think of all the social situations he is put in every single week. Most introverts would shudder at the thought.

Magnus Carlsen is in a special position. The Norwegian who has achieved the most outstanding results across all sports through the ages. He is neurodivergent.

# Capitalizing on Autism

## In what roles do individuals with Autism thrive?

Autism a neurological developmental disorder, characterized by repetitive patterns of behaviour and difficulties with social communication. This means that people with autism looking for jobs may struggle with application processes and be unsuccessful. However, people with autism can offer great benefits in several areas.

No definition can truly capture the range of characteristics people with autism have, but many individuals share similar characteristics and experiences that can make them suited to certain jobs. They often show strengths in areas such as logical thinking and retention. Other common strengths of people with autism include:

## Attention to detail

People on the autistic spectrum often have great attention to detail and focus. This means they can search through a lot of information for specific content.

## Efficiency

Efficiency is another common strength. They are usually very good at following rules, sequences, and orders, meaning that with the right structure they can be super-efficient.

## Logical thinking

People with Autism are generally logical thinkers, as they can struggle to consider emotional factors. This brings an innovative and objective approach to problem solving.

## Retention

People with Autism also build encyclopaedic knowledge on topics of interest, retaining lots of information. Visual memory is often also strong in a similar way. Where information retention is important, their abilities are second to none. Which means, they are capable of excelling in a shole plethora of such roles.

## Web developer

Having such a strong attention to detail, as well as the capability to retain information well, makes web development a great career path for someone with autism. With the job frequently touching on set rules and sequences, this also matches well with the efficiency associated with autism.

## Data officer

Similarly, there are lots of roles in data for people that have a strong attention to detail. Being able to spot errors and replicate, change and identify information efficiently makes data a strong area for people with autism to consider.

## Policy adviser

Having great retention on specific topics allows people with autism to build great knowledge banks. This makes them extremely useful as policy advisers. The ability to build an area of interest, alongside viewing things logically, allows them to add great value to discussions.

## Copywriter

Writing content for websites, products and more is an essential part of marketing. People with autism are often intelligent and can write brilliantly, making this role an area to thrive in for those who also work efficiently and can notice errors.

To succeed with employees with Asperger's in a job situation, you as a leader must ensure the following:

- Be specific and accurate in messages and instructions
- Avoid irony and sarcasm
- Be solution-oriented
- Do not take it personally if the employee does not always understand or participate in social settings.

# 3.7: BUSINESS AND NEURODIVERSITY?

Recruitment is largely about reducing uncertainty. From this aspect, there is reason to believe that divergence is interpreted as having increased risks which few organisations are willing to take. Divergence is in many ways a 'risk' versus 'reward' issue where most people end up wanting to reduce uncertainty. They choose the safe over the unsafe option even though there is huge potential for a higher upside and downside if they take a risk.

Through a stronger focus on values and a desirable behaviour associated with these as well as expanded use of personality tests in the recruitment processes, one will most likely get more focus on balanced personality profiles and therefore a balanced team. However, balanced personalities provide balanced behaviour and performance, and with all probability reduce the opportunity to create something extraordinary. This, of course, depends a bit on which values you choose, and how you choose to interpret the personality profiles. But reducing uncertainty seems to be the most important driver, even with the consequences it often has.

There are many indications that managers are looking for qualities they themselves appreciate, or even think are important. Often these are qualities they possess themselves. Focusing on certain behavioural traits and seeing them as valuable can naturally lead to a higher degree of simplicity.

Special people and those with 'unbalanced personalities and appearances' may have been weeded out long before they reach the final round of a recruitment process. If you are different and want a career, you have to show this through good results over time, but this will be before anyone dares to invest in them. This can be a little difficult if you never get the opportunity in the first place.

It is time to do something with the acceptance and tolerance levels for different behaviours and be less judgemental of peculiarities as these are often the side effects of being a genius. If you manage to live with and lead diversity, the potential is far greater.

I remember I was once involved in recruiting an insanely good marketing manager. The person in question took up an enormous amount of space, was at times demanding and others perceived him as headstrong. Nevertheless, that one person created results that no one else before or since had created in a similar position. If you as a leader manage to get such people to work in a team and in a company, the potential is enormous.

# Capitalizing on Neurodiversity

### 'The Kahoot Case'

Johan Brand is a creative technology entrepreneur & investor based in Oslo, Norway. He co-founded Kahoot! one of the fastest growing learning brands in the world, used by millions every day in over 200 countries. Kahoot! grew from a research project to become a company that captures 1/3rd of US classrooms every month and with millions of business users too.

He is also the Founder & Chief Entrepreneur at EntrepreneurShipOne, a pay-it-forward platform for the Nordic startup community and a Founding Partner at We Are Human where he creates purpose driven organisations striving for sustainable social and commercial impact.

As a Fellow of the Royal Society of Arts, he has been awarded 'Founder of the Year' at the Norwegian Nordic Startup Awards, 'Digital Leader of the Year' by Financial News E24 as well as being named as one of the top 100 most influential leaders in EdTech, globally.

While no longer involved in the management of Kahoot, Johan remains an active owner and strategic advisor.

Johan was told he was dyslexic at the age of 16, although he says he inherently always knew that he was different and that he saw the world differently. He has ADHD, and recently came to understand he was more neurodiverse. Johan is passionate about the concept of inclusive design, which is not about disabilities, rather designing for the unserved no matter what it is, be it a disability, cultural, or otherwise.

Johan dedicated his companies such as Kahoot to exploiting the untapped potential that lies in the utilization of neurodiversity. He works extensively with diversity and continues to raise awareness of inclusion. Recently he agreed to appear on stage with the former Prime Minister Erna Solberg to talk about equality and diversity, challenging what he calls the 'the old ways of thinking about equality,' which is still very relevant but still lacking any focus on neurodiversity. Johan does not see neurodiversity as a handicap.

*You are left-handed, I am dyslexic. I have ADHD right? I hate the labels of being disadvantaged whether I have learning difficulty, I simply learn differently. I write differently. I'm actually ambidextrous which is even funnier.*

*I don't see any of those neurodiverse things in myself as a problem. I see them as a superpower because it's a minority thing. I'm not better than others but the fact that I'm different to the majority of them in the situation I am in, means I have a superpower in that thing.*

## To capitalize on neurodiversity

- Start seeing the potential in neurodiversity.
- Try to employ different profiles, not just 'balanced' profiles of people who think like you.
- Seek to divert from homogeneity by employing people who have different profiles to build an excelling team, accommodate divergent behaviour and views in the workplace.
- Endeavour to create psychological safety in the workplace.
- One size does not fit all, not in management so be flexible.

# PART 4
# PRACTICAL
# TOOLS &
# ADVICE

# 4.1: PUTTING TOGETHER A TEAM

## Diversity

### Competence Diversity

There seems to be a consensus that diversity in terms of competence, skills and character in a team will strengthen performance. Most boards therefore have a lawyer, an economist, and someone with relevant operational business understanding, based on the idea that the combination of different experiences and skills is important for the result.

Further down in an organisation, however, the priorities seem to be different. People who are similar are often chosen to a greater extent, often with the same experience, as this seems to reduce the managers' own insecurities.

What is needed, first and foremost, however, is someone with strengths and skills in the areas where you are weak which will enable the team to deliver the overall work requirements with far better results. Complementary competencies are underestimated in many organisations from the management team downwards.

Few are surprised that we are different in terms of personality and preferences. Every person has work tasks they prefer, enjoy and are good at. There are also those work tasks that are postponed because they require too much energy or are perceived as boring, unchallenging, or simply do not fit our priorities. Most of us have experienced that the tasks we do not like are often tackled by others with great zeal and enthusiasm. The art is to use this difference in the best possible way for both the company and the individual so the right result is achieved. In a team, you will be able to take care of these different tasks if the diversity in the team is broad enough to cater for the work requirements.

In working life, we often use the term - someone has ended up on the right or wrong shelf or they are a square peg in a round hole. Such statements say something about how well you feel that person suits the job they have been allocated. The person and the company will both achieve better results if there is a match between the work tasks and the person's skills, characteristics, and preferences. Both the company and the individuals will be better served by finding the best match between the demands of the work and the individual's capacity and characteristics.

To create a high-performing team, there must primarily be a correspondence between the work requirements that the team must deliver on, and the individual's skills. As a rule, the requirements are diverse in their uniqueness and therefore it will be natural to look for people with slightly different profiles and preferences so that you can take care of the entirety of the work requirements in the best possible way.

The saying, 'birds of a feather flock together' certainly has great relevance when choosing your own circle of friends. In a work context, it is almost the opposite. Here you must recruit people who are good in areas you yourself are bad at so that the 'final total' of skills is as high as possible. Unfortunately, the opposite is easier to do. Researcher Jon Rogstad has been a fly on the wall during 67 job interviews. He found that managers subconsciously look for someone who 'fits in', not necessarily the strongest academically or with complementing skills. Psychologically, we like those who are like us best.

In other words, we must make sure we build a team of both complementing qualities and skills, preferably with the support of various tools that can identify the preferences and personalities. The team must possess the wide experiences and the skills that the tasks require.

## Functional Diversity

To have a well-functioning and high-performing team, we depend on people with different preferences and personality characteristics. We need the visionary strategists who can set the direction, we need the innovators who can develop new and better solutions, those who can organise the work and make sensible goals and action plans, and not least those who can carry out the work in practice. In addition to this, we need those who can check, and quality assure that the work is in accordance with procedures, regulations and to good enough quality, as well as specialists in various important disciplines such as advisory support functions along the way. It is not the case that there are human types who are good at everything, or even find all the above tasks very stimulating. To maximize team performance, we need people with different personality traits and preferences to make the best possible results.

To have a well-functioning and high-performing team we need:

- Visionary strategists to set the direction
- Innovators to develop new and better solutions
- Organisers to set sensible goals and action plans
- The people on the ground who do the actual work
- Quality assurers to check quality, procedures, and regulations
- Advisory support functions.

Football teams are good at taking advantage of diversity related to personalities and preferences. Not everyone has the right personality characteristics to be a successful striker. There seems to be a type of person who thrives and succeeds best in such a role. Some are better suited in defence; some are suitable as midfield and some as goalkeepers. The important thing is that everyone can use their strengths more often, and that the team or group consists of complementing personalities and skillsets to achieve the goals - literally.

It is better for both the employer and the employee to know what they are suitable for and what they most prefer to work with. In this way, they can put their best foot forward more often for the benefit of both themselves, and the company. There seems to be a focus by some where they think that almost anyone can learn anything given the right training and influence. True enough, development opportunities are great for most people in many areas, but they are still better if you are working to your natural strengths. It requires awareness and understanding of the difference between the two ways of looking at it to exploit this for the benefit of the employees and the company.

# The right person in the right position

People have different preferences as to which hand they prefer to write with. If you write with the 'wrong hand', the result is often far worse and harder work than using the preferred one unless you are lucky enough to be ambidextrous. You will spend far more time and energy to get the same job done and the result will not be as good. If you choose a job, you are not suitable for, the result can be the same as writing with the wrong hand. Not all people are suited for tough sales roles. It might be an advantage to be socially bold rather than shy for example. In a typical customer service role, one will succeed better if you are warm and sociable rather than cold and reserved. In an analytical role it is better to be cooler and more fact based rather than warm, enthusiastic, and driven by emotions. In other words, personality and preferences will affect suitability and potential in relation to different types of work tasks.

A high priority in a company or organisation is to ensure that you have the right person in the right position at the right time. An assessment of personality and preferences will, in such a context, be important input into a comprehensive assessment of what is often described as, suitability for the task. People who succeed well in one type of job do not necessarily succeed in another where the work requirements are different. One can also rightly claim that training and skills development in various forms can counteract the lack of suitability in personality. Nevertheless, there is little doubt that you can go further in areas where you have the best of both. Therefore, insight in this area will be profitable for the individual employee and the company. It is even claimed that you should train more to one's strengths to make yourself even more competitive and unique as an employee. This is a correct observation if you can fill critical gaps which act as a barrier to development at the same time.

Many people make poor judgements in their own choices in adolescence. They choose directions and specializations influenced by family in particular, friends and social pressure to the detriment of their own preferences and suitability. Study and career guidance is therefore extremely important and should be given even more attention. It is important for both society and the individual that as many people as possible, end up on the right shelf.

In 1900, Carl Gustav Jung developed a psychological type of theory that is used by many companies today called Theory of Personality. The results of these tests give good indications of which tasks you enjoy and how you prefer to work. People have different preferences and Jung has divided them up into sixteen different types based on four different dimensions. Jung's type test and MBTI (Myers Briggs Type Indicator) are widely used in business today:

| What gives you energy? | Extroversion (E) vs. Introversion (I) |
| How do you gather information? | Sensing (S) vs. Intuition (N) |
| How do you make decisions? | Thinking (T) vs. Feeling (F) |
| How do you like to organize your life? | Decision (J) vs. Experience (P) |

If you use the results of such tests in a business context, you can get a good overview of who is suitable for various tasks as shown below. Are you an innovator, communicator, idea developer, entrepreneur, implementer, quality assurer, maintainer, or supervisor? What do you prefer? It is easy to understand that you are not suitable for all these tasks and that you are most served by having different types in a team.

## How different preferences can be best used in a composite team or group

Business is a bit like football. It is not made up of only strikers to succeed. The best business has the best composed team, where everyone contributes with their expertise, and it is they who lift the trophy over their heads in the end. The British Psychological Society has adapted Carl Jung's original preference test related to job situations called the Team Management system (TMP).

Helge Lund former CEO of Statoil was known for choosing leaders who were quite different from himself and had the good combination of being a very demanding but caring leader.

# The best foot forward theory

Some people choose to practice and develop the strengths they do not have; others think this is very unreasonable. A best foot forward theory is about training more on what you are naturally good at rather than spending a lot of time training non-preferred skills and weaker qualities. If you do that, you can be unique and competitive in an area where you have the best conditions. The theory also links the individual's interest in helping others. It relies on the success of a team being based on the best use of the complementary skills and building team potency. Team potency is defined as the collective belief in the ability of the team to be successful. Where there is a strong shared vision drive and shared group will, there will be a strong team potency. In such a scenario, each individual puts their best foot forward in a collective effort while operating in their zone of excellence. According to organisational research, team potency is one of the strongest predictors of team performance (Pearce & Ensley, 2004).

The best foot forward theory is well in accordance with research, for example as presented in Yukl (2012), an important prerequisite for team learning is for members to understand each other. Members that understand each other's perceptions and role expectations are better able to coordinate their actions more easily. It takes away the guesswork and uncertainty.

Everyone must respect what the others can do and create the conditions for them to succeed. In a team, everyone must be willing to acknowledge those who are better, and not be jealous. This agrees with the theory that a high-performing team consists of people with different preferences who all work together to complement each other and form an unbeatable team.

*You become good by making the others good,*

is a phrase that one former football coach used when describing his football philosophy.

It is important to go on the field aiming to be the best that you can possibly be, but it is even more important to go on the field to help your teammates look good. A successful football club follows a prolonged and laborious process which involves continuous quality improvements at all levels to create a dynamic culture – which is a winning culture. For this to happen everyone must participate, from the secretaries of the clubhouse to the goal hunter of the Champions League team. To perform great achievements and solve complicated problems, all the players in the community must want the same. With mutual help and support they can bring out the best in each other, create a culture where the positive willingness to interact comes from within - and with the right desire and mood to win.

## The power and potential of a personality diverse team

Working in a team with different personalities requires flexibility, patience, and a great degree of openness. The ceiling for disagreement must also be high and one does not always have to find a compromise. You can simply agree to disagree if you understand and accept each other's views. Facilitating and playing on each other's strengths is a prerequisite for success as a team. If you are good at this, you can help your team reach its full potential.

Although it is far easier to lead simple one type teams, most of us would get tired of working in groups where everyone had the same personality. The fact that a team consists of several personalities with different strengths makes the work much more stimulating and interesting. Therefore, learn from this, bring in different types of personalities and use everyone in the areas where they are good. Let those who are skilled on-stage shine on stage. Let those who are skilled with analysis and numbers work with analysis and numbers. Let those who are good at sales, sell. Let those who are good at negotiations be those who negotiate and so on. By understanding what your employees are good at and passionate about, you will both increase efficiency and strengthen your team. It is better to focus on and further develop employees' strengths rather than criticise their weaknesses.

It is not uncommon for alliances, or smaller groups, to form within larger teams, based on who gets along best, or who has the best chemistry. This helps to build invisible walls in the communication and can create unnecessary misunderstandings because the communication is blocked. Break down those invisible walls. Consciously place employees who either do not work together very much in daily life, or have a challenging relationship with each other, into small groups. Then they will have to learn to cooperate and gradually build trust in each other. That way, they will usually see each other in a new light.

Leaders who are skilled at creating strong teams with different personalities focus on the results everyone achieves, rather than trying to get them to achieve results in a specific way. To do this delegate the tasks and allow your employees to take the initiative and find a way to solve them in such a way that every member of the team contributes significantly to the team effort.

It is not always easy to work together where there are big differences in personality, but those who succeed can achieve something huge. Examples of this can be found in various rock bands. Anyone who knows their music culture knows that personal and creative friction is part of the DNA structure of any band - especially in a band that has been going on for a long time. In rock 'n' roll, many will say that friction is more than half the idea, and even in a pop band it should be a bit jarring if the result is to be something more than rosy idyll and 'synthetic chewing gum pop'.

A-ha, the most successful Norwegian band was made up of individuals with different personality types.

There was an obvious conflict between Paul and Morten; two fundamentally different personalities who were almost tied together in the band A-ha in a sometimes-forced marriage. At times, they almost considered each other as necessary evils. Nevertheless, they managed to support each other well and used their complementing personalities for the good of the band. And no other Norwegian band has even been close to the international success that A-ha has had.

*Personality diversity is at times very demanding but can also give fantastic results if you manage to play on each other's strengths. The result is greatest if you get teams with a wide range of personalities to work together.*

# 4.2: SUCCEEDING AT DIVERSITY LEADERSHIP

The skillsets required for successfully leading diversity have been discussed earlier however, in this section, we would like to look at why some leaders, despite having relevant skills, the best of intentions and the right competence still fail at diversity leadership. Leadership failure has often been an issue of poor sensemaking and situational awareness. According to Professor Arjen Boin, one of the leading researchers on international crises in the world, effective sensemaking requires well-rehearsed information processing, sharing, analysis, creating and efficiently communicating a comprehensive dynamic picture with possible 'futures' and potential consequences which are understandable to everyone.

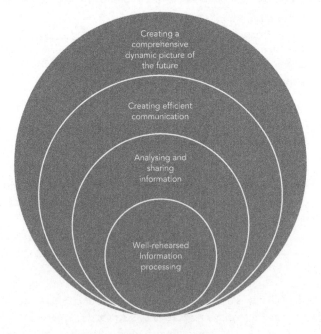

*Figure 21: Crisis leadership*

Professor Boin has extensively researched crisis leadership in the public domain. Boin (2019) iterates that the solution effective leadership sensemaking may not lie in the development of new management technologies. It is rather in the development of the ability of managers' skills to gather, analyse and make sense of information from multiple sources and make sound decisions under highly dynamic, uncertain, and complex decision-making environments (Alison et al., 2015; House et al., 2014).

Lack of diversity and inclusion is, in many ways, a creeping crisis which has manifested in many of society's symptoms. When people do not feel included in society, there are many consequences. Earlier on we discussed social unrest and demonstrations resulting from injustice, lawsuits against firms, mental health issues from unhealthy working environments, and so on. If we think of this lack of diversity as a crisis which we must deal with head on, then we can start to see the prerequisites for good diversity leadership.

From the diagram above, we can see that good sensemaking and leadership requires good social and cognitive skills, and this is where most of the problems in leadership lie. Many leaders fail, not due to wilful misconduct, negligence, or unlawful behaviour but rather because of a failure to decode the landscape and apply the correct social skills.

Social and cognitive skills are important for all human relations, and it is during uncertainty and change that such skills become fundamental. We often see people progressing in their careers assuming management positions because of their expertise in a particular role, but without possessing any of the social skills required for leadership. As an engineer, I have seen many engineers progress to management roles for which they are not socially skilled. Just because one is a good engineer does not mean one is capable of being a good engineering manager with personnel responsibilities to develop others.

They may have the technical skills but lack what is called Non-Technical Skills (NTS). Non-Technical skills are defined as 'the cognitive, social and personal resource skills that complement technical skills, and contribute to safe and efficient task performance' (Flin et al., 2008).

Where there have been disasters such as in healthcare, aviation, offshore sector, extensive research points consistently to the root cause being failures and omissions due to cognition rather than hard skills. Major surgical accidents are rarely due to the inability of the surgeon to operate, but rather more likely will be due to miscommunication, misunderstanding of the situation or extreme fatigue. The same applies to aviation disasters and offshore catastrophes. Miscommunication is the most common cause in all these.

The main components of NTS are Situational Awareness (SA), decision-making, communication, teamwork, leadership, and the ability to cope with stress and manage fatigue. This will be discussed in the coming section.

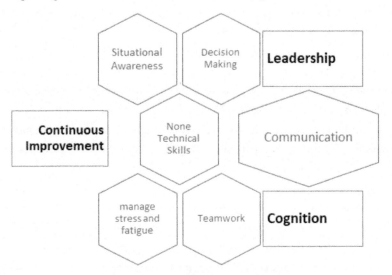

*Figure 22: NTS and Situational Awareness*

# Clarity: Sensemaking and Situational Awareness

The number one reason most businesses fail is due to lack of clarity: internal clarity such as finances, performance, ethics about the business, and external clarity about the business environment and competition. To have clarity, one needs to fully understand the operating conditions; that is to say, one must develop situational awareness.

Situational awareness is defined as the 'perception of the elements in the environment within the volume of time and space, the comprehension of their meaning, and the projection of the status in the near future' (Endsley, 1995; Rosenman et al., 2018).

In the early days in the context of war, situational awareness was the warrior's habit of being in a constant state of alertness and being prepared. Taking lessons from Sun Tsu's legendary book on the art of war, the warrior's ability to read the surrounding environment accurately, allows him to correctly decipher signs of danger so he can act and react with a temporal and tactical advantage (Krasmann & Hentschel, 2019; Sun, 1963).

We live in a world of constant change and uncertainty which requires the same kind of situational awareness approach. Without being in a state of preparation, knowing and understanding the business context and what is moving inside and outside the organisation, leaders will fail. Ignorance is not bliss; in fact, poor knowledge is dangerous.

The first level of situational awareness involves systematic information gathering from multiple sources, from inside and outside the national borders. Sensemaking is not made in a vacuum. How I see and understand a situation is based on my experience, background, knowledge, and other history that has shaped my perception. In reality, no two people can perceive the world in an identical manner.

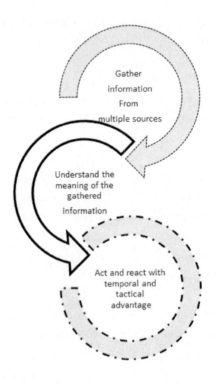

Gather
information
From
multiple sources

Understand the
meaning of the
gathered
information

Act and react with
temporal and
tactical
advantage

*Figure 23 Three levels of Situational Awareness*

Thus, situational awareness is a form of active, embodied preparedness. At the same time, situational awareness grows out of preparedness, to act beyond that which can be predicted, calculated, or rehearsed. In the case of diversity, without understanding the status of diversity in your organisation, and how it is affecting performance or lack of performance, as well as the goals and directions set out, it is hard to say one is aware of the state of affairs. How do you solve a problem before you are aware of the problem, or understand it?

Top management has often failed due to this lack of awareness of what is happening at the lower levels in the organisation, particularly when middle management 'filter' the upward communication and information flow.

The second level of situational awareness is about comprehension of the meaning of gathered information and events. To decipher signs of trouble, available data must be synthesised, interpreted, and prioritised to create an understanding of the current state of the system. Without understanding raw data, you cannot make good decisions to support a strategy. Many organisations gather statistics and employee surveys but fail to fully synthesise the data properly.

A question I often ask is,

'What is missing in the data?'

For example, when an employee survey has no mention of safety hazards, is this because there are no observable hazards, or are they afraid to report them?

As discussed earlier, the absence of reporting on bullying and harassment in the workspace does not mean that it does not exist. It may be an indication that there is no confidence in the management to resolve such grievances hence there is no point in reporting them. It could also mean that the whistleblowing points are functional, or trusted, or worse, part of the problem. Hence, proper synthesising of the data is crucial.

The third level is about being able to act and react with a temporal and tactical advantage (Krasmann & Hentschel, 2019; Sun, 1963). This requires the skill of adaptability. It also requires you to be able to project future states and possible trajectories to allow for contingency planning for probable events and anticipation of next steps (Rosenman et al., 2018). When you know the state of affairs and have a clear enough understanding of the meaning of the information, then you can act or react to any situation with a higher degree of success.

Often top management is not aware of the misconduct of their employees or suppliers and sub-suppliers until it becomes headline news. By then, it becomes a firefighting mission, which is far harder to manage than to prevent it happening in the first place. It is said prevention is better than cure, that also goes for leadership scandals.

*One morning, as I went through security at Oslo international airport, I realised I had forgotten to pack my toothpaste. I was heading to the Offshore fare ONS in Stavanger on the first flight. I was tired, it was way too early for me, which my state of appearance possibly showed. I walked into Heinemann for a tube of toothpaste. There I met a very friendly Pakistani lady. She took one look at me and smiled, asking me where I was travelling to and why.*

*When I told her, she looked at me and said kindly:*

*'Then you need to look your best!'*

*She then led me by the hand without asking what I needed. She sat me down and offered me a glass of water.*

*She went on to apply my make-up and sprayed me with a fragrant perfume. By the time she was done, I looked and smelled my best but also felt much better. Then she asked me what I needed.*

*I only bought the toothpaste that day but I had also made a friend.*

*For years, every time I was at the Oslo airport and needed to buy anything travel related, I went straight to Heinemann, hoping to find her there. Often, I called her to find out if she would be working that particular day. Because she made me feel so great, I still wear the perfume she recommended that day. I can buy similar cosmetics anywhere, but I always return to this memory, to the sense of service with a joyful smile.*

*To me, this lady embodied the art of using situational awareness. She observed me, gathered information from me, processed the information I gave her wisely and proceeded to act with tact, and that won her and the store a loyal customer for years.*

# Decision Making

Figure 24: Make a decision

Decision making is a crucial skill because often, they are made in highly unstable environments which are rapidly changing and unpredictable. According to the American psychologist Janis, the basis of high quality decision-making is correct situational awareness from gathering and evaluating complete information, examining all aspects of multiple options in order to settle on a decision (Janis, 1989).

While that sounds simple and straight forward, extensive research from Nobel Laureates Daniel Kahneman and Tversky reveal in various publications such as 'Thinking Fast and slow' that there are cognitive limitations and biases that preclude individuals from making fully value-maximizing choices when making decisions (Kahneman, 2011; Kelman et al., 2017; Tversky & Kahneman, 1974).

The level and diversity of skills required to lead complex organisations are so wide that no leader can encompass them all because their own problem-solving methods are biased and therefore, ill equipped. Good decision making requires powerful leaders to listen to their advisors and heed recommendations even if they don't like them. Decisions made must be concretely assigned and timely in execution otherwise it becomes a case of everyone's responsible and no one is accountable.

In their research, Alison et al (2015) found that decision tasks which are not time specific, involve multiple agencies and had no clear strategic direction, were more likely to fail as a result of indecisiveness and interagency action.
Hence, we ought to ask ourselves, what are the ingredients or processes for a good decision making system?

*Figure 25: Good decision making processes*

Slow decision making is symptomatic of political and bureaucratic processes in many organisations where there are unclear roles, muddled strategies, and lack of task communication. It is not uncommon for a political party to make grand promises during political campaigns, but those promises will never be fulfilled post elections.

Tragically, often, there may be clear understanding and good situational awareness, but many leaders still struggle to make the decisions due to a sort of decision anxiety - this is particularly true if the decision will prove unpopular. By avoiding making those decisions about a potential problem, a leader is no different from an ostrich that sees a predator and sticks its head in the sand. Lack of decision making is leadership by 'ostrichism'.

## Teamwork

Managing a team in one jurisdiction is hard enough whereas the challenges and complexities of internationally spread out and diverse teams makes it even harder to manage. While managing a seemingly homogenous team, even in one location is hard, managing a diverse team requires even better cognitive skills and teamwork.

Extensive research has shown that institutions and teams become dysfunctional when there are no clear roles, no identifiable ownership of those potential roles, and no established strategic direction. Such teams will experience reduced ability to coordinate concerns or to communicate effectively across team borders (Alison et al., 2015; House et al., 2014; Van den Heuvel et al., 2014; Waring et al., 2018).

As spread out and diverse teams may not be confined to a single territory, they require leadership at multiple levels, sometimes with decentralised command and control settings. Measures must be taken across a wide landscape, rife with complexity and the scattered teams will have a varying degree of shared understanding. Those measures will need to facilitate team coordination and task performance, as well as manage organisation structures and team leadership.

A challenge in working with diverse teams is that they often have different approaches to problem solving, strategies and goals which makes the potential coordination of tasks risky, with potential to fail unless there is a common understanding and good team leadership. Since we all perceive things differently, there may still be a lack of clear and shared understanding of roles, responsibilities, and information. Sometimes, it is better to go over things one more time even if it may seem like a waste of time.

According to extensive research by Carter et al (2020), research on team leadership has often focused on internal team processes and objectives. With the global working environment, teams are no longer a 'physical' cluster of people in one location. Many are working from multiple locations, across diverse boundaries. So even what should be considered internal team processes now go beyond the boundaries of what used to be the traditional team walls.

*When I was the Chair of the Quantafuel Danish entity, if I consider the board as my team, I had the following clusters of complexity. There were six members living in two different countries. There was gender, language, dialect, competence, age, race, religion, social status, personality, and interest diversity which sometimes made chairing a meeting a challenge. I would be chairing a meeting in which three different Danish dialects were spoken plus Norwegian while I took minutes in English which exacerbated my fear of missing any important details. Sometimes there were various interests and agendas being run by different board members.*

*I have sat through many learning experiences over the years but my tenure on this board stands out as the most challenging but also the most educational on diversity leadership.*

## Communication and Information in Diversity Leadership

Successful performance of a diverse team requires clarity of information, communication, and leadership. Communication is essential to all stages of leadership and must be at the core to enable the establishment of joint situational awareness, decision-making processes, and teamwork. In a diverse team, especially with members spread over a wide geographical area, clear communication across boundaries and levels is crucial.

### What is communication?

We often assume that communication is the spoken word, or emails, or the policies and procedures we send around. True communication in this context means <u>all social interaction</u> including speech, gestures, texts, discourses, body language, symbols and other means that transmits a message from one person to another. You can communicate an entire situation without knowing you have; body language can reveal everything, that is true communication. Even the absence of communication is communication as it reveals an anomaly.

As you are reading this book, I assume you speak English but which version do you speak? There are apparently over 160 different versions or variants of the English language. Two people speaking English may fail to communicate effectively, because even within the language they share, there are complexities and potentials for misunderstandings.

I was leading contractual negotiations for a contract in West Africa and at that point, I was in Oslo, with legal support from a lawyer in Oslo as well as my General Counsel in France who was Spanish Italian. My client's lawyer was Nigerian, based in West Africa. During one telephone session, I decided to sit back and watch how the meeting would pan out. Normally I acted as the bridge between English, legal, technical, cultural, and whatever other role I needed to fill. Here I took on a social experimental observant role.
Indeed, within a very short time, the meeting disintegrated into chaos with three furious gentlemen nearly screaming at each other while I sat back with a devilish smile.

You see, thanks to different accents, they had failed to understand that they were actually all in agreement. All three learned men were communicating in what they thought was the same language and context but were failing miserably. Here are some elements of effective communication, not all, but some of the most important.

Communication is interactive as in both giving and receiving information. It is a form of continuous interactions at multiple levels and with multiple potential outcomes because we all make sense of situations differently. To succeed with a diverse team, a leader ought to be a good listener, interlocuter, as well as a good conveyor of his message.

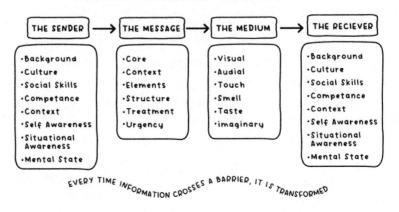

*Figure 26: The transformational nature of information*

When communicating across boundaries such as language, dialect, cultural, or even religious, information must be communicated concisely by the sender and in a such a way that the receiver can understand and recognise the relevance of it. One must acknowledge and recognise the importance of lingual, cultural, political, technological, and institutional environments of organisations and how they shape the way we communicate.

> ❝ *Always remember that whenever information crosses a barrier from a sender to a receiver, it is transformed* ❞

It is essential to realise that how it is understood by the recipient may well be far from what the sender intended. How information is received, understood, interpreted and the urgency with which it is acted upon depends on the factors and differences between the communicating entities. According to research by Waring et al (2018), often unclear communication, limited situational awareness and poor articulation have delayed expected cooperation between different teams and people.

It is said that actions speak louder than words, and such is the case with diversity leadership. The behaviour of the leaders and their teams sends a message to everyone else; if the leaders can communicate well with the rest of the organisation, it is likely the same will happen within the organisation. Passivity of leaders will influence subordinates and others to believe that passivity is the appropriate response. A culture of communication only through top down emails will lead to a culture of bottom up emails. Such communication robs the leader of the other unwritten mediums of communication such as directly getting feedback or information verbally or through observations, smell, touch, and imagination.

Diffusion of responsibilities when communicating may lead to passivity and chaos in the team because defuse roles and responsibilities create lack of psychological 'ownership' of a problem. When communication becomes messy, empires will fall.

An illustration of the power of communication comes from the biblical story about the tower of Babel. The story says the people wanted to build a tower to the heavens. From the book of Genesis chapter 11:3-8 we see the following:

> *3 They said to each other, 'Come, let's make bricks and bake them thoroughly.' They used brick instead of stone, and tar for mortar. 4 Then they said, 'Come, let us build ourselves a city, with a tower that reaches to the heavens, so that we may make a name for ourselves; otherwise we will be scattered over the face of the whole earth.'*

*⁵ But the Lᴏʀᴅ came down to see the city and the tower the people were building. ⁶ The Lᴏʀᴅ said, 'If as one people speaking the same language they have begun to do this, then nothing they plan to do will be impossible for them. ⁷ Come, let us go down and confuse their language so they will not understand each other.'*

In this story, one can see that the people knew how to construct the tower and they had the manpower to do it. God did not destroy any of that, all that was distorted was their ability to communicate because their ability to accomplish any task was dependent on their ability to communicate. Any other issues could be solved with communication. Destroying communication was enough to derail the entire project. How often has poor communication brought down a team, company, or even governments?

Without good clear communication and actions, there is a risk of pluralistic ignorance.

> *Pluralistic ignorance is a state in which a group of people misinterpret what each other believes and then uses that misinterpretation as evidence about what must be true.*

*(Sabini, 1992, p.44).*

Make your popcorn and look no further than the next political change season and enjoy pluralistic ignorance, conspiracy theories and misinformation at its best.

## GRIPS Methodology

Without clear communication, despite the best efforts, failure is inevitable. A GRIPS (Goals Roles, Interactions Processes, Styles) methodology can be recommended as a mechanism to check understanding and perception.

Here one may ask the following set of questions to establish shared situational awareness and understanding:

| Goals: | Do we have a common understanding of the team goals? |
|---|---|
| | Do we have an agreed understanding of the team goals? |

It should be noted that just because a goal is commonly understood does not mean it is commonly agreed.

| Roles: | Are the roles clearly allocated? |
|---|---|
| | Do you have the right person in the right position? |

Without clear understanding of roles, not only will communication falter but performance will suffer.

| Interactions: | Is communication clear and open? |
|---|---|
| | Do we actively listen to what is actually being said? |
| | Are we constructive about listening to what is said? |
| | Are the appropriate people involved in the communication and decision making? |

Interaction is key in human processes, and imperative for diversity and inclusion. We must be willing to willing and active communicators with the best of intentions to build trust.

| Processes: | Are we planning our tasks well? |
|---|---|
| | Are we using the correct tools for the right jobs? |
| | Are we using the appropriate resources in the right places? |

One must not assume that success in managing a team whether diverse or not comes without planning. Planning allows us to stop and evaluate/validate where we are and make necessary adjustments.

| Style: | Is the management style appropriate for the particular team, task, or process at hand? |
|---|---|

There is no one size fits all in leadership, period. Know the context you are working in and adjust the style.

# Cognition Stress and Fatigue

Leadership and decision-making are not made in a void but are susceptible to a wide range of individual, social, and environmental influences such and stress and fatigue. Let us just face it, being a leader today is a lot more stressful than ever. The volatility, uncertainty and complexity of the world makes it a high-risk operation.

Several researchers such as Kahneman have concluded that stress has a profound effect on cognitive functions. It is it very hard to correctly process information while experiencing high levels of stress (Kahneman, 2011; Maitlis et al., 2013).

It is hard to be cheerful, patient, in control of one's temper and be an understanding leader when experiencing high levels of stress. Nor is it easy to make good sense of a situation when experiencing such levels.

Leadership is, in general, a protracted and exhaustive process with stress cumulating over time, particularly when in a state of crisis or major organisational change. The complexity of leading diverse teams, especially those scattered all over the place, means that the volume of information and communication alone is massive.

Many of us are already suffering from information overload, some of us have long accepted that we can never win the war against the content of our overflowing inboxes. No sooner do you respond to one email than ten more appear. Sometimes just keeping afloat feels like fighting Medusa where every serpent head you cut grows seven new ones.

Important emails get lost in the pile of unimportant stuff. This further contributes to cluttering the decision-making landscape. Vital information is lost in all the clutter of emails, publications, commercials and so on. Information overload increases cognitive load while reducing the capacity for information processing. Then we get stressed further because we are aware we are not on top of everything, which leads to more stress and the resultant poor decision making.

Leadership requires constant decision-making, which during uncertain periods of change and turbulence can lead to a phenomenon known as decision fatigue (Pignatiello et al., 2020). In short, we get tired of making hard decision after hard decision after hard decision. Decision fatigue is simply the impaired ability to make further decisions and control behaviour because of repeated acts of decision-making. This is a result of mental resources becoming depleted and/or motivation to exert mental effort declining over time. This results in a measurable shift toward easier, safer, or more gratifying decisions and actions (Allan et al., 2019; Pignatiello et al., 2020).

In the 1980s classic comedy 'Airplane', we see the character Steve McCroskey going into a decision fatigue spiral to more and more gratifying actions in the middle of a dramatic series of events.

*Looks like I picked the wrong week to quit sniffing glue!*
*Looks like I picked the wrong week to quit amphetamines!*
*Looks like I picked the wrong week to quit smoking!*
*Looks like I picked the wrong week to quit drinking!*

At the individual level, there is inherent risk of fatigue linked to the high intensity response required over a longer period of time. Burn out is not uncommon among people exposed to stress over a long period. This is not just relevant for leaders, but leaders must be mindful of their people with high workloads, especially high performers. They will often go the extra mile deliver on their job even to the detriment of their health.

There are several physical and psychosomatic diseases that are linked to work stress and the accumulated fatigue. These diseases have a tremendous cost impact to the companies, as well as to the state. As with most things, prevention is better than cure. We should all be mindful and take care of each other.

As you can see, the ability to manage stress and fatigue both at individual as well as group level is vital not only for performance but for safety and reliability.

# Traits that Impede Diversity Leadership Performance

It is often said that your strength can also be your weakness. For example, high self-esteem can turn into arrogance, enthusiasm can turn into anger and frustration, and scepticism can be perceived as negativity if there is too much of it. It is usually your most important strength that has the greatest potential to become your biggest weakness. Under normal circumstances, your characteristic personality traits will usually be a strength, but when you are tired, pressured, bored, or distracted, the same traits can impair your effectiveness and / or impair your chances of performing well in your leadership role.

The psychologists Robert and Joyce Hogan created what we call an inventory of traits referred to as the 'dark side' traits because taken to the extremes, they turn into personality disorders that result in pervasive dysfunctional behaviour. Based on their extensive analysis involving the profiling of millions of employees, managers, and leaders, it is known that most people display at least three of these dark-side traits, while about 40% score so high on one or two putting them at risk of disruption in their careers (Chamorro-Premuzic, 2017).

It is rare to hear that a CFO was fired in a company because he or she knew too little about finance. On the other hand, it happens very often that those who fail as leaders have counterproductive behaviour patterns that can create a distance between themselves and the people they lead. According to Dr Robert Hogan's research on why leaders fail, it is concluded that this is largely due to derailment tendencies based on personality (Hogan et al., 2007; Hogan et al., 1996). Most people have traits with a potential to repel people. The important thing in such situations is that you know them and can regulate them.

From an economic point of view, it is important that managers, board members or owners tolerate some derailment tendencies amongst their managers. Completely normal and balanced personalities are likely to create normal results at the other end. Without some derailment tendencies in the personality, one does not achieve the big upsides, and if one does not recruit them because of a slight impact on the personality profiles, there is a risk of missing out on the best. It is possible to manage ingenious people with derailment tendencies but much more difficult to get completely ordinary people to come up with ingenious ideas.

Somewhat special people need to be coached so that their special features can shine out and not become a burden on the environment. If you achieve this, you have a great potential for results over time. This topic is further discussed in the section on neurodiversity. However, it is important that candidates have enough self-awareness to understand their potential for counterproductive behaviour so that they can regulate it.

## Excitable

To be excitable is to have the tendency to develop strong enthusiasm for people or projects, only for the enthusiasm to fizzle out in time and end up in disappointment. They will seem unsustainable due to mood and energy fluctuations. This can make it difficult for employees to know where they stand with their manager. At any one moment they will oscillate between over-engagement and lack of engagement, good mood and bad mood, laughter, and irritation and so on. At their best, they can create an enormous commitment as they are good at speaking from the heart and attracting people's feelings, but they can in turn break down the trust they have built up relatively easily.

Leaders who score highly on this dimension can charm people quickly and will infect them with their committed enthusiasm, but they are in great danger of wearing people out with over-commitment coupled with a little rough temperament and short temper in the long run.

## Sceptical

This is about the tendency to have good social insight in combination with being sensitive to criticism. The result of this is that one can easily be perceived as suspicious. Too much time is spent on speculation of the motives behind words and actions, and it takes a lot for such a leader to give you confidence. At best such a person can be insightful and a little cunning when it comes to the political game in the workplace. At worst, they can be suspicious, cynical, hold grudges and are often on the lookout for poor treatment.

Leaders who score highly on this dimension can, individually, be beneficial in a team as they easily find weaknesses, errors, or shortcomings in suggestions. One must avoid the other extreme though which is to be too gullible. If there is too much scepticism or too many sceptics on the team, they create a defensive climate in the group where one is primarily concerned with covering one's back. Nobody dares to make suggestions for fear that they will simply be shouted down by critical voices.

## Cautious

Caution is about being very anxious about being criticised. The result is that one is reluctant to change things or take chances. Leaders who doubt themselves until decisions are made will consequently spend a long time on issues that should be concluded relatively quickly. An evasive leader is often a 'bottleneck' in the system, and their lack of clarity often spreads down throughout the organisation. Doubt at the top often creates even more doubt and frustration further down the chain. As the leader's main objective is to avoid being criticised for making mistakes, the result will be a lack of desire to think outside the proven beaten tracks, and they will seek approval from others before deciding.

Our experience with elusive leaders is that decisions are eventually made after a long time. You really do not know where you are with them because they can never give you a straight answer. They avoid risky choices and decisions or send others into battle without giving them proper backing for when problems arise.

They often push problems under the rug, and do not address challenges, problems, and conflicts as quickly as they should. Leaders who are very cautious are also very concerned about their power, reputation and future careers and will have a strong incentive to avoid blame by not making any decisions (Kuipers & Brändström, 2020; Moynihan, 2012). From their research on political leaders, Boin et al found that the biggest fears public leaders had was particularly related to those actions that are public, irrevocable, and hard to undo or disown (Boin & t' Hart, 2003; Weick, 1988). This fear extends beyond public leadership and is well identified amongst overly cautious leaders.

## Reserved

Reserved is about the tendency to lack interest in or attention to the feelings and needs of others. The result is that you seem to be particularly bad at communicating and that you withdraw a little from other people. Reserved leaders can frustrate others and weaken their ability to create engagement. They can withstand tough situations, but often underestimate the needs of others for, among other things, security.

Our experience with leaders who score highly on this screen is that they handle pressure and criticism in a controlled manner. It is hard for them to get out of hand. At the same time, they may seem insensitive to other people. Since they do not show sympathy, nor consider other people's feelings to any significant degree, they are prone to hurting other people without even realising it. In a downsizing process, they communicate around the company's challenges and rationale to cut costs on a fact-based basis without necessarily showing care for the people who will be affected.

The positive effect of this trait is that they are good change agents. They can execute strategies and follow through tough calls without being too overly affected by other people's opinions and feelings. In implementing a diversity and inclusion strategy, this is a good ability as it enables a leader to perhaps not take too much consideration of the resistance to change from the majority and push forward an inclusive agenda, albeit unemotionally charged.

## Leisurely

It is about the tendency to be independent, ignore other people's opinions and get annoyed if they insist. Unlike a combative person who takes up the boxing gloves in a conflict situation, a passive aggressive person chooses to oppose those he or she disagrees with in silence. Alternatively, they do not help people who need it or simply ignore them. A leader with this disposition seems stubborn, slow, and uncooperative, and tends to follow his own agenda.

Our experience with leaders who score highly on passive-aggressive is that instead of telling you what the problem is by being open and honest about challenges, they tend to choose to oppose you through backbiting, tactical opposition, and various other types of sabotage.

For example, a passive-aggressive employee may tell his new manager that 'you are doing just fine as a manager, given that you are so young.' Through small verbal or non-verbal drips, hostility seeps out. Passive-aggressive people can, for example, use tactics to make you angry.

In this way, they can then blame you, and thus get an outlet for their own unrest and dissatisfaction. Passive aggressive people find it difficult to take feedback. They become as slippery as a wet bar of soap which is difficult to grab a hold of. They are otherwise tactical in nature and are good at staying in with the right people in an organisation as a survival mechanism.

This trait is particularly counterproductive in trying to build a well-functioning diverse team. Lack of trust will infuse the team and points of cooperation soon become points of contest.

## Bold

Being bold is about the tendency to overestimate one's own competence and value. The result of this is being unable to admit mistakes or learn from experience. A leader with this tendency tends to ignore the input of others and may be reluctant to actively listen to anyone else. They think that they have all the right answers, and therefore do not pay much attention to the other views. The starting point for a discussion is: 'I am right, and you are wrong, and now I will show you that this is the case'.

Our experience is that this is perhaps the most common derailment trend among top executives in general. I have tested a few hundred leaders in high positions, and this is the dimension that gets the highest average score. Strong belief in one's own ability has been the strength which got them to where they are today, but it is a weakness in relation to actively listening to the views of others. Many leaders are aware of this trait in themselves and can regulate their own behaviour so that they become better at listening than the 'starting point' they have in their personality.

## Mischievous

This is about tending to be charming, thrill-seeking, and willing to take chances. The result is a problem with long-term obligations and learning from experience. Leaders with this tendency are often better at making the big hairy and ambitious goals, than delivering on them.

While the ability to manipulate facts can be an advantage in some contexts, it is detrimental to trust. In politics, it can sometimes be good to be able to speak out on difficult questions from the press, to wing it but that is a high-risk operation. Taking things too lightly is likely to lead to mistakes, errors and omissions that will leave long term blemishes to the reputation. They manage to 'spin the plates', but as soon as one plate falls, there is a risk that the entire house of cards will collapse. So, all credit to #metoo. Bill Clinton's statement: 'I did not have sex with that woman' must be said to be one of history's most manipulative manoeuvres but we all know how it backfired.

When working with people in general, trust is of fundamental importance. A leader that does not fully recognise the value of diversity but tries to play diversity as a token is likely to end up in a situation with a non-functioning diverse but not inclusive team. The diversity figures in the annual reports will look great but the benefits will be absent.

## Colourful

This quality is about being overly attention-seeking whereby one is concerned about being noticed but may lack the ability to maintain focus over time. Leaders with such a trait tend to steal all the limelight and let others in, to a certain extent. While this trait is the result of insecurity, it projects a sense of confidence instead.

Our experience with such leaders is that they love to dominate in social situations, and they like to share 'bragging rights' on social media with an army of 'fans' around them. They seem colourful, quick-thinking and take on many assignments. Because they are very focused on how they are perceived, they tend to have little interest in understanding others unless it serves their own agenda. They will jump on the diversity bandwagon for the clicks and likes but the likelihood of them working on inclusion and the wellbeing of their crew is minimal.

Some of them are not ashamed to take credit for the achievements of others as long as it can give them what matters most to them, namely attention. The urge to share their feelings with others, even if this may be unreasonable for tactical reasons, is done from time to time without a sufficient 'filter'. This is likely to be intimidating to those new to his/her circle as they feel the need to be receptive cheerleaders only.

While being colourful and attention-seeking may have some advantages, the major side effect is that one is in danger of taking up too much space and not knowing when to stop. An open personality makes it easier to make contact with others, however, lack of humility and willingness to listen to others and let them in, becomes the ultimate hinderance to inclusion.

## Eccentric

This is a term for people who have unusual or fixed ideas, or who display conspicuous behaviour, appearance or perceptions that clearly differ from what is usual and common. It's about the tendency to think and act in interesting and unusual ways. The result is that you seem creative but can sometimes also lack good judgement. Eccentric leaders are seen as a bit 'far out' in some contexts, and working with them can pose challenges, yet eccentricity has the enormous potential to provide outside the box thinking, resulting in innovative and creative problem solving.

Eccentric leaders are more often going to engage in thinking outside of traditional constraints. This can push the team to great heights. Focus on the goal may appear compulsive, impulsive, and even egocentric which can create friction, yet it is those very values that push the team to greater results than they otherwise would have achieved.

Because eccentric leaders are often obsessed with goals, they are less keen to engage in ideal leadership of others. If they do not get things done exactly as they want, they are likely to throw tantrums and have temper outbursts. Hence, people working under eccentric leaders often report walking on eggshells as a survival mechanism. The nurturing and people focus required to manage diversity is often lacking in eccentric leaders.

## Diligent

Being diligent is not a bad trait, however, when taken to the extreme, it can be highly detrimental. It is the tendency to be overly conscientious, a perfectionist and extremely difficult to satisfy. This can incapacitate others. In females, some people have chosen to call it the 'good girl syndrome'. The need to exceed expectations and deliver perfection becomes crippling because of the extreme efforts always required to deliver. Good enough is good enough in most cases.

Leaders who score highly on this have an attitude like the following:

*The best way to get things done is to do them yourself*

They have difficulty trusting others and therefore find it difficult to delegate responsibility and authority to anyone else. High demands on oneself can be incredibly stressful. If you can never rest assured that things are good enough, you are in danger of being burned out eventually. The demands you make on yourself quickly become greater than the capacity you have to meet them. I have had many conversations with leaders who must learn to reduce the pressure on themselves so that they do not end up hitting the buffers.

In the context of diversity, being dutiful can be detrimental to integration. A dutiful manager struggles to let go of responsibility and task. A lack of trust in others to do the job well enough, particularly someone he deems very different from him or herself leads to a state of constant micromanagement. Micromanagement does not build trust in a team, and without trust, inclusion is virtually impossible.

Being diligent is one of my dark sides I have had to work with. Earlier in my career, I sought perfection in everything I did. It meant that I worked much harder than my colleagues. Yes, my results were good, my track record was good, but I paid a high price for it.

I recall sitting up until 4am in the morning to re-write a test procedure that an engineer had sent me for checking. Instead of returning it with comments, I spent my night writing a new one which he later, gladly, submitted for approval, in his own name of course. I have had to learn that good enough is good enough and letting those who work with me make mistakes is part of growing together.

## Dutiful and people pleasing

Being dutiful is the tendency to be willing to please others and showing reluctance to act independently. The result is that one is nice and compliant but unwilling to support subordinates if it conflicts with expectations from leaders higher up in the system.

Our experience with leaders who score highly on dependence is that they always seem to agree with superiors as a type of survival strategy. Many people literally submit to authority or shift with the winds in a manner that is baffling. I well remember situations where I agreed with another leader until Helge Lund meant something else. Then the leader turned 180 degrees in the matter of seconds. Integrity is not always present for tactical reasons, but a 180 degree turn in a matter of second does not give the best credibility.

In our experience, dutiful leaders are great at top-down strategy adoption but poor at giving negative feedback to top management from the bottom. It is their desire to always please the leadership. This is a dangerous trait as top management is blind to what is going on within the organisation. Stupid decisions and strategies will be forced down through the organisation with the best of intentions.

I worked in an organisation where the middle management were so afraid of the top management at headquarters that they dared not point out flaws, misunderstandings, and poor decisions. This resulted in major blunders, and some executives were eventually forced to leave. They were simply too out of touch with the market and the rest of the organisation and yet remained oblivious because they were never given honest feedback.

A blind tendency to deal with diversity because it is mandated by management is to go after the visible diversity that can be easily presented as statistics in the annual report. A dutiful manager will of course seek to please and jump at the mandate. Rather than evaluate diversity holistically, especially looking at performance enhancing cognitive diversity which may not be easily presented in statistics, a dutiful manager will do as told. How the team works together, how inclusive it is may be is a matter of interest as inclusion is not a measurable parameter.

## Self-insight and self-regulation

By testing one's own potential for derailment tendencies, one usually ends up with some negative and positive findings. The downside is that the vast majority have up to several different derailment tendencies that emerge under pressure. The positive is that you can do something about them. You cannot change personality, but you can regulate your own behaviour by becoming more aware of the situations where you tend to offend people, and then find other better reaction patterns.

Through a better insight into one's own counterproductive aspects, one will be able to regulate behaviour in situations where it may be appropriate and thus make more of one's strengths stand out and be visible.

You become a far better leader if you master the art of regulating your own weaknesses. I had a score of 99% on the colourful dimension, and 360 evaluations in the company indicated that listening skills had a potential for improvement. In our own development plan, we should regulate the desire to speak, and become better listeners. Personally, it was not easy because it was almost unnatural for me to keep my mouth shut. Since I was now aware of this weakness, I was able to regulate my own behaviour, and thus let the others speak first and more often as part of my own development plan. The result was a more effective leadership and a higher score on the ability to listen at the next 360 evaluation.

# 4.3: THE STRENGTH OF DIFFERENT ATTITUDES

It is not uncommon to associate with people with similar attitudes as oneself. It reduces uncertainty and is probably more comfortable for most people than the alternative. It is even claimed that equal children play best, and much research documents that we tend to seek out environments that, to the greatest possible extent, justify our own attitudes (Rajecki: 1990).

Given the social arena, it is understandable that a certain degree of equality in attitudes may be preferable. The challenge is that this is also largely preferred for employment in companies and organisations. You can place too much emphasis on hiring people with whom you get along well with in favour of the type of people the company really needs and who could have contributed with other important supplementary views.

A team of people with different attitudes can provide a better basis for a more holistic approach to issues because it can be looked at from different angles. In addition, most companies will have customers with different attitudes. The understanding of how these can be attracted is better with a wider range of attitudes at higher levels where important decisions about positioning and more are made.

Different attitudes at higher levels are also important for internal communication. What, for example, may for some seem like a logical and rational piece of information to all employees may to others seem cold, unempathetic and maybe even a little cynical. I cannot count how many times I have had to stop letters or emails being sent out to employees in order to change the wording. It would have simply created a huge storm if the letter had been sent as it was originally written. Better to avoid it in the first place.

If you manage to balance a message or a decision with elements of vision from people with different dispositions of attitudes, you have, as a starting point, a far greater probability of achieving the best possible result both in decision-making processes and with communication internally and externally. The nuances, process and shape are important to get right for as many people as possible.

For example, if you get 50% of the organisation against you, you have failed with your message. This is easily done if the message has nuances of political and ideology in it. There is a greater danger of excluding a large proportion of the employees. It is all about getting as many people as possible involved and motivated for the tasks while building a good reputation externally.

# What is an Attitude?

An attitude is a relatively persistent readiness we as humans have, to react positively or negatively to social ideas, values, objects, and other people. They may be based on knowledge or be acquired through experience, but often left relatively unaltered by parents, friends, or other groups you have chosen to identify with. An attitude is normally expressed through perceptions and expressions of opinion, emotional reactions and through concrete actions (Rajecki: 1990).

Attitudes consists of three components:

## Our thoughts – the cognitive component

Thoughts are a person's knowledge, opinions and information about an object of attitude (what one has an attitude towards). Here reference is made to a process in which one reasons logically in relation to the attitude object.

Examples of this could be:
- If I eat a lot without exercising, this can lead to increased weight and poorer health.
- If I am good at saving money, I can afford to buy a nicer car.

## Our emotions – the affective component

Now it is not the case that our thoughts seem to be the most important in terms of what we choose to do ultimately, in other words our behaviour. Emotions such as like, dislike, love, hate, desire and fear seem to be more fundamental for most people in terms of the choices they make. It is also the case that our emotions tend to drown out the logical content of an expression of opinion if it is presented by a person with whom we have a negative relationship. For example, most of what Donald Trump says will probably be interpreted negatively by most Europeans, regardless of content, simply because he basically lacks confidence and many do not like his way of behaving. Many people regard the affective component of the attitude as the very core of the attitudes – what a person's feelings are towards the object of attitude.

Examples of this could be:

- I feel a tremendous sense of pride when I hear Norway's national anthem.
- I react with disgust when I see someone with the burqa.

Emotions largely control our thoughts. Lyndon B. Johnson was not a particularly popular president, and in the end it did little good to try to strengthen his popularity in his home country. There were negative headlines no matter what he did. Finally, he made the following comment: 'If I walked on water today, the headline in American newspapers tomorrow would be as follows: Lyndon B. Johnson cannot swim'. In other words if you have first had an emotionally bad relationship with a person, it does not help much what the person does or says after that. It will always be interpreted in the worst sense.

> Had I walked on water today, the headline in the American media tomorrow would have been as follows: Lyndon B. Johnson cannot swim.
> (Lynden B Johnson)

## Our behaviour – the behavioural component

Here, reference is made to the person's behavioural tendency in relation to the attitude object. We usually find similarities between unspoken attitudes and behaviours, such as in opinion polls before political elections in what you vote for, but it also happens that people also act differently from what their attitude would suggest. One can, for example, express attitudes one does not stand for as a way of adapting to social expectations.

From time to time, someone may express opinions they do not have just to impress an audience such as in a Miss Universe pageant; 'I am for peace in the world, and I think the environment is important.' One can also use attitudes to defend oneself against unpleasant truths (we are smarter than them). Other situational barriers that prevent an attitude from becoming an action can be, for example:

- Do you train enough in relation to the ambitions you have?
- Do you dare to criticise people you think deserve it?

## Consistency and inconsistency

The three different parts of the attitude – thoughts, feelings, and behaviour – are usually intuitively related. It seems logical that if a thought about a case changes, our feelings towards the same case will change at the same time, and the behaviour will be adjusted.

Many of our decisions and opinions need to be understood in terms of the need for consistency. Most people are more comfortable with a certain degree of coherence about what they say and do. If this is inconsistent and you are acting against your own convictions, you will experience discomfort and will want to redress the balance or ignore or downplay the contradictions. It can be difficult to admit that you have done something meaningless, worthless, or stupid. In such situations, it is easy to be tempted to develop views and opinions that justify your behaviour.

In addition to this, it is not common and normal to regulate one's attitudes; in other words, socially adapt or even express positive values (your self-realisation function) which do not necessarily correspond to one's own attitudes. For example, a person who is not racially prejudiced may in a situation where prejudice is the accepted norm assume that attitude just to fit in. A common adaptation of attitude among teens is often linked to peer pressure. One assumes a certain attitude in a certain environment.

# An Attempt to Categorise People with Different Attitudes

By analysing which values characterise the same people, one can roughly divide the population into four main groups:

1. Modern Materialists
2. Modern Idealists
3. Traditional Materialists
4. Traditional Idealists

## Modern Materialists

Modern materialists tend to be young men living in big cities where the joys of the moment are being at the centre of everything. They crave status goods; luxury and pleasure are key elements, and they score highly on values such as contempt for norms and law, the freedom to do what they want, consume what they desire, enjoy taking risks, are materialistic, desire high status, are non-religious and urban.

A Modern Materialist is known for:

- Being concerned about appearance
- Things becoming a goal in themselves
- Thinking short-term
- Liking action, partying and fun
- Using the internet for entertainment
- Shopping a lot online and at high end stores
- Wanting to impress others by showing off so living a public social media packed life
- Accepting that to be rich means being successful
- Liking the American style of life
- Accepting special treatment.

## Modern Idealists

The Modern idealist is characterised by their tolerance and claim they are willing to put consideration for others at their own expense. They are concerned with self-realisation, protecting the environment and are to a small extent, obedient to authority figures. A typical member of this group is a woman in her 40s with a high level of education who will often be employed in the public sector. They score highly on equality, self-realisation, individuality, tolerance, altruism, emotion, and novelty.

A modern idealist is known for:

- Seeking excitement
- Self-realization
- Reading widely and often
- Going frequently to concerts, opera, and museums
- Accepting that things are means, not goals
- Emphasising usability and flexibility
- Informality
- Preferring traditional broadcasting networks and channels instead of popular culture channels
- Their culture and elite power
- Preferring to live in old houses
- Being well internationally travelled.

## Traditional Materialists

The Traditional Materialist is characterised by a focus on material security and economic growth but has little sense of self-realisation, has limited environmental consideration, and makes few radical changes. A typical member of this group is a man over the age of 50 with lower education. They score highly on reason, traditional gender roles, conformity, traditions, security, distance, and authoritarianism. Popularly called 'traditional industrial culture.'

A Traditional Materialist is known for:

- Having a preference for low prices and offers
- Having relatively low income or bad financial control
- Low education level
- Watching commercial TV
- Low activity level;
- Living in sparsely populated areas
- Being a member of a Labour/Trade Union
- Little use of the internet.

## Traditional Idealists

The Traditional Idealist is often religious with a high respect for morals, law, and rules. They prioritise health, everything in moderation and sensible action and they have a clear negative attitude towards consumption, pleasure, and materialism. A typical member of this group is a woman over 60 with a medium education. This group scores highly on austerity, law and order, Puritanism, security, anti-materialism, religion, health, and intolerance. Popularly called 'pre-industrial peasant culture'.

A Traditional Idealist is known for:

- Prioritising church and country
- Having low alcohol consumption
- Little to no presence on social media and online platforms
- Emphasising quality over quantity
- Being guardians of norm and morality
- Being overly law abiding
- Being family centred and oriented.

A main feature of the development in Norway since 1985 is the move towards materialism in the nineties, with the shift back in the idealistic direction after 2003. Men are on average more materialistic than women and older men are more traditional than the younger.

To attract customers, it is important to understand their attitudes and patterns of behaviour so that companies can best position themselves to reach their important target groups. You need to be careful about cultivating a too narrow type of ideology in a company, as this will mostly exclude large segments of the population.

## Attitude versus Fear

It is not so difficult to express desirable and socially acceptable views to make an impression on the surroundings. Politically correct attitudes create acceptance and respect in society, and it is usually fairly easy to see which way the wind is blowing if you follow the times. Expressing views in line with the direction of the wind is one way of adapting to society and of acceptance.

It is harder for those who want to go against the tide of emotions. Most leaders are not always able to challenge our collective mindsets. I If you attempt to go against the tide of emotions then media and social media will respond quickly and at times quite viciously, to bring you back in line. The court of public opinion is at best ruthless, at worst, lethal.

Many of those who are active in social media have an opinion of their own, they do not always act so much in line with their own beliefs but rather jump on the bandwagon of what is 'in' at that particular time. They are quick to judge and mercilessly crucify others without considering their own actions. It is a case of *'seeing the speck in thy brother's eye and not the log in thine own eye.'*

'Walk the talk' is perhaps too little valued, and words without practical content are given too much weight in a society where social media dominates more and more. Today, social media has even become a kind of 'court', the undisputed court of public opinion where people risk becoming almost lawless.

Leaders and people in key positions of trust are largely restricted in their room for manoeuvre, especially when it comes to their opinions. Is there really any freedom of speech in the world at present? Or are we all so conformist that there is little room for difference?

If that is the case then in the future, we risk getting leaders who will become too cautious, afraid to have any original thoughts, afraid of their own shadows so much so that instead of delivering outstanding results, they become too preoccupied with watching their backs to achieve anything worth achieving.

*We have Freedom of speech.*

*Freedom **AFTER** speech, now that's different story*

*(Allegedly said by Idi Amin Dada)*

It is admittingly clear that leadership in the public sphere is more challenging with the unfiltered influences of social media. It is harder to take controversial and unpopular actions that may be deemed necessary because of fear of public judgement. There has not been a lack of criticism, ridicule, and blame. Several research studies point towards the conclusion that fear is a hindrance for public leaders taking bold actions (Arjen Boin et al., 2013a), in particular those actions that are public, irrevocable, and hard to undo or disown (Boin & t' Hart, 2003; Weick, 1988). Someone out there has a record, a photo, a tweet of whatever was said or done, and the willing masses are ready to use that information.

It can feel as if the business community has moved towards being like a 'Miss Universe' competition where everything is a popularity contest, a reputation building competition because moral resentment has become the new currency of the media economy. Do the leaders and key shop stewards of the future need be more sacred than the pope to survive in their future roles?

Those who want a position in public life or a position at a senior level in organisations in the future must be even more adept at expressing attitudes that are socially acceptable and politically correct and avoid anything that seems a little unpopular. It has almost become a requirement or a qualification today. You can like or dislike this, because as a leader and a centrally elected representative, you have to relate to the outside world as it is not as we would like it to be.

Own opinions that are not socially acceptable must be kept to oneself. You cannot spend time getting worked up by what is put out on social media, norm conformity and political correctness. Behaviour outside the norm could easily become a so-called CLM or career limiting move. What is of concern is whether greater conformity could become a constraint on performance-enhancing diversity. To achieve something extraordinary, you have to be able to think outside the box and go upstream at times, but is the climate quite right for this at present?

## Can One Change Attitudes?

Attitudes are formed over many years through influence and learning. Through countless signals of what is right and wrong, children are made aware of their parents' perceptions and assessments from an early age. Attitudes develop because of this direct influence. As children grow, influence from others will give children new attitudes. School, mass media, social media, sports clubs, and groups of friends are usually important sources of influence.

It is easy to understand why the interest in how attitudes change is so great. Politicians want to capture your vote and the business community want you as a customer. Both advertising agencies and political parties work on the basis that a change in attitude will lead to a change in behaviour.

Nevertheless, it can be claimed that attitudes are well vaccinated against change as they have been built up over many years. In some cases, however, a change of attitude can occur over a relatively short period of time if, for example, you are disappointed by someone very close to you. Infidelity is a good example of something that can lead to a change in attitude relatively quickly.

The business community wants to greatly influence their employees' attitudes to values, customers, and colleagues to, for example, create a value-based performance culture. To manage this, you have to work systematically over time with education and training requirements while motivating and managing expectations. Changing attitudes often starts with the knowledge of why we, for example, should do things differently in the future.

Let us say you want to improve sales in your company by getting clerks to become salespeople. It is not the case that imparted knowledge or training will immediately lead to behavioural change. You must first and foremost make sure that the employees have understood the message and are receptive. This can be done, for example, by testing the employees in the most important areas and thereby ensuring that the new competence can be acquired.

Even if they have understood the message, it is not certain that everyone will believe in it. It can often be useful to lead by example and / or to have examples to show how changing behaviour is profitable or beneficial for the employee and the company. Some may argue that it is a disadvantage to be too sales oriented and that customers will quickly feel cheated – though this can be seen as an excuse for not asking customers about sales more actively. Even if one both understands and believes in it, there is no guarantee of changed behaviour.

It takes courage and self-confidence to change your own habits, and you must be motivated to change. One can make demands on the behaviour, but it will have side effects. It tends to be a behaviour without empathy, almost like a 'robot service' without having 'their heart' in the action.

In years gone by Statoil Retail had a campaign that gave the customer a free car wash if they were not asked if they wanted one. Although sales of car washes doubled, in fact as many as 4% of employees chose to report in sick. If you manage to persuade people to want to change where the heart is involved, then this will be reflected in a new behaviour. Then the probability of more sales increases considerably.

The road to attitude change is long and difficult but is entirely reachable.

## Pragmatism versus Ideology in Business

Ideology can be a mindset based on political, philosophical, or religious ideas about how the world and society should be understood and arranged. Pragmatism is based on the practical utility and focus on the usefulness of ideas.

What works best in practice usually trumps dogmas and ideologies, but despite this it is seen that different philosophies and ideologies in some contexts almost override pragmatic decisions. Many people become too attached to a type of ideology or philosophy of life rather than being more concerned with what actually works in practice. In politics, it will sometimes be the case that an idea from the Conservative Party works best, other times the idea from liberal is far better. It really does not matter where such an idea originated or what kind of ideology it is based on, as long as the idea is good and works in practice.

Important decisions are often made at the expense of practicality and more rational assessments, even in large professional companies. Could it be that too many decisions are coloured by feelings, values or ideology often wrapped up in a rational disguise? Are we in danger of using 'emotions' rather than deeper cognitive processes when important decisions are to be made, cf. Kahneman's well-known theory of system1 and system2?

You would think that research was an area where there was a large degree of factual knowledge free of the more ideological thoughts, and this probably is the case in most areas within biological and natural science and mathematical subjects. Within social science topics, on the other hand, there are often political and ideological undertones, and the search for answers that support your own political message, or your own ideological beliefs is often present.

# Attitudes

## Do we develop attitudes that suit us best?

Do we act in accordance with our attitudes, or do we develop attitudes that justify previous actions? It is probably a bit of both, but you may not be aware that previous actions are often justified through changes or adaptation of your own attitudes. Either way, it is difficult to admit that you have done something meaningless and stupid. It is often easier just to look for arguments that justify previous behaviour and decisions. In that situation, people will usually look for evidence that supports their own claims rather than actively listening to their opponents, and thus their attitudes are to some extent vaccinated against change unless the changes are in their own best interests.

*Those who say that the most important thing is not to win but to participate have probably lost.*

*(Martina Navratilova 1980)*

## Attitudes and ethical dilemmas

Let us say you are in a car with your best friend driving at 80 in a 60 zone. Unfortunately, he hits a pedestrian who later dies from his injuries. After a while, you are called as a witness in a court case in which your best friend faces several years in prison. The family of the victim / or the lawyer for the victim's family asks you what speed your friend was driving at when the accident occurred.

What do you answer?

This is an ethical dilemma. On the one hand, you want to help your best friend in a very traumatic situation. On the other hand, you do not want to lie either. If you tell the truth, your friend will face several years in prison, and it will not help to bring the pedestrian back from the dead.

Research in this area shows that how you respond in such a situation will largely depend on your cultural background. In so-called monochronic societies such as England, Norway, Sweden, where right or wrong is the actual truth, one tends to tell the truth in such situations.

In polychronic societies such as Italy, Spain, and Brazil, you are expected to support your friend 100%. It would be seen as stabbing your friend in the back if you told the truth here.

In a diverse setting, it is important to understand how cultural attitudes shape ethical behaviour, because sooner or later, unethical behaviour will affect the organisation if left unchecked.

## Attitudes towards business ethics grey areas and corruption

As a leader, you are put to the ethical test many times throughout your working life, and so it is important to keep up with the times and have clearly documented requirements for business practice and behaviour. The changes in the business community in relation to corruption have been rapid, and not everyone has been able to keep up. Times have changed. Some of what was previously considered customer care is today considered corruption.

In 1995 a trip to Switzerland covered by the supplier was a perk but became a so-called grey area in the year 2000. By the year 2005, the same 'perk' had turned into corruption. Today, you risk a prison sentence by offering such undue benefits to decision-makers before a tender.

This shows that we as a society have developed in an ethically stricter direction here. The difficulties for many arise in situations when they work in countries which have not come so far in this area as others.

As a manager, you must set the requirements for business practice and personal behaviour in a way that employees avoid ending up in these grey areas or in situations which can be described as corruption. You should prepare some ethical guidelines which describe the company's ethical issues and link this to the expected behaviour. The intention is to make the guidelines as clear and direct as possible when it comes to difficult issues that the company's employees may encounter. In addition to this, the employees must be trained so that they know how to deal with ethically difficult dilemmas.

There are various areas of ethics that employees should be trained in dealing with to avoid all conflict.

# Lack of Compliance in Practice

Most companies today have all encompassing governing documents including ethical guidelines, rules, routines, and laws that employees must not only comply with figuratively but in practice. However, they are not always complied with in practice, and when violations or unethical behaviours occur, it is usually a minority who spoil it for the majority.

There are always those who follow their own assessments or intuition rather than the company's rules and guidelines. There are those who feel it is okay to manipulate the truth a little or even be a little excited by an element of risk but choose to do this in the wrong area.

These people always think they are invincible and allow themselves to cut some corners to get to the goal faster or make far more money.

Charming manipulative personalities with a lower degree of conscience and sense of order are those responsible for breaches of ethical guidelines or internal routines. Sometimes you can blame the whole culture in the company, but often there are just a few that ruin it for everybody else. Lack of compliance with rules and routines by the few has led to some of history's biggest scandals and disasters.

## Case Study: Tenerife Accident

The Tenerife accident of 27 March 1977 claimed a total of 583 lives and is the deadliest plane accident crash of all times. The captain, who in many ways caused this accident, was the experienced Dutch pilot Jacob Veldhuyzen van Zanten from KLM. He ignored the warning that the runway was not ready and overruled the flight engineer who was in the cockpit with him. The investigation report established that he had taken off without permission from the air tower.

What happened was that two Boing 747s (KLM and Pan AM) collided on the runway in the fog. Both planes were going to Las Palmas but had been forced to land on Tenerife because of a bomb threat on Las Palmas. The bomb threat turned out to be false, and the KLM plane was about to take off from Tenerife on its way to Las Palmas when the accident occurred.

At full speed on the runway, the KLM pilot suddenly realised his mistake and tried to lift off the plane. However, it was too late, and the undercarriage of the KLM aeroplane collided with the roof of the PAN AM aeroplane. None of the 234 passengers or crew on the KLM flight survived. The PAN AM plane caught fire, and most of the 396 passengers on board died. 61 miraculously did survive, including the three flight crew in the cockpit.

Many reports have concluded that the captain's excessive self-confidence and the co-pilots' total respect for him was one of several important underlying causes of the accident.

## Case Study: Bhopal Accident

The Bhopal accident is considered the world's largest industrial accident and took place in 1984 at a pesticide factory owned by the American Dow Chemical Company. At around midnight between 2nd and 3rd December 1984, the gas plant inadvertently released several tons of the toxic gas methyl isocyanate along with other toxins, into the atmosphere, which resulted in more than 500,000 people being directly exposed to these environmental toxins. It is estimated that 8,000 died during the first weeks and that another 7,000 later died of gas-related diseases.

Several serious human errors were subsequently discovered in addition to system failures at the factory. Some employees at the factory were sentenced to short prison terms.

## Case Study: Banking Errors

Fines of a staggering NOK 1800 billion were recorded in the banking sector from 2009-2015. KBW made the list of the 175 largest fines the banks globally have been fined in the period 2009-2015. In total, this amounts to just under NOK 1,800 billion which is equivalent to the expenditure for a Norwegian state for 18 months. It is about everything from tax evasion, corruption, insider trading, misleading customers, loans to bad payers, breaches of competition rules, tampering with information and more.

There are many indications that this has largely been driven by greed as the motive, with the potential for sky-high individual bonus agreements. In most countries, maximum ceilings for bonus payments of around 50% of basic salaries in the financial sector have now been introduced. So far, it seems that this has been pushing the financial sector in the right direction.

Banks often find themselves in situations where they and their customers have conflicting interests. Let us say that a customer with a high loan inherits 1 MNOK, and wonders what to do with the money. Should he repay the loan, put the money into a high-interest account or invest the money in an index fund? From the customer's point of view, he will probably be better off repaying the loan as it provides a risk-free return and reduces the high debt. The banks will of course, not benefit from the customer repaying the loans as they lose interest income on the loan as well as the income from savings in a high-interest account or index fund. The question is whether your customer advisor has your interest or the bank's interest at heart. Bank of America was convicted of 34 offences and fines over USD 70 billion.

# How to Strengthen Compliance with Proper Behaviour in the Workplace

Most companies today have written down their values, ethical guidelines and more which employees must adhere to and comply with in practice which is in line with national compliance legislations. Many also have forms of training which will ensure the employee's understanding of the ethical issues and dilemmas is clear and explain how to best comply with the guidelines in practice. Nevertheless, there will still occur some breaches of rules and internal guidelines, and with it a lack of compliance with procedures and breaches of the law. As a result, most companies end up investing even more time and money in training. However, I am not sure if this is necessarily the right medicine in all contexts.

If an employee repeatedly arrives late for meetings – does it make sense to send them on a course to teach them how to tell the time? Hardly. Compliance is not the same as knowledge, although knowledge can naturally contribute to increased compliance. However, courses and gatherings also have their clear limitations - knowledge and behaviour are two different things. My manager in Statoil ASA was annoyed that people constantly arrived late for his meetings, so he simply locked the door when the meeting was about to start. After that, no one arrived late.

When I started as HR director in Statoil ASA, I was first quite surprised at how extremely careful everyone was in the HSE area. I remember being scolded for not holding on to the railing when I went downstairs to the head office. Furthermore, I was told to back the car into the parking lot so that I had a better overview when I had to drive out again. All meetings began with information about where the emergency exits were, and the first item on all agendas was HSE.

To a former retailer, this seemed almost absurd to begin with, but soon I realised that this was about building a culture of security. If you work in an oil and gas company, an airline, nuclear power and more, the consequences of non-compliance can be so catastrophic that safety must always be in high focus. By being accurate on more everyday events, one created an increased awareness of safety, and therefore limited the potential for future accidents. As a result, the number of incidents fell sharply as people worked more systematically with HSE, on everyday tasks. HSE was the focus of everyone in the building and became the new routine.

Impact management is quite effective in making people aware of their own behaviour. I remember that I had once forgotten to lock my locker with, among other things, sensitive information in it. I received a clear message that my accumulated bonus would disappear if this were repeated. It did not happen again.

Compliance is not just about ethics and safety. It can also be the behaviour the company wants more of, for example, to increase sales in meetings with customers. It is not an unknown issue that companies want to change employee behaviour with respect to enhanced sales. Money is often invested in sending employees to motivational gatherings with sales as a review theme.

The gatherings are often both exciting and entertaining, but when the employees return to work on Monday morning, the vast majority will go back to their normal behaviour.

> ❟ *If you want to change behaviour, you must practice new behaviour until you feel comfortable with the new way of doing things.*❟

We often talk about 20-30 repetitions with good coaching and guidance for it to become instilled. In other words, for them to become established habits as habits take time to change. Courses and training are hardly sufficient. You learn through doing - not by seeing and hearing as it is too easy to switch off.

Finally, many accidents and challenges with non-compliance in practice could have been avoided with a strengthened recruitment process. Often, as previously mentioned, it is the few who in practice spoil it for the rest. Those who score highly on charming manipulative, but low on propriety and low on security are often the most non-compliant. By changing the recruitment routines, a distribution company in the USA managed to reduce the number of accidents by more than 80%. It is about recruiting people with the right attitudes or in other words:

## *'Hire for attitude - train for skills'*

To capitalize on behaviour diversity, you must:

- Seek pragmatic solutions as they are more profitable in practice.
- Capitalise on different dispositions of attitudes in a team or a group.
- Refrain from the philosophy of one size fits all.
- Be willing to listen actively to and familiarize yourself with other people's perspectives.

- Create a good culture for compliance with ethics and regulations in practice.
- Set aside time to practice good behaviour.

# 4.4: DIVERSITY MANAGEMENT

Diversity management is about linking people together across differences as well as capitalising on complementing skills in practice. You need to create an inclusive workplace where people can collaborate, share information and knowledge, solve problems together, build good relationships and feel like 'insiders' in the organisation. In an inclusive workplace, employees should feel a sense of belonging, in other words they are part of the organisation and at the same time see themselves as unique. With a heterogeneous workforce, more attention, competence and work are required from the manager, but at the same time it offers greater potential for creating the best results.

A good diversity manager must be aware that people are unique in many aspects and be careful about putting employees in a box. Society and our social understanding of the world are made up of social identities and groups. We place ourselves and others in these boxes, such as doctor, economist, vegetarian, northerner, Muslim, nerd, right-wing populist, left-wing radical and more. These group memberships become part of who we or they are. It is important to remember that not all groups and differences are equally valued. In most countries social groups have different places in the status hierarchy. This affects whether people want to share their different social identities and to what extent they like to be connected to it.

Good diversity management is about having a conscious relationship with the language managers use. Words and expressions that are used often have great significance for the work environment and community building. When the manager talks about how 'our new compatriots' or 'our minorities' work in the warehouse or with cleaning, the statements show two things: that the manager sets a distinction between his employees, and that most employees with multicultural backgrounds work at the lowest level in the company.

To be a good diversity leader, however, one must ensure that all employees are treated fairly, are valued for who they are and are included in relevant decision-making processes. Make sure that some individuals do not fall outside that process just because they are different. It can be a difficult balancing act to define a set of values that should apply to everyone, preferably operationalised with examples of desirable behaviour, and at the same time stimulate diversity. Here you must understand that *'one size never fits all'*. There must be room to adapt the company's values to the position and the person, otherwise the results will be that some will have to behave in a manner which is unnatural for them. It is important that the values are also chosen to contribute towards creating a diverse culture not pulling in the opposite direction. In practice they need to contribute to more simplicity.

## Genuine Interest in Creating Diversity

The leader who succeeds in motivating people can bring out the best in them. A desire to help and inspire others would ensure that those leaders took many steps in the right direction. It is important to show sincere interest in all the various employees - not only as employees but as people with their own unique history and personality. The employees will take it as a compliment and feel more significant if the manager spends time and energy getting to know them regardless of whether their name is Albert, Jennifer, or Ali. A smile and positive attention will be understood by all people across all nationalities.

There are several principles that are universal and which bind us humans across culture, personality, gender, age and more. If you want to become a good diversity leader, it may make sense to start here. Once we have built a common platform of relationships that bind us together, differences can flourish on top of that solid foundation. The foundation of all leadership is about trust and respect for each other. Without this, you will not succeed as a leader - and certainly not as a diversity leader.

In addition to trust and respect, most of us appreciate feedback in the form of praise, encouragement, and constructive guidance. Unfortunately, it is often the case that you rarely get clear feedback before something has already gone wrong. A leader who is genuinely interested in other people is usually better at finding the strengths of their various employees which they can then capitalise on. Showing gratitude for good effort or positive initiatives on top of trust and respect will put you well on the way to succeeding as a good diversity leader. Most of us are more driven by emotions than we might like to believe, and we basically find it easy to like the person who likes us. We also find it easier to go that much further for people we like. Therefore, it is a good investment to really take the time to get to know your employees.

A leader's most important task is ultimately to create results through the efforts of others. How you treat your employees is therefore of greater importance than the results you create on your own. Your own job performance cannot compensate for the lack of effort total from the employees. The most crucial thing for a manager is to find the key to bringing out the best in each individual unique employee. To help with this it can be helpful to ask yourself the following questions:

1. Do I know my employees?
2. Do I trust my employees?
3. Do I like my employees?

If the answer is negative or partially negative to one of these questions, you have a challenge on your hands. First, the answers to these questions are usually mutually correlated. Firstly, if you are sceptical of an employee, they are probably also sceptical of you. Secondly, it is difficult to delegate responsibility and authority for job performance if trust is not present in the first place. In other words, the basis for good leadership is a good mutual trust and respect for each other, and it all starts with the leader's curiosity and interest in his employees.

## Motivating a Diverse Workforce

Motivation includes all the driving forces behind will-driven actions. We are talking about absolutely everything from primitive instincts and drives to more complex needs and motives. Motivation can be a long-term trait, or a short-term condition. Some people are almost always positive about working hard and getting involved over time. In such cases, motivation is a long-term trait. If there is a specific situation that motivates, we use the term short-term condition.

Our motivation is greatly influenced by what we consider to be significant and insignificant. In other words, it is related to our own basic values and attitudes such as materialistic prosperity vs. idealistic business; excitement seeking vs. security increase; new vs. traditional and more. It is also intricately linked to our basic personality as introvert vs. extrovert; social vs. antisocial; impulsive vs. calm and more. What motivates us will therefore vary greatly from individual to individual.

It will be difficult to find definitive answers to what motivates employees in the work situation, precisely because they have quite different needs, and in a diverse work environment, this tendency will naturally intensify. Most people still agree that human behaviour has some general similarities and commonalities. For example, most people appreciate positive attention. Below you will find a list of words that can be related to motivation in a work context. You will see that motivation spans a large field.

Based on several surveys, the following seems to be most important for motivation for many:

| | |
|---|---|
| Skilled management | They have an interest in the employees, give frequent feedback, give help when needed |
| Good feeling of mastery | Feeling of success, feeling of making a difference |
| Responsibility and authority | To have influence and self-determination within clarified frameworks |
| Interesting work assignments | Stimulating content of the work assignments, preferably with some challenges |
| A good working environment | Surrounded by people who contribute positively to your well-being |

## Understanding needs and wishes

After considering the more general principles of motivation that apply to most people, it is important to identify, consider and capitalise on the differences. Although there are similarities that are universal in terms of motivation, it is important to realise, as we've stated, that one size does not fit all. You should carefully consider the diversity of different needs and desires, which is especially important if you want to become a good diversity leader. It is almost a prerequisite in a world where diversity is the new normal.

It can be fateful to assume that others have the same needs as yourself. It is also dangerous to think that you can predict what others will think - without asking or listening to them. We are all created with a different starting point, and all have different life experiences. This gives us different wants and needs.

A manager who has problems motivating his employees often has too little knowledge of what the employees actually want. It is not always appropriate to bombard unmotivated people with 'stand-by-speeches' and instructions. Better to ask questions and listen actively.

To understand other people better, it is important to look at how their background differs from your own. At the same time, keep in mind that human needs change over time. The way in which employees are motivated must constantly be adapted to their new needs. The author George Bernard Shaw is quoted as saying that:

The only person who behaves sensibly is the tailor.

He takes new measurements every time.

Everyone else assumes that

the measurements

still hold.

## Taking individual considerations into consideration

It is important that you as a leader take individual considerations into account. At the same time, you should not discriminate in a way that is perceived as unfair. This can be a difficult balancing act. The biggest danger in treating employees differently is that it is easily perceived as favouring someone. At the same time, we know that different employees are motivated by different things. Thus, it will be most optimal to facilitate an approximate 'tailoring' for everyone. This becomes especially important across different geographies where the differences are greater.

Let us say you have employees from India who lose one of their loved ones. It is reasonable to give welfare leave with pay for a funeral. The difference between a funeral in Norway and in India is that in India including travel it takes about a week. The most appropriate thing in such a situation would be to give welfare leave for a week, even though it may be stated in an old personnel handbook that a day's welfare leave is granted at a funeral. If you use your head, you will understand that this is not sufficient for a funeral in India.

Another simple example is how to organise a Christmas party so that this can be a pleasant experience for all employees across different cultures. You do not necessarily have to ban alcohol, but you can set some restrictions and at the same time ensure that there are more exciting alternatives than just mineral water for those who want to stay alcohol-free. In this way, you can gather people together and create a pleasant atmosphere across different cultures and desires. It is also an advantage to be able to offer different foods at a Christmas party as otherwise you can exclude a lot of people for religious reasons. It costs so little to think about, and yet it gives so much at the other end.

There are also areas where it makes sense to treat everyone equally. When it comes to compliance with the company's regulations, laws and ethical guidelines, there should be few individual adjustments - if any. If a leader treats someone more gently in such a case, one will rightly be accused of being unfair. Fixed attitudes in connection with compliance with laws, rules and guidelines are important. The reactions to those who commit any violations should be strict and consistent to create a good corporate culture.

## Expecting the best from everyone (building trust)

Several psychological studies show that the expectations we have of other people largely control their performance. We can either bring out the best or the worst in people using our expectations. The reason for this is simple. It is not so easy to believe in yourself unless others do. Positive expectations help to increase the employee's self-confidence in the job situation and so job performance improves. A manager who, on the other hand, has a lack of faith in their employees will have a noticeable negative influence on their performance. Employees' expectations of success or failure are fundamental to their motivation. No one is motivated to work with things they or others do not believe in, nor will they perform at their best if they are convinced that their abilities are not good enough.

Unfortunately, some leaders still try to take on a 'police type role'. They want to control everything and think that it is their role to look over people's shoulders, looking for faults and revealing incompetence. By being a watchdog, a leader quickly creates conflict with his employees. If you are sceptical of certain employees, such as those from a minority background, the result will be a lack of self-confidence and poorer performance from those same employees. The leader will also lose the trust of his team as trust is usually mutual. It is extremely easy to notice whether a leader has confidence in their team or not through body language, comments and behaviour.

Most employees can achieve success in some areas. It is important that we as leaders are aware of this. It is amazing what people can achieve with hard work. However, a prerequisite for working hard is that the motivation is in place. And it is only strong enough, if you think that the effort you put in will give a positive return. That you as a leader expect good results in certain areas will be seen as a vote of confidence. The manager's belief in the employees' abilities and possibilities will stimulate effort and initiative, and it will strengthen the employee's motivation and improve the results.

If people do not perform well, or make mistakes, it is important to give them the opportunity to improve. You must also pick up immediately on any improvements so that the previous mistakes do not end up as an issue. Once a thief - always a thief should not be the feeling. In other words, errors can be fatal if improvements are not noticed. If you first get a certain reputation, it is often difficult to get rid of, and then motivation will decrease. If improvements are not noticed for a long time - why then improve?

## Empowering your employees

Having opportunities to be able to control one's own work situation is truly motivating. On the other hand, it's very demotivating to be controlled in every detail or to get things rammed down our throats - at least for most of us. With increased responsibility and a greater degree of self-determination, the employee feels more significant and gains a sense of self-worth. Increased responsibility is also a declaration of trust that works better than any oral feedback. The manager shows through action that they believe in the employees. Actions speak louder than words.

Research on job autonomy shows that the agreed parameters should be as broad as possible, especially if high productivity and good performance are the goals. This emerged from a statistical overview analysis that included a total of 259 individual studies and a total of 219,625 people (Humphrey et al., 2007, Journal of Applied Psychology).

In larger companies, it can sometimes be difficult to see the connection between the work you do yourself and the company's results. However, it is extremely important that the employees understand this connection so that the work they do becomes meaningful. If a manager does not emphasise how important everyone's effort is, the employee will easily feel like a small piece in a big puzzle, or a small cog in a big wheel. The challenge for you as a leader is to make all employees feel significant.

A general piece of advice like this applies to most, but not all. On several occasions, I have found employees who want to be controlled and have less freedom. They simply like to be told what to do and expect their leaders to be clear and controlling. We also know that a more masculine leadership style is expected to a much greater extent outside this country's borders. Norwegian leaders abroad who delegate a lot of responsibility run the risk of being seen as weak.

## Expressing recognition

Recognition must be genuine, direct, and clearly specified, preferably as soon as possible after the action has been completed. It should also focus on the behaviour that was the basis for a good result rather than the result itself. What you want to do is reinforce a desired behaviour so that it is maintained or even further improved.

To get the most out of positive feedback, it may from time to time make sense to praise the employee while others are listening. This gives them a stronger sense of importance in the eyes of their peers. Some people are shy and may feel embarrassed when they are picked out in public as a good example. Still, it is extremely rare to meet anyone who does not like to be praised. When the boss mentions who has made positive contributions to the company it induces a sense of joy for the person or persons concerned, and they will feel proud.

Success can be a pretext to celebrate. Why not treat all the staff to dinner one evening? Here it needs to be emphasised that this dinner is well deserved, because of good performances. This way, employees can link positive emotions with good performance. The leader will create an important emotional connection to effort and achievement, a life experience.

*An appreciation in the form of a gift can also underline your recognition. A written compliment is still what perhaps gives the best result. At least if you are good at specifying what the appreciation is for. There is almost a magical power in that short letter, especially if it is handwritten not typed. It makes the employee feel important, noticed and appreciated when the boss takes the time to handwrite a letter of thanks. I remember receiving a letter from my former head of Statoil Retail; Jacob Schram. This was in conjunction with a tough restructuring process for which I was responsible, a difficult process which included a downsizing process. After the process was concluded, I received a letter in the mailbox from the boss.*

*In this handwritten letter, he not only specified how important my efforts for the company had been, but also what behaviour he had particularly appreciated during such difficult times. In addition, I got a free dinner at a restaurant of my choice with my wife as a thank you for my extraordinary effort. My eyes teared up as I read the letter, and the words from the boss left a strong and lasting impression on me. In fact, I went on to work for him for another eight years and for the most part I found my skills and qualities were well appreciated.*

## Giving negative feedback

Contrary to praise, negative feedback should be given with as few people present as possible. There is nothing worse than criticising an employee in the presence of colleagues, friends, or customers. Criticism should take place in calm and controlled form, behind closed doors and between the two of you.

Getting an employee receptive to criticism can be difficult. If you face criticism, you will often become defensive. The most important thing in this context must be the starting point for the criticism - which should be intended to help that person - not to put the person in their place. If this is clearly stated at the outset, then the defensive response can be averted. The best advice in connection with criticism of employees is to use 'coaching'. Instead of telling them what they did wrong, you can ask questions and listen.

*'Based on the experience you have now gained in this project, what would you do differently if you started again today? '*

With such a question, it is overwhelmingly likely that you will get the same answers you would have chosen to ram down their throats. The employee will recognise what mistake they made and be more motivated not to do it again than if you had simply pointed it out. Self-awareness is far more productive.

It also matters how the employee responds to leadership and criticism.  Some will like you to be honest and direct - and will dislike various forms of vacillation, others you will need to be more careful with and handle them with kid gloves. You will find out quickly enough which employees need which style, and if you are ever in any doubt, then simply ask them.

## Being firm as a manager

Many who talk about motivation are primarily focused on treating employees in a positive and encouraging way. You should definitely build on their abilities and listen to their needs and desires and more. However, this does not mean that a skilled leader should be soft and gentle. On the contrary! Most leaders who are good at motivating can be as tough as steel when it comes to skill requirements. A person I know very well once said in a job interview when asked how she would describe her leadership style.

'I am G-strict..... Good but strict'. - That is the combination you are often looking for when recruiting managers. They need to be cosy but demanding. By the way, she ended up getting the position as CEO of Baby shop at that time.

From school we all remember the stern teacher, who made us tremble a little with nervousness. But when we look back on their demand that we do our best, it will be with a certain degree of gratitude. Kind leaders who do not care enough about performance are rarely respected. If you as a leader require skill or results, then you show that you care about the company as well as your employees. There is nothing more demotivating than a leader who does not care about skills or results. Imagine a leader who reacts indifferently to the fact that you have done your absolute best and have performed insanely well and achieved more than your targets.

The principle of setting requirements for skill is just as important in an international perspective. Here you risk losing their confidence completely if you are not clear on what results you expect. Too democratic a leadership style will often be interpreted as weak leadership in most other countries in the world.

Creating a performance culture requires a strong leader - not a dominant and ego-driven leader - but one who has a firm, unwavering belief in their team to achieve good results and who expects everyone to do their best. We know that parents who have a determined and fair attitude create the safest children. Even if the children protest the rules, they as adults will become more confident in themselves, more ambitious and more adaptable as they get older.

It is otherwise a cultural misconception that we would all be happier if we were not in such a hurry, that everything would be better if we did not work so hard and did not have so much homework and that everything would be fine if we could just relax and taken longer vacations. When people hate their job, one may ask - why? It's rare because work requires too much of them.

It is also important to be aware that expectations for work-related efforts are often greater in other countries compared with Norwegian conditions. In the United States, it is not uncommon to work from early in the morning until late at night with only one week of vacation a year.

I have also found that both English and American owners are happy to call you at all hours of the day and expect reports. Public holidays they do not acknowledge, and they expect you to be available whenever they call. Some are quite upset about Norwegians who turn off the phone when on holiday, and who do not even show up when precarious situations arise. In many other countries it is expected that the job to a greater extent is a number one priority over private life.

# Using The Competitive Instinct as a Driving Force

If you look at how children play and all the competitive elements which are naturally part of it, you will understand the natural urge many of us have to compete. This is certainly the case in the world of sports and in working life. We live in a society where competitiveness is crucial to companies' existence. Without being competitive, companies in the worst-case scenario will go bust and employees will lose their jobs. We don't like to look competitive because Ideological reasons do not find it attractive.

However, it makes sense that the individual element of a competition is biased in favour of the collective. In a company, we will, after all, create good results through collaboration. I have experience with individual sales competitions in both Statoil retail and pharmacy1. The result of only measuring an individual's achievements is that the good get better, while the less good grow inferior. In both companies, the sum of both types of salespeople has become the status quo with an average overall economic effect on the entire organisation. I do not have good experience with the other extreme (collective competition and collective profit sharing). With such a solution, one could easily lean on other people's achievements, and there will be a smaller relationship between their own achievements and the results by which you are being measured.

My experience of what works best in practice is in fact a hybrid solution where the collective and individual counts equally. Then we avoid the pointed fingers suggesting that some people largely lean on other people's achievements rather than perform at the top of their game. The perfect balance is maintained by recognising that both good individual and collective achievements are important.

Finally, it is important to compete against the external and internal competition. The focus should therefore be on how we must outperform our competitors together. By creating a common 'enemy image', using all your combined strengths as well as utilising the competitors' weaknesses, you strengthen your own competitiveness. This type of community feels the best basis for motivating most employees to increase their efforts. From one time in Norway, I remember that on several occasions we used Rema 1000 as a kind of picture of the enemy. This improved the strength of the cohesion better between the chains internally and coordinated the attack against the most important competitor in a far better way. In many ways one can say that NorgesGruppen has succeeded in this work, perhaps with good help from Rema 1000's strategy.

The competitive element is used to a greater extent in American owned companies as against Scandinavian owned. In Scandinavian countries, we have a greater focus on the collective than the individual and less focus on talent cultivation. Whereas in the United States it is the opposite. However, we see clear indications that US business culture is having an influence on the Norwegian to a greater and greater extent. At least it has made the Norwegian trade movement wake up. Performance management systems with individual measurements, ratings and characters which have been imported from the United States have created great interest, but also great despair amongst some.

## Using comparisons for inspiration

Comparing yourselves with each other to awaken the competitive spirit must be done properly. Using comparisons to inspire can give a positive effect, but it also can do the opposite depending on how it is done. There can be very little difference between what seems inspiring and what seems demotivating. Let me illustrate it with two different ways to communicate that your sister has better grades than you.

*'Why can't you manage it when Jørn gets it?'*

*'When you see that she gets it, it's obvious that you can do it too. What do you think? I'm absolutely sure that you too can get it?'*

The essence here is to use comparison to inspire others, not to make them feel ashamed or slighted. Therefore, it is extremely important not to put people in degrading positions through extensive ranking work. Feel free to praise the best or the top 3 so everyone can learn and be inspired by them but avoid showing up the bottom 3 in front of colleagues. The goal of comparison is to inspire - not to belittle someone.

Don't always use comparison as a starting point to inspire. Jack Welsh - voted 20 years in a row as top leader in GE - used ranking systems to get rid of what he called the 'Low Performers'. The 5% worst performers simply got fired every year. I am not recommending this in Scandinavian businesses, but there is a reason for this even though the philosophy may seem cynical. It is not necessarily caring to have people in positions where they consistently not perform. It is neither good for the company nor for the employee.

# A Common Responsibility for Creating a Good Working Environment

A good environment is not just a means of increased productivity, but also an important goal. After all, we spend almost half our waking life at work, and many of us have just as much contact with colleagues as with family and friends.

A good working environment is characterised by a strong community feeling and a common responsibility across inequalities. In such a group with a strong cohesion, there are no passengers. The group stands together and takes shared responsibility - also for things and conditions that are not the goal. We can use the term support climate for environments where members of the group support each other and take common responsibilities. They all stand together to solve common issues, and the environment is characterised by good team spirit. If there is insecurity and mutual competition, we call this a defence climate. A good working climate is often characterised by:

1. Social Climate: That it is high on the agenda, there is humour and a good atmosphere in the workplace.

2. Cooperation: The people of the organisation all pull in the same direction, to achieve common goals.

3. Intimacy: Everyone knows each other well and it is easy for them to contact each other when they need help.

There is an argument which says that workers thrive best in jobs with a steady even gender distribution. In both men and women, the well-being increases when there is a balance of genders in the workplace. Øystein Gullvåg Holter in the Nordic Institute for Women's and Gender Research, stands behind the report *Gender equality and quality of life 2007* where the feeling of well-being corresponded to the degree of gender distribution.

Everyone is responsible for a good working environment. Those who complain probably should look at themselves in the mirror and ask what they have done to contribute to the good working environment. Nevertheless, the leader must take an overall responsibility and make it easy for it to happen. It can sometimes be difficult for someone from a minority background to be the one who takes the initiative. For various reasons, they may not have the social self-confidence to take the initiative needed. So, it is particularly important that managers ensure that those from minority backgrounds are integrated into the working and social environment so that they feel valued and safe. Then it becomes easier to be able to take the initiative next time.

Good relationships between people are essential for creating a good working environment, but it is also important for doing business. Many Norwegian managers have previously underestimated the importance of building relationships with people in companies in other countries before doing business with them. For many, it is almost a prerequisite that one has a good personal relationship before it is relevant to enter into any agreements. In this area Norwegians generally have much to learn. Many contracts have gone to companies in other countries just because the relationship building and small talk was undervalued.

# 4.5: OBSTACLES TO INCLUSION

## Obstacles which Must be Resolved Immediately

### Back-biting and isolation

Backbiting is one of the most common environmental problems in the workplace, and few things can destroy an environment more quickly than this. It is not uncommon for minority groups and people who are slightly different from the majority to become the starting point for backbiting with the attitude, *'We are better than them'*. It is said that backbiting damages three people at the same time; the one who backbites, the one who gets backbitten and the one who listens.

A good principle in the workplace is, of course, that we should be talking to each other, not about each other. Some claim that what you do not know, does not hurt you, to justify that backbiting of others. But no one gains from this. It will come back to haunt them. In such situations, it is normal to act dismissively or evasively. Or even the opposite, with spasmodic and unnatural goodness. Both types of behaviour are hiding a bad conscience. The one who was the target of the backbiting will eventually feel that something is wrong. They do not need to hear anything negative being said but they will sense it from the working environment.

We must accept and benefit from the fact that everyone is different. If we understand that we are all different, then it is easier to accept other people's opinions. Here I have good experience when using preference tools such as a Jung / MBTI test. Through an increased understanding of differences, the ability to accept a greater range of inequality is reinforced. You react with understanding rather than frustration at different behaviours and meaningful changes and are therefore far better at using complementing skills in practice.

## Bullying

There was a large study involving a sample of 10,627 employees from 96 Norwegian organisations, Nielsen et al (Nielsen et al., 2020) from the Norwegian National Institute of Occupational Health. They examined the protective effects of supervisor, colleague, and non-work-related social support on the associations between workplace bullying, mental distress, and medically certified sickness absence. Their findings showed that social support, and especially supervisor support, was beneficial for reducing the negative impact of workplace bullying on the health and work ability of those exposed.

As managers and colleagues, it is our duty to intervene where there is bullying. Often, we tend to mind our own business and turn a blind eye to that which does not directly affect us, especially with regards to people we do not know very well.

Because many people perceive succumbing to mental distress as a sign of weakness, they do not report such issues immediately. Instead, the bullying continues to hurt even long after the actual encounters are over.

In another extensive study to determine the relationship between workplace bullying and mental distress in Norway, almost 2000 Norwegian employees, recruited from 20 different organisations, answered questions regarding workplace bullying and mental distress as a baseline and a follow-up two years later. The study showed that workplace bullying predicted mental distress for at least two years. The finding also showed that mental distress was also a predictor of bullying (Finne et al., 2011). The Norwegian Labour Inspection Authority reports that bullying and harassment in the workplace is an ever-increasing problem, as it leads to increased sickness absence.

As a leader, you have responsibility for the total health, safety, and security of the working environment and for averting negative behaviour. It is impossible to ensure that work is being organised in a satisfactory manner, that good communication is established and that the scheme of safety representatives works in accordance with the work environment act without tracking.

There must be tracking and traceability to capture these improper acts - and prevent bullying. It is also an advantage to be proactive through anonymous employee surveys with clear communication to build a company culture that makes it possible for all employees to thrive.

You must dare to ask uncomfortable questions, and to deal with uncomfortable situations immediately you find out about them. Bullying does not simply disappear; it must be tackled head on. In addition, it is imperative to offer the right kind of support to both the bully and the bullied.

## Sexual harassment

Sexual harassment has proven to be a far bigger problem than anyone was aware of. This can be anything from conversations charged with sexual insinuations, to actual physical violations. Where the boundary is between innocent kidding or flirting, and what is perceived as harassment, is difficult for some people to decide, and this will also vary from person to person.

If a victim of sexual harassment suffers in silence, their work performance begins to suffer. In the worst case, the person will quit to escape their unwanted persecutor, which costs the employer money in terms of employment and the training of a successor - in addition to losing the employee.

*As a young female employee in male dominated industries, I had my fair share of good jokes, funny flirts, men falling in love with me and to the extreme case of aggressive sexual harassment by a member of the senior staff. While my plight was known to several colleagues, there was no easy way to deal with the situation, particularly because he was a member of the senior staff, and very visible within the organisation and industry. There were known cases of unwanted sexual behaviours within the company which was instead swept under the rug or confined to 'girls' lunches' where the problem was discussed but never officially dealt with. It got to the point where I was personally broken in spirit and so I chose to resign.*

Elements of sexual harassment can include:

- Repeated comments and coarse personal remarks
- A remark that is far beyond the limit of what is considered normal behaviour
- Unwanted physical, digital, verbal approaches and contacts and a refusal to accept no for an answer
- Unacceptable, unwanted, and reciprocal actions.

It is a fact that many find a way into the workplace. However, the rules are completely clear: The interest must be reciprocal and unequivocal. The one who falls in love with or desires a staff member who does not share the same feelings must refrain from showing interest right away. If not, there is great danger that the next approach is perceived as harassment.

As with bullying, sexual harassment tendencies must be nipped in the bud. The culture within the company must be such that it is totally unacceptable. There must be channels and mechanisms to report such acts. Once reported, investigations must happen quickly, and swift action must be taken.

Sexual harassment is a pertinent issue affecting women in male dominated workplaces, and as such a hinderance to their full integration and participation. Once the word is out that a company has poor culture in that respect, recruiting female employees becomes difficult.

It can also work the other way when men can be victims of unwanted female attention. Remember if the attention is unwanted, it is sexual harassment.

Disagreement and conflicts can simply arise because of diversity. We have different interests, responsibilities, education, experiences, languages, culture, age and so on. These differences must not lead to conflict but do arise when things are not as we think they should be - seen from our perspective.

Conflict and disagreement are a completely natural part of working life. When you think about it, disagreement can also be positive for the company. It can be a source of learning and development, and you may have some ingrown habits that often occur which need to be ironed out. You might find new and better ways to work as a result. If a conflict, on the other hand increases in intensity and is no longer about a simple issue it can become harmful. Such conflict takes up unnecessary time and requires a lot of energy and resources to cure and can result in a bad atmosphere in the workplace. It becomes a burden on employees and managers, and threatens good relationships, good cooperation, and good financial results.

The way we deal with the difference is crucial for worsening conflicts. In a culture with high ceiling height for inequality, participants can take up matters they disagree about. Employees listen to each other's views and examine what the disagreement is about before it becomes a full-blown conflict. Such an open culture makes it possible to prevent, handle and resolve conflicts in a good way. Conflicts do not end by themselves, and it is the manager's responsibility to deal with it quickly. To solve a conflict, you must work on both the situation and the relationship. A solution must be found which both parties can live with, and at the same time, you need to work on the relationship between the two parties. Often it will involve them reconciling with each other. But it is not always necessary that the parties be friends or that all disagreements are solved. One can agree to disagree.

To deal with a conflict, it is important to find out what type of conflict it is. Conflicts can occur in different dimensions. It can be a professional disagreement, a disagreement about the distribution of resources, a disagreement about working hours or the distribution of benefits. Conflicts can also turn into personal conflicts. What kind of conflict is it?

- What does the conflict entail in difference of opinion?
- What is important for each side in the conflict?
- Is it a communication problem?
- Is it possible to find a fair solution?
- Is there a basis for compromise?
- Can we limit the disagreement?

The worst thing we can do when conflicts arise is to avoid talking about the problem. Refusing to relate to and accept that there is a conflict usually leads to helplessness, and misery. Everything tends to go wrong if communication stops. To avoid unnecessary sparks and confrontations, it is important to have these moments as a starting point with those you conflict with:

- I want to understand your viewpoint in the best way I can.
- I respect you.
- I will be considerate and honest.

When you take up a problem or a conflict it must happen in such a way that you do not upset anyone else's self-esteem in the process. Maybe even let the other side get the feeling they have gained something. Problems will usually grow and blow up in everyone's faces which causes polarizations in the workplace shown below.

*Figure 27: The conflict staircase*

The conflict staircase above can also be a useful tool for understanding conflicts. It highlights the different levels of visibility and illustrates how a conflict can develop from a small disagreement to genuine hostility. At each step there is the possibility of either going up or down the stairs.

# 4.6: CREATING A HIGH-PERFORMING TEAM

To create a high-performing team with complementing skills, we must be better than the competition at recruiting, developing and retaining competent and motivated people with skills adapted to the organisation's needs. This is easy to say but difficult to achieve. To be successful in practice, we must move away from the traditional ways of recruiting through advertising positions internally and externally so that everyone can apply – as normally the best self-promoters eventually end up getting the most business-critical jobs. They may not be the best fit.

Those who are best at self-promoting are often extroverted men in the 35-45 age bracket with excellent sales abilities selling themselves and their skills, but they are not necessarily what will serve the company best. Although introverts are unable to market their excellence in the same way as an extrovert – they can nevertheless have the ability to deliver in practice far better.

The same can be said of women. They are not, on average, as good at self-promoting as men and find it difficult to boast of their own achievements or excellence. Their conscience also makes it more difficult for them to manipulate facts to paint themselves in a better light to achieve the position. They are also more honest about weaknesses linked to the position. In a self-promoting competitive game, they simply are not up to it in the same way as men.

An open recruitment process usually ends with the candidate who made the best impression in the interview - winning the job regardless of the complementing skills required by the overall team. This may not be the best solution for the company.

The alternative to open recruitment is a more controlled process where you promote those who perform best in business-critical positions, and you match the defined position profile and the candidate. It is through this controlled process that you can get a greater range of diversity in the workplace. It is also motivating for the current employees to know that if they consistently achieve their best there is potential for advancement within the company.

# Recruiting for Diversity of Skills

One of the most important individual measures to ensure good job performance and organisational success is a solid and well thought out recruitment process. Once you have followed a bad recruitment process and appointed the wrong candidate, it is incredibly difficult, if even possible, to compensate for this through training, targeted leadership or any other measures.

Recruitment is largely about reducing uncertainty. This was covered in the sections on Neurodiversity and Autism. From this aspect, there is reason to believe that being different is interpreted as being increased risk which few are willing to take. Difference is in many ways a 'risk versus reward' issue where most people end up on the side of reducing uncertainty. You choose the safe over the unsafe even though there is potential for a higher upside than downside.

## Planning and executing a recruitment process

To recruit the right employees, recruiters must make many important decisions: whom to target, what message to convey and how to reach the right candidates.

James Breaugh, the world renowned industrial and organisational Psychologist has conducted a great deal of research on recruitment, consulting with many companies, and has worked on (Breaugh, 2009):

- developing realistic job previews
- creating selection systems
- instituting 360-degree feedback programmes
- evaluating recruitment strategies
- conducting attitude surveys
- validating testing programmes
- dividing a strategic recruitment process into four sub processes.

The four sub processes in recruitment are:

| First process | Establish a recruitment objective. Why and what are we recruiting for? |
|---|---|
| Second process | Establish a recruitment strategy. How are we going to reach the people we need to reach? |
| Third process | The recruitment itself. What tools are best suited to attracting the best candidates to us and then picking out the best for interview? |
| Fourth and final process | The evaluation How did we do in our recruitment process? Did we succeed with the recruitment objectives? |

By strengthening the quality of the recruitment process at each stage with well thought out objectives and strategy, we are better placed to reach the targets. One needs to use the right tools such as:

1. Screening tests
2. Interview guides
3. Assessments
4. Reference checks
5. Effective recruitment administration solutions to increase the likelihood of successful recruitment.

The process must take into consideration such blind spots and hurdles that can hinder good candidates from recruitment. This has already been touched upon with regards to interviews and neurodivergent applicants.

| | |
|---|---|
| Establish Recruitment Objective | Number of positions<br>Need-by date<br>Number of applicants desired<br>Qualifications and skillsets of applicants<br>Job performance goals for new hires<br>Expected retention rate of new hires |
| Establish Recruitment Strategy | Type of individuals to target<br>Where are they?<br>When should the process start?<br>How best to reach target audience?<br>How to communicate best with target audience?<br>Who do I use to recruit?<br>What should the job offer entail? |
| Execute Recruitment | How best can I execute the recruitment process to get the best possible candidates?<br>What tools and evaluation methods are best suited for this recruitment?<br>How do I make the position attractive enough for the desired candidates? |
| Evaluate success of Recruitment | Did we hire the right person with the right competence?<br>Are we a reputable employer of choice?<br>Number of diverse candidates? |

A solid recruitment process begins by uncovering the strategic objectives and the need to recruit in a holistic manner. Beyond defining what is required about the tasks to be completed in the position, you should also define what complementary skills are required by the company or department and what the need is with regards to expertise, experience, skills, personal qualities and more, and then create an announcement that intends to attract those matching this profile.

It is important to have a clear understanding of the target profile needed for the job, where you expect to find the candidates, how best to shape the narrative of the communication to attract the right profiles. Recruiting for diversity also entails being conscious of the context and finding avenues to reach a wider audience. Today, in principle, one can recruit with the whole world as a starting point.

## Attracting the Right Candidates

Unless you attract the attention of the targeted individuals, a recruitment process is bound to fail. For example, if an objective is to increase the gender balance in the workplace, you should ask yourself:

'How can we attract qualified female candidates?'

'How can we generate their interest in this opening? '

Here the wording and presentation of the vacancy is important. How is it portrayed? It is said a picture paints a thousand words, so think about who or how is the organisation fronted.

The point is to make the position as attractive as possible to the targeted individuals so that they will apply. The applicant has to make the decision to apply, then remain a candidate during the entire recruitment process and finally to accept a job offer if one is extended (Breaugh, 2009). If you do not attract the right profiles, then the recruitment process fails.

## Use of tests

Use of test tools as a supplement in recruitment has become increasingly more important in line with the development of more sophisticated and accurate recruitment tools. Some tools have a higher correlation today than standard interviews considering the percentage share of successful recruitments. Anyway, you would think that the use of several different methods overall should give the best result.

Different universities in the world have different standards so it can be difficult to know how to assess the grades of candidates across the world. This means that cognitive ability surveys can be an excellent addition to the process to ensure that cognitive skills are in line with the skills required for the job performance. Testing of cognitive abilities may be fair across different cultures, but it may also pose challenges for neurodiverse candidates.

Objective tests do not discriminate as compared to more subjective assessment methods. Testing of cognitive skills is more and more common where intelligence is required for the job performance.

In addition to testing cognitive abilities, it is common to create different variations of personality testing. This does not say anything about expertise or skills, but it can say something about the suitability in relation to the tasks to be completed in the position. It can also provide good indications of whether candidates possess character traits which may seem complementary in a team or group.

## Unstructured interviews

When it comes to strategic recruitment, unstructured interviews may not be sufficient, unless of course a strategic analysis shows that this is the right method of communication for the target population. With unstructured interviews, much of the assessment relies on subjective experiences and gut feeling with extraordinarily little accuracy. Personal biases and preferences can play a significant role in one's choice of candidate as objective criteria are less central to the process.

With unstructured interviews it is likely that there will be deviations from the core interview subject area on some occasions (Bryman, 2016). For some roles, this should be encouraged as it may highlight areas not thought through and it can be an open channel for creative ideas, angles, and insight. Upon analysis of the interview data, follow-up interviews would be needed to focus on the core issues identified.

Unstructured interviews are diligently used in Norwegian business and industry with the limitations it entails. Minority groups of introverted and different people often under perform in such interviews as they may portray a sense of uncertainty. Language barriers, cultural differences and preferences may create a sense of unease that makes it harder to show the confidence required in the context of an unstructured interview.

## Structured interviews

To increase accuracy, structured and well thought out interviews should be implemented and evaluated along the way. Structured interviewing is likely to give more in-depth insight into the interviewees point of view and experiences.

In such interviews, the concern is about how the candidate has performed in the past in their previous relevant jobs. Actual achievements in previous jobs are a good indication of what you can expect in the future. If they can prove that they have delivered well in previous jobs, the probability that they will succeed in future endeavours is higher than if they have a record of failures.

The role of the interviewer is to guide the interview by asking open-ended questions and allowing the candidate to express their views. The interviewer should try to remain neutral and nondirective especially when asking follow-up questions to avoid introducing personal biases.

However, it is important to verify a candidate's credentials and achievements following an interview. Well-structured interviews have shown in the table under the highest correlation of the various recruitment methods. One sees the correlation between recruitment methods and how accurately they are to lead to a great recruitment.

### Assessment / Assessment Centres

Another method sometimes used, which is, in fact, the most accurate is an assessment centre. Here the candidates are given concrete tasks or challenges to solve. These tasks are designed to be relevant to the job being applied for and often it will be in collaboration with others. The candidate is then evaluated on how well they solved the challenge how much they involved and cooperated with the others.

A slightly different variant of this is to give the candidates a case they need to present to the decision makers of the recruitment process. I recall when we were to hire a new marketing manager in Statoil Retail that after a long-drawn-out process, we had narrowed the selection down to two candidates, but were uncertain which one to select. We decided to give them a practical case where they would present how Statoil retail could take up a market position in the breakfast sector. When the candidates had presented their cases, there was little doubt about who to offer the job to. One candidate had made a such an impressive analysis, coming up with suggestions that should be implemented almost immediately. The second candidate was grabbing thin straws from the air with very little concrete to offer.

# Overall Performance Management Systems

For all managers and employees to understand what is expected of them, and so that the internal competition for attractive positions would be seen as transparent and fair, it makes sense to introduce a comprehensive performance management system. Such a system is essential to ensure that the right candidates are found for any position rather than just those who are good at self-promotion. These are the candidates the company most needs to secure its future success.

Overall performance management systems will also make it much easier for minorities to build careers. There will be less internal politics, fewer self-promoting games, less informal networks, and more fact-based evaluation as well as a far more predictable way to drive career development.

Those who like such systems best are those who perform best over the rest. Those who underperform are not as excited about it, and often refer to research that criticises such systems claiming they have a negative impact on inner motivation. There are naturally downsides to everything but overall, a business over time will be served better by a good performance management system as previously mentioned than from a more comprehensive assessment.

In any system, it should be recognised that how you deliver is as important as what you deliver. It does not help if your deliveries are outstanding, but your ethics operate in grey areas or have such management behaviours which are not in accordance with the company's values. Your company is, of course, depending on good deliveries to be competitive and in compliance with good business ethics, procedures, and practices. It is of little use if the behaviour is great, but deliveries are not up to expectations either. Both deliveries and behaviour must therefore be in place for the achievement to be considered good.

All managers and employees should design a performance contract consisting of different goals and measures. Goal achievement is weighted and evaluated from defined measurable targets usually categorised within the following 4 areas:

- Economy
- Market
- Quality & environment
- People & organisation

In order to easily access good goals, one can develop a KPI Bank where one collects all good measurement indicators in one place. Delivery goals will be something like this:

## Behaviour

Conduct is often considered by each leader based on input from, among other things, 360/180-degree evaluation, employee surveys, implementation of development plan and observations of behaviour. There is not necessarily a direct correlation between a 360-degree evaluation and which evaluation one ends up getting overall, but it is nevertheless an important input. You may have a responsibility to carry out something that is slightly unpopular, such as a downsizing. Then it can be difficult to simultaneously score well in a 360 evaluation or employee survey. The leader must therefore make the fairest comprehensive assessment of achievements where everything is taken into account and is reflected in the overall assessment.

## Use of Scales in Evaluations of Achievements

It is difficult to know how well an employee really performs without using a monitoring scale. It is also difficult to compare achievements without a system that says something about how well an achievement is compared to others. To give clear feedback it will make sense to rank an achievement. Not everyone is thrilled about this, and especially those who score under par. At the same time, it is important to remember that children are graded at school. If it is acceptable for children at school, then it should be acceptable for adults at work. There are various types of scales, but it is recommended to use a scale of 1-5 with 3 as an average.

## Biases and prejudices in recruitment

Unfortunately, it is still the case that many are excluded in a recruitment process purely because of their name and nationality. Many large companies which operate internationally still do not have employees of different nationalities at the top management levels. There can be many reasons for this, but it often boils down to bias and prejudice.

A bias is a flaw in our own reasoning that leads us to wrongly interpret or understand information from our social world which makes us make wrong decisions. The brain stores, sorts and manages tons of information which constantly floods in, so it develops short cuts to help us make quick decisions, these short cuts are the so-called heuristics.

Here, past experiences, conditioning, and old beliefs play an important role. Our past experiences or even our lack of them form our expectations of people or events and create our probable future scenarios. Simply put, it is all about sensemaking. The philosophers of constructivism Guba and Lincoln (2013) argued that sensemaking is simply the act of interpretation. As humans we do not merely experience events but create them in reflection with our attempts at making sense of that experience.

If we have had a negative experience working with ethnic minorities, we are likely to avoid that in the future. If we have been brought up to believe that people of a certain race or culture are dishonest, we are unlikely to hire them.

Koval and Rosette (2020) recently published a research based on four studies that demonstrated a clear bias against black women with natural hairstyles such as afro, braids, cornrows or dreadlocks in job recruitment.

In the first Study, participants were told to evaluate profiles of Black and White female job applicants across a variety of hairstyles. According to the study, black women with natural hairstyles were perceived to be less professional, less competent, and less likely to be recommended for a job interview than black women with straightened hairstyles and white women with either curly or straight hairstyles. When they replicated the study, black women with natural hairstyles received more negative evaluations when they applied for jobs in an industry with strong dress norms.

There are similar biases towards people with excess weight who are often perceived as lazy, or lacking will power, so even when qualified for a job will not be hired because of that assumption.

Hijab phobia is a bias towards Muslim women wearing hijabs. Because the hijab is often viewed as a representation of oppression by western cultures, women wearing hijabs are often viewed as being unable to make their own choices and subjected to social control, thus they may not be considered during recruitment processes despite their qualifications.

We need look no further than 2001, when there were in fact large companies in Europe that still saw the recruitment of people with different ethnic backgrounds as a risk factor. For that reason, they chose not to hire them. The uncertainty is probably still present, but it is probably not true of most employers in Europe today.

# Global Recruitment: Opportunities and Challenges

In a hiring process, one can recruit with the whole world as a starting point. There is little to suggest that the best candidates for a job are within an extremely limited geographical area of the world. Performance variations follow a gaussian curve across areas of the world. It will naturally be best for a company to choose those that are as far to the right of the gaussian curve regardless of name or nationality. If you consider people as individuals and not as groups, then you will have a good starting point for strengthening the competitiveness of your organisation.

Performance variations in individuals within the business world follow a Gaussian-shaped curve across geographies. If you look at people with a minority background as individuals, and not as a group and have the ability to recruit those who are furthest to the right in the normal distribution curve, you will be the winner tomorrow.

Large international corporations with greater elements of multiculturalism seem to adapt better than those who have people of all the same nationality at top management levels. For example, Korean corporations with a larger spread of nationalities in higher management levels have, on average, shown a far better profit than, for example, the Japanese, where the top management levels are mostly occupied by older Japanese men. There are many examples of American companies with a large element of geographical diversity and economic success. Most large American corporations are multinational both in terms of distribution and in terms of managers at higher levels. The philosophy is to recruit the best regardless of nationality. They are also willing to pay well for high skills.

Uncertainty, fear, prejudices, and biases all probably contribute to a large extent to the fact that many companies refuse to recruit from abroad or from people with different cultural backgrounds. It requires a great deal of the leaders to lead a wider range of geographical diversity, but the gain is present if you master this. The prospect of 33-35% greater probability of success (ref. McKinsey studies) should create curiosity more than uncertainty in managers. To lead an ever-increasing geographical diversity, one must first and foremost focus on what binds us together. Firstly, which common denominators can create good contact and help create a larger community and a stronger team? Secondly, how can you promote differences as a strength of performance. A good diverse workplace is characterised by diversity being the normal state, and that inequality is used as a resource. The problem is that many European leaders today lack the competence to lead diversity properly.

European leaders do not always have much knowledge, nor interest in the cultures in which they will do business. They are a bit ethnocentric. They have the basic attitude that their own culture is the best. Foreigners can see that Europeans think they know best about a lot and lack the interest in other cultures.

Photograph 3: Official France squad photo. Twitter/equipedefrance

Professional football clubs are skilled at putting together teams consisting of complementing skills from across different geographies. The business community is not as skilled in this area.

# Helpful markers for diversifying your recruitment:

Your organisation is likely to succeed with talents from multiple backgrounds when you:

- Are an attractive employer for potential job seekers from a minority background. They need to feel welcome and have psychological safety in order to perform.
- Have geographical diversity in the management team that reflects the diversity of customers that the company has.
- You as a leader are able to lead a geographically diverse organisation.
- The company utilises the potential that lies in recruiting with the whole world as a starting point. it is very unlikely that the world's best managers and employees you will employ come from the same country.
- You show enough interest in corporate cultures in other countries.
- You adapt the leadership style to accommodate different cultures and contexts.

# CONCLUSION

In Part one, we sought to provides a general introduction to the concept of diversity and profitable and a necessity, not a burden we must tolerate. It is our hope that we have managed to make a reasonable case for diversity and inclusion as something to be sought after. Inclusion starts with each of us, how we meet and see each other and treat each other. Therefore, we saw it as necessary to bring out the importance of character. If we become more aware of our character traits, we are better able to meet different people and situations appropriately.

In Part two, our goal was to address the visible aspects of diversity, that which we see and aften address in our statistics; gender, ethnical, social, physical disability, age, class and cultural diversity. This is the part of DEI that is most discussed, however, due to large geographical disparities in gender diversity, we explored the differences between Norway and USA as a study case. The objective is to take learnings across geographies. We can take that which works elsewhere and apply them, where possible and applicable.

In Part three, our goal was to address the less visible elements of diversity. The traits, and characteristics, personality diversity and Neurodiversity. Invisible diversity is proving to be the most challenging area for inclusion, this is still an area laced with taboo, shame and non-acceptance. Invisible diversity is like an umbrella over all other diversity because all races, classes, genders, people in general have invisible differences. It has been our goal to address different diagnoses not just as challenges but rather to lift up the potential that resides in these individuals. Such potential is vital for business idea generation, creativity, resilience and entrepreneurship.

In Part four, we shared practical tools and advice from our vast experience to help you to build and lead a diverse team successfully. Here we want to highlight how to recruit and retain diverse talents, the dos and don'ts and what key issues must be addressed without delay, what to nip in the bud, what to water and cultivate.

At the end of the day, it is all about people. It is about creating an environment where we can all feel safe and thrive to our abilities and capabilities doing what we are good at. It is not about offering others a seat at the table; it is about having a table where we are all automatically welcome as we are. It is recognizing how interconnected we are, as explained by the Nobel Laureate Bishop Desmond Tutu, 'I am because we are'.

*Come as you are, as you were*

*As I want you to be*

*As a friend, as a friend.*

Kurt Cobain,
Nirvana

That is what diversity equity and inclusion is all about.

# ABOUT THE AUTHORS

Olav Haraldseid is the Managing Director of Olav Haraldseid AS, a consultancy specializing in enhancing organisational performance, diversity, developmental assessments, and management training. He has more than 20 years' experience working as a CHRO/HR director in large multinational companies such as Equinor ASA, NorgesGruppen ASA, Circle K, and Apotek1.

Olav holds a master's degree in sports psychology from the Norwegian University of physical education and sports specializing in attitudes, motivation, and self-confidence. He was the Norwegian national team coach in table tennis for 7 years, building an exciting generation of athletes who have asserted themselves very well internationally.

Olav has always had a great passion for what lies beneath outstanding results, both individually and as a team. He holds lectures for various companies and organisations on topics such as performance culture, changes management, leadership development, motivation, sales management etc, and has received ANFO's Owl - best speaker in Norway award, voted by participants. He has also been awarded the HR Norway's competence prize.

In recent years, he has taken a keen interest in an area where companies and organisations have great potential for improvement, the opportunities that lie in enhancing diversity in organisational performance, an area not fully explored currently. Today, diversity is first and foremost a theme in reputation building. However, Olav believes that diversity is first and foremost an important tool for strengthening competitiveness, and one which provides clear competitive advantages for the future of any organisation. It is imperative to understand what diversity is, and that it goes beyond that which is visible to the naked eye or easily categorized such as gender, sexual orientation, faith, and ethnicity. While these are important dimensions within the concept of diversity, the most important elements in diversity are in the minds of people, elements such as knowledge, experience, personality, attitudes, character strengths, skillsets, and more.

Today it is challenging to enhance diversity in practice simply because we appreciate the people who are relatively like ourselves far too much. Unfortunately, in a company or an organisation, we do not need 'clones'. We need people who are skilled in areas we are not good at - also called complementary skills. In football, managers are good at putting together teams of complementary skills, but this is not used to the same extent within the business community today. A wider range of diversity strengthens customer service, employee satisfaction, decision-making, innovation ability, and the recruitment of top talent in a company. It is no longer about tolerating diversity; it is about capitalizing on diversity by building stronger teams with complementary business skills.

# Winifred Patricia Johansen

Winifred Johansen is the senior vice-president for commercial affairs for Quantafuel ASA, she sits on multiple boards in the UK, and Norway. Winifred is an engineer, business strategist, and lead researcher. With more than two decades of industrial experience (Automotive, Oil and Gas, and Circular Economy), and she has vast experience both in business development and working across cultures. Winifred has a strong passion for social justice, ethical business, environmental sustainability, and education. She is a director of the social enterprise and ethical trade auditing consultancy Partner Africa (PA). The vision of PA is to improve the livelihoods of workers and producers across Africa and facilitate access to local and international markets.

Winifred holds an M.Sc. in Mechanical Engineering from the Norwegian University of Science and Technology (NTNU) and Politecnico di Milano, an MBA from the Robert Gordon University, Aberdeen, and is currently an extramural doctorate researcher on Crisis leadership at the University of Bradford. She uses sensemaking as a tool to engage with people to develop products, partnerships, initiatives, and market entry strategies.

Passionate about entrepreneurship as a tool for improving the quality of life, she serves as an Advisor to emerging entrepreneurs in Antler, a global early-stage VC enabling and investing in exceptional entrepreneurs. She has helped several start-ups to develop their business concepts and approach to the market.

When it comes to understanding diversity, Winifred is the ultimate underdog, a black woman and an immigrant who has spent the last twenty years working internationally in male-dominated industries. She has first-hand experience with the pertinent issues surrounding diversity. As a sensemaking researcher, she brings insight and hands-on knowledge in the implementation strategies for diversity as a profitability tool and unique competitive advantage.

# TABLE OF FIGURES

# TABLE OF PHOTOGRAPHS

Photograph 1: An all male business leaders' lunch at the Munich Security Conference Photographer Michael Bröcker

Photograph 2: The then Prime Minister Erna Solberg in conversation with Michael Moore Energy Broker with severe visual impediment

Photograph 3: Official France squad photo. Twitter/equipedefrance

# ENDNOTES/REFERENCES

Abascal, M., & Baldassarri, A. (2015). Love thy Neighbor? Ethnoracial Diversity and Trust Reexamined. American Journal of Sociology, 121(3), 722-782.

Alison, L., Power, N., den, v., Heuvel, C., Humann, M., Palasinksi, M., & Crego, J. (2015). Decision inertia: Deciding between least worst outcomes in emergency
responses to disasters. Journal of Occupational and Organizational Psychology, 88, 295-321.

Allan, J. L., Johnston, D. W., Powell, D. J. H., Farquharson, B., Jones, M. C., Leckie, G., & Johnston, M. (2019). Clinical decisions and time since rest break: An analysis of decision fatigue in nurses. Health psychology : official journal of the Division of Health Psychology, American Psychological Association, 38(4), 318-324. https://doi.org/10.1037/hea0000725

AlSheddi, M. (2020). Humility and Bridging Differences: A Systematic Literature Review of Humility in Relation to Diversity. International journal of intercultural relations, 79, 36-45. https://doi.org/10.1016/j.ijintrel.2020.06.002

Boin, A. (2019). The Transboundary Crisis: Why we are unprepared and the road ahead. Journal of Contingencies and Crisis Management, 7(1), 1-99. https://doi.org/10.1111/1468-5973.12241

Boin, A., & t' Hart, P. (2003). Public leadership in times of crisis: Mission impossible? Public Administration Review, 63(5), 544-553.

Breaugh, J. A. (2009). Recruiting and Attracting Talent: A Guide to Understanding and Managing the
Recruitment Process. Strategic Human Resource Management Foundation.

Bryman, A. (2016). Social research methods. In (5th ed.). Oxford, United Kingdom: Oxford University Press.

Cancer, A., Manzoli, S., & Antonietti, A. (2016). The alleged link between creativity and dyslexia: Identifying the specific process in which dyslexic students excel. In M. Besson (Ed.), Cogent Psychology (Vol. 3). https://doi.org/10.1080/23311908.2016.1190309

Carter, D. R., Cullen-Lester, K. L., Jones, J. M., Gerbasi, A., Chrobot-Mason, D., & Nae, E. Y. (2020). Functional leadership in interteam contexts: Understanding 'what' in the context of why? where? when? and who? Leadership Quarterly. https://doi.org/10.1016/j.leaqua.2019.101378

Chamorro-Premuzic, T. (2013). Why Do So Many Incompetent Men become Leaders? Harvard Business Review.

Chamorro-Premuzic, T. (2017). Could Your Personality Derail Your Career? Harvard Business Review(September-October), 138-141.

Clance, P. R., & Imes, S. A. (1978). The imposter phenomenon in high achieving women: Dynamics and therapeutic intervention. Psychotherapy: Theory, Research & Practice, 15(3), 241-247. https://doi.org/https://doi.org/10.1037/h0086006

Collins, J. (2001). Good to Great. Random House.

Costa, A. C. (2003). Work team trust and effectiveness. Personnel review, 32(5), 605-622. https://doi.org/10.1108/00483480310488360

Costa, A. C., & Anderson, N. (2011). Measuring trust in teams: Development and validation of a multifaceted measure of formative and reflective indicators of team trust. European journal of work and organisational psychology, 20(1), 119-154. https://doi.org/10.1080/13594320903272083

Costa, A. C., Fulmer, C. A., & Anderson, N. R. (2018). Trust in work teams: An integrative review, multilevel model, and future directions. Journal of organizational Behavior, 39(2), 169-184. https://doi.org/10.1002/job.2213

Costa, A. C., Roe, R. A., & Taillieu, T. (2001). Trust within teams: The relation with performance effectiveness. European journal of work and organizational psychology, 10(3), 225-244. https://doi.org/10.1080/13594320143000654

Crossan, M. M., Byrne, A., Seijts, G. H., Reno, M., Monzani, L., & Gandz, J. (2017). Toward a Framework of Leader Character in Organizations. Journal of management studies, 54(7), 986-1018. https://doi.org/10.1111/joms.12254

Doyle, N. (2020). The world needs Neurodiversity: Unusual Times Call For Unusual Thinking. https://www.forbes.com/sites/drnancydoyle/2020/03/24/the-world-needs-neurodiversity-unusual-times-call-for-unusual-thinking/?sh=1c1c00d46db2

Duckworth, A., Peterson, C., Matthews, M., & Kelly, D. (2007). Grit: Perseverance and Passion for Long-term goals. Journal of Personality and Social Psychology, 92(6), 1087-1101. https://doi.org/10.1037/0022-3514.92.6.1087.

Dunning, D., Johnson, K., Ehrlinger, J., & Kruger, J. (2003). Why People Fail to Recognize Their Own Incompetence. Current Directions in Psychological Science, 12(3), 83-87. https://doi.org/10.1111/1467-8721.01235

Eagly, A., & Carli, L. L. (2019). Women and the Labyrinth of Leadership. In W. E. Rosenbach, R. L. Taylor, & M. A. Youndt (Eds.), Contemporary Issues in

Leadership (7th ed., pp. 320). Routledge.
https://doi.org/https://doi.org/10.4324/9780429494000
Eagly, A., & Karau, S. (2002). Role Congruity Theory of Prejudice Toward
Female Leaders. Psychological Review, 109(3), 573-598.
Endsley, M. R. (1995). Toward a Theory of Situation Awareness in Dynamic
Systems. Human Factors, 37(1), 32–64.
Finne, L. B., Knardahl, S., & Lau, B. (2011). Workplace bullying and mental
distress – a prospective study of Norwegian employees. Scandinavian Journal
of Work, Environment, and Health, 37(4), 276-287.
https://doi.org/https://www.sjweh.fi/show_abstract.php?abstract_id=3156
Flin, R., O'Connor, M., & Crichton, M. (2008). Safety at the Sharp End: A Guide
to Non-technical Skills. Aldershot.
Flynn, J. R., & Shayer, M. (2018). IQ decline and Piaget: Does the rot start at
the top? Intelligence, 66, 112-121.
https://doi.org/https://doi.org/10.1016/j.intell.2017.11.010
Fransen, K., Steffens, N. K., Haslam, S. A., Vanbeselaere, N., Vande Broek, G.,
& Boen, F. (2016). We will be champions: Leaders' confidence in 'us' inspires
team members' team confidence and performance. Scandinavian journal of
medicine & science in sports, 26(12), 1455-1469.
https://doi.org/10.1111/sms.12603
Georgiadou, A., Gonzalez-Perez, M.-A., & Olivas-Lujan, M. R. (2019). Diversity
within diversity management: country based perspectives. Emerald Publishing
Limited.
Gibson, M. A. (2001). Immigrant Adaptation and Patterns of Acculturation.
Human Development, 44(1), 19-23.
Grewal, D. (2016). Does Diversity Create Distrust? Doubts about a Harvard
Professor's landmark finding. Behavior & Society(November 29).
https://doi.org/https://www.scientificamerican.com/article/does-diversity-
create-distrust/
Hewlett, S. H., Marshall, M., & Sherbin, L. (2013). How Diversity Can Drive
Innovation. https://hbr.org/2013/12/how-diversity-can-drive-innovation
Hogan, J., Barrett, P., & Hogan, R. (2007). Personality Measurement, Faking,
and Employment Selection. Journal of applied psychology, 92(5), 1270-1285.
https://doi.org/10.1037/0021-9010.92.5.1270
Hogan, R., Hogan, J., & Roberts, B. W. (1996). Personality Measurement and
Employment Decisions: Questions and Answers. The American psychologist,
51(5), 469-477. https://doi.org/10.1037/0003-066X.51.5.469
House, A., Power, N., & Alison, L. (2014). A Systematic review of the Potential
Hurdles of Interoperability to the Emergency Services in Major Incidents:
Recommendations for Solutions and Alternatives. Cognition, Technology and
Work, 16(3), 319-335. https://doi.org/10.1007/s10111-013-0259-6

Huselid, M. A., Becker, B. E., & Beatty, R. W. (2005). The workforce scorecard: Managing human capital to execute strategy. Harvard Business School Press.

Janis, I. L. (1972). Victims of Groupthink. In. Boston: Houghton Mifflin Co.

Janis, I. L. (1982). Groupthink: Psychological Studies of Policy Decisions and Fiascos (2nd ed.). Houghton Mifflin Co.

Janis, I. L. (1989). Crucial Decisions: Leadership in Policymaking and Crisis Management. The Free Press.

Kahneman, D. (2011). Thinking, Fast and Slow. In (pp. 504). London: Allen Lane.

Kelman, S., Sanders, R., & Pandit, G. (2017). "Tell It Like It Is": Decision Making, Groupthink, and Decisiveness among U.S. Federal Subcabinet Executives. Governance, 30(2), 245-261. https://doi.org/10.1111/gove.12200

Koval, C. Z., & Rosette, A. S. (2020). The Natural Hair Bias in Job Recruitment. Social Psychological and Personality Science, 1948550620937937. https://doi.org/10.1177/1948550620937937

Krasmann, S., & Hentschel, C. (2019). 'Situational awareness': Rethinking security in times of urban terrorism. Security Dialogue, 50(2), 181-197. https://doi.org/10.1177/0967010618819598

Kuipers, S., & Brändström, A. (2020). Accountability and Blame Avoidance After Crises.

Lagarde, C. (2018, September 5th). Ten Years After Lehman - Lessons Learned and Challenges Ahead. Insights & Analysis on Economics and Finances. https://blogs.imf.org/2018/09/05/ten-years-after-lehman-lessons-learned-and-challenges-ahead/

Langdridge, D. (2007). Phenomenological Psychology: Theory, Research and Method. Pearson Education Ltd.

Laverty, S. M. (2003). Hermeneutic Phenomenology and Phenomenology: A Comparison of Historical and Methodological Considerations. International Journal of Qualitative Methods, 2(3), 21-35. https://doi.org/10.1177/160940690300200303

Lewin, K. (1947). Field Theory in Social Science. In. New York: Harper & Row.

Lincoln, Y. S., & Guba, E. G. (2013). The constructivist credo. Left Coast Press, Inc.

Lincoln, Y. S., Guba, E. G., & ProQuest (Firm). (2013). The constructivist credo. Left Coast Press, Inc.

Lorenzo, R., Voight, N., Tsusaka, M., Krentz, M., & Abouzahr, K. (2018). How Diverse Leadership Teams Boost Innovation. Retrieved 8 Jan. 2022, from

Lumpkin, A., & Achen, R. M. (2018). Explicating the Synergies of Self-Determination Theory, Ethical Leadership, Servant Leadership, and Emotional Intelligence. Journal of leadership studies (Hoboken, N.J.), 12(1), 6-20. https://doi.org/10.1002/jls.21554

Madsbjerg, C. (2016). Sensemaking: The Power of the Humanities in the Age of the Algorithm (Vol. 263). PWxyz, LLC.

Maitlis, S., Vogus, T. J., & Lawrence, T. B. (2013). Sensemaking and emotion in organizations. Organizational Psychology Review, 3(3), 222-247. https://doi.org/10.1177/2041386613489062

McKinsey. (2020a). Diversity wins: How inclusion matters.

McKinsey. (2020b). Diversity wins: How inclusion matters.

Moynihan, D. P. (2012). Extra-Network Organizational Reputation and Blame Avoidance in Networks: The Hurricane Katrina Example. Governance, 25, 567-588. https://doi.org/10.1111/j.1468-0491.2012.01593.x

Mueller, J. (2012). Why individuals in larger teams perform worse. Organizational Behavior and Human Decision Processes, 117(1). https://doi.org/10.1016/j.obhdp.2011.08.004

Murase, T., Carter, D., DeChurch, L., & Marks, M. (2014). Mind the Gap: The role of leadership in Multiteam System Collective Cognition. Leadership Quarterly, 25(5), 972-986.

Nielsen, M. B., Christensen, J. O., Finne, L. B., & Knardal, S. (2020). Workplace bullying, mental distress, and sickness absence: the protective role of social support. International Archives of Occupational and Environmental Health, 93, 43-53. https://doi.org/https://doi.org/10.1007/s00420-019-01463-y

Pennycook, G., Ross, R. M., Koehler, D. J., & Fugelsang, J. A. (2017). Dunning–Kruger effects in reasoning: Theoretical implications of the failure to recognize incompetence. Psychonomic bulletin & review, 24(6), 1774-1784. https://doi.org/10.3758/s13423-017-1242-7

Peterson, C., & Seligman, M. E. P. (2004). Character Strengths and Virtues: A handbook and classification. APA Press and Oxford University Press.

Pfeffer, J., & Sutton, R. (1999). The Knowing-Doing Gap: How Smart Companies Turn Knowledge into Action. Harvard Business Review.

Philips, W. K. (2017). How Diversity Make us Smarter. Retrieved July 26, 2021, from https://greatergood.berkeley.edu/article/item/how_diversity_makes_us_smarter

Pignatiello, G. A., Martin, R. J., & Hickman, R. L. (2020). Decision fatigue: A conceptual analysis. In (Vol. 25, pp. 123-135). London, England: SAGE Publications.

PricewaterhouseCoopers. (2016). Annual corporate directors survey. https://www.pwc.com/us/en/

PriceWaterhouseCoopers. (2020). Annual Corporate Directors Survey: Turning Crisis into Opportunity. https://www.pwc.com/us/en/services/governance-insights-center/library/annual-corporate-directors-survey.html

Putnam, R. D. (2007). E Pluribus Unum: Diversity and Community in the Twenty-First Century-The 2006 Johan Skytte Prize Lecture. Scandinavian Political Studies, 30(2), 137-174.

Rosenman, E. D., Dixon, A. J., Webb, J. M., Brolliar, S., Golden, S. J., Jones, K. A., . . . Cloutier, R. (2018). A Simulation-based Approach to Measuring Team Situational Awareness in Emergency Medicine: A Multicenter, Observational Study. Academic Emergency Medicine, 25(2), 196-204. https://doi.org/10.1111/acem.13257

Sabini, J. (1992). Social Psychology (First Edition ed.). W.W Norton and Company.

Salgado, J. F., & De Fruyt, F. (2017). Personality in Personnel Selection. In A. Evers, N. Anderson, & O. Voskuijl (Eds.), The Blackwell Handbook of Personnel Selection. https://doi.org/https://doi.org/10.1002/9781405164221.ch8

Sandberg, S. (2013). Lean in: Women, work, and the will to lead (First Edition ed.). Alfred A. Knopf.

Saridakis, G., Lai, Y., Muñoz Torres, R. I., & Gourlay, S. (2020). Exploring the relationship between job satisfaction and organizational commitment: an instrumental variable approach. International journal of human resource management, 31(13), 1739-1769. https://doi.org/10.1080/09585192.2017.1423100

Schutz, A. (1967). The Phenomenology of the Social World. Northwestern University press.

Seijts, G., Byrne, A., Crossan, M. M., & Gandz, J. (2018). Leader character in board governance. Journal of management and governance, 23(1), 227-258. https://doi.org/10.1007/s10997-018-9426-8

Shuffler, M. L., & Carter, D. R. (2018). Teamwork Situated in Multiteam Systems: Key Lessons Learned and Future Opportunities. American Psychologist, 73(4), 390-406.

Sjöberg, S., Svensson, C., & Sjöberg, A. (2012). Measuring and Assessing Individual Potential. Elanders Sverige.

Solhaug, T., & Kristensen, N. N. (2020). Gender and intercultural competence: analysis of intercultural competence among upper secondary school students in Denmark and Norway. Educational psychology (Dorchester-on-Thames), 40(1), 120-140. https://doi.org/10.1080/01443410.2019.1646410

Solhaug, T., & Osler, A. (2018). Intercultural empathy among Norwegian students: an inclusive citizenship perspective. International journal of inclusive education, 22(1), 89-110. https://doi.org/10.1080/13603116.2017.1357768

Sun, T. (1963). The Art of War. Oxford University Press .

Tulsshyan, R., & Burey, J. (2021). Stop Telling women they have Imposter Syndrome. Harvard Business Review.

Tversky, A., & Kahneman, D. (1974). Judgement under uncertainty: heuristics and biases. Science, 185, 1124-1131.

Van Aswegen, A. (2015). Women vs. Men—Gender Differences in Purchase Decision Making. Guided Selling, 29.

Van den Heuvel, C., Alison, L., & Power, N. (2014). Coping with Uncertainty: Police Strategies for Resilient Decision-Making and Action Implementation. Cognition, Technology & Work, 16, 25-45. https://doi.org/10.1007/s10111-012-0241-8

Van Manen, M. (1997). Researching lived experience: Human Science for an action sensitive Pedagogy (2nd ed.). The Althouse Press, University of Western Ontario.

Waring, S., Alison, L., Carter, G., Barrett-Pink, C., Humann, M., Swan, L., & Zilinsky, T. (2018). Information sharing in interteam responses to disaster. Journal of Occupational and Organizational Psychology, 91(3), 591-619. https://doi.org/10.1111/joop.12217

Washington, E., & Patrick, C. (2018). 3 Requirements for a Diverse and Inclusive Culture. Retrieved 9 Jan. 2022, from

Wei, Y. S., O'Neill, H., & Zhou, N. (2019). How Does Perceived Integrity in Leadership Matter to Firms in a Transitional Economy? Journal of business ethics, 167(4), 623-619. https://doi.org/10.1007/s10551-019-04168-x

Weick, E. K. (1988). Enacted Sensemaking in Crisis Situations. Management Studies, 25(4), 305-317.

Yu W, W. J., & A., P.-L. (2021). ADHD Symptoms, Entrepreneurial Orientation (EO), and Firm Performance. Entrepreneurship Theory and Practice, 45(1), 92-117. https://doi.org/10.1177/1042258719892987